Hermann Von Holst

John C. Calhoun

Hermann Von Holst

John C. Calhoun

ISBN/EAN: 9783337398637

Printed in Europe, USA, Canada, Australia, Japan

Cover: Foto ©Andreas Hilbeck / pixelio.de

More available books at **www.hansebooks.com**

American Statesmen

JOHN C. CALHOUN

BY

DR. H. von HOLST

BOSTON
HOUGHTON, MIFFLIN AND COMPANY
NEW YORK: 11 EAST SEVENTEENTH STREET
The Riverside Press, Cambridge
1892

CONTENTS.

CHAPTER VIII.

CHAPTER IX.

CHAPTER I.

YOUTH.

LIFE is not only " stranger than fiction," but frequently also more tragical than any tragedy ever conceived by the most fervid imagination. Often in these tragedies of life there is not one drop of blood to make us shudder, nor a single event to compel the tears into the eye. A man endowed with an intellect far above the average, impelled by a high-soaring ambition, untainted by any petty or ignoble passion, and guided by a character of sterling firmness and more than common purity, yet, with fatal illusion, devoting all his mental powers, all his moral energy and the whole force of his iron will to the service of a doomed and unholy cause, and at last sinking into the grave in the very moment when, under the weight of the top-stone, the towering pillars of the temple of his impure idol are rent to their very base, — can anything more tragical be conceived?

That is, in a few lines, the story of the life of John C. Calhoun. In spite of his grand career, South Carolina's greatest son has had a more hapless fate than any other of the illustrious men in the history of the United States. With few exceptions it is probable that the readers of these pages will consider this a strange or even an absurd assertion, and thereby themselves will furnish another proof of its truth. Alexander Hamilton, America's greatest political genius, has been obliged to wait three quarters of a century to have a statue erected to his memory, and then it had to be done by his own offspring. Calhoun has not had to complain of the same neglect, though nobody could have been justly accused of ingratitude if this honor had not been vouchsafed to him; for he has no claims upon the gratitude of his country, although his name will forever remain one of the foremost in its records. But, in common with Alexander Hamilton, he is still waiting for the only monument worthy of his memory, a biography which does him full justice; and he will probably have to wait much longer for such a memorial, — *œre perennius*, — which indeed, it is not unlikely, may never be erected. As yet it is hardly possible to pass an unbiassed judgment upon him, because the wounds of the terrible conflict, in which he was during the lifetime of a whole generation the acknowledged leader, have not fully healed, and therefore those passions have not completely died away which were engendered by the catastrophe in which that conflict ended. Meanwhile, it becomes every day more difficult really to understand that struggle. Even the present generation, which has grown into manhood since the civil war, hardly realizes that it is not a soul-stirring romance, but sober history. The next generation will find it easier to form an adequate conception of the life of the ancient Indians and Egyptians than of that of their own grandfathers; for there is no other instance in all the history of the world, where the civilizations of two different ages, with their antagonistic principles and modes of thinking and feeling, have been so intricately interwoven as in the United States during the times of the slavery conflict. It is only the part played by Calhoun in this conflict which puts him into the very first rank of the men who have acted on the political stage of the United States, though he has done enough else to secure for his name a permanent place in the annals of his country.

As the years roll on, the fame of Daniel Webster and Henry Clay is gradually growing dimmer, while the name of Calhoun has yet lost hardly anything of the lurid intensity with

which it glowed on the political firmament of
the United States towards the end of the first
half of this century. Nor will it ever lose
much of this. The fact is easily explained,
though it may seem strange to the superficial
student. The number of Calhoun's admirers
in his later years was insignificant in comparison with the enthusiastic hosts who knew no
more powerful charm than the captivating voice
of the eloquent Kentuckian, and to-day it will
not be seriously questioned that Webster was
intellectually more than the peer of Calhoun.
Neither of the three can lay claim to the name
of a statesman in the highest acceptation of the
term without more than one qualifying restric-
tion, but Calhoun is certainly less entitled to it
than either of his great rivals. Moreover, these
had so many peculiar traits of character, habits,
and fancies, that their lives are a rich source of
pleasant anecdotes; and from the background
of the general historical development, their fig-
ures spring forth in bold relief with a vividness
equalling that of Washington, Jefferson, and
John Adams. Of Calhoun the man, on the
contrary, but very little is to be told. Even
his contemporaries, with perhaps the exception
of his nearest neighbors, did not know much of
his doings as a private individual, or at least
do not seem to have thought them of suffi-

cient interest to be handed down to posterity. Whether his private correspondence, which is still withheld from the public, will throw much light on this side of his life, cannot be told. I have to state with régret that, according to my information, not very much is to be expected. I was assured in Charleston, by an intimate younger friend of Calhoun, that he had not been in the habit of carefully preserving his private letters, and that many of his papers, which are at present intrusted to Mr. Hunter of Virginia, were lost during the civil war. However that may be, the newspapers of the times and the published private correspondences of his co-actors tell hardly anything of the personal relations and the home-life of the man, whose slightest public act was watched with interest by the whole nation. We hear that he was a just and kind master to his slaves, that he was possessed of an uncommon conversational talent, and that he exercised an especial fascination upon young men. This is about all.

From the historical standpoint it is, of course, deeply to be regretted that we are so little informed about the every-day life of so remarkable a man; and yet one cannot help feeling at the same time a certain satisfaction that we learn no more about it. There is no better proof of the personal purity of a public man than the complete stillness of all gossipping tongues, among friends as well as foes. The consequence of this silence is, however, that so soon as the grave closes over such a public personage, the figure begins to assume a shadowy appearance. A well-read student of the history of the United States may often easily imagine himself seated next to Webster and Clay at the social board, or walking with them in the lanes of their farms, though he may have been born after their eyes had been closed forever. But no one who has not actually grasped Calhoun's hand and looked into the depth of those steady and keen eyes, will ever be tempted to indulge for a single moment in such an illusion with regard to him. Twenty or thirty years hence there will not be a single person left to whom he is or ever has been fully a man of flesh and bone. The Representative, the Secretary of War, the Vice-President, the "great Nullifier," the Senator, our posterity like ourselves may be perfectly acquainted with; but the Calhoun off the political stage, the Calhoun who ate and drank like other mortals, who laughed, chatted, and sorrowed, who enjoyed life and battled with its small and great cares, is long ago dead, and no pen will ever be able to recall him to life in the same sense in which Webster and Clay still are and will remain alive so long as the American people cherish the memory of their great men.

Yet it is unquestionably true, as it was asserted before, that the name of Calhoun already conveys a much more definite idea to the American people than that of either Webster or Clay, and that this difference will be steadily increased in his favor. The simple explanation of this remarkable fact is, that Calhoun is in an infinitely higher degree the representative of an *idea*, and this idea is the pivotal point on which the history of the United States has turned from 1819 to nearly the end of the first century of their existence as an independent republic. From about 1830 to the day of his death, Calhoun may be called the very impersonation of the slavery question. From the moment when he assumes this character, his figure towers far above all his contemporaries, even Jackson not excepted; while up to that time he is, in spite of his uncommonly brilliant career, only an able politician of the higher and nobler order, having many peers and even a considerable number of superiors among the statesmen of the United States. These introductory remarks seem necessary in order to justify the brevity with which we are compelled to treat the youth of Calhoun and the first period of his public life.

In 1733 James Calhoun is said to have emi-
grated from Donegal in Ireland to the United
States. He first went to Pennsylvania, then
settled on the Kanawha, in Virginia, and at
last, in 1756, removed to South Carolina. In
1770 his son Patrick married Martha Caldwell,
the daughter of a Presbyterian emigrant from
Ireland. John Caldwell Calhoun, the third son
of Patrick and Martha, was born March 18,
1782, in the Abbeville District, South Carolina.
Though his father died while he was still a boy,
the ardent temper of the zealous revolutionary
patriot seems to have exercised a marked influence on the formation of the character of the
son. John remained with his mother on the
farm. There he led a quiet and simple life, for
his father had left the family in very modest
circumstances. No opportunity was offered him
to attend regularly a good school, and his solitary rambles in the woods had to serve in
lieu of systematic instruction. Being from his
early childhood of a meditative turn of mind,
the youth learned to think before his memory
had become burdened with the thoughts of other
people. This defective education in his boy-
hood made itself felt through his whole life.
In spite of the diligence with which he applied
himself later, for some years, to his books, the
stock of positive knowledge which he had to

fall back upon was never large, and the peculiar kind of narrowness which is inseparable from onesidedness was among the most prominent traits in his mental and moral structure. But what he lacked in breadth of view he fully made up by penetrating intensity, bold independence of thinking, and a keen instinct for the true nature of the things which fell within the limited circle in which his mind moved.

Calhoun had completed his eighteenth year, when he began an uninterrupted course of systematic study in order to fit himself for the higher walks of life. Under the direction of his brother-in-law, Dr. Waddel, a Presbyterian clergyman, he prepared himself for college, and after two short years he was able to enter the junior class at Yale. In 1804 he was graduated with high honors, and then devoted himself for three years to the study of law, spending eighteen months of the time at the law school at Litchfield, Connecticut. Of much more importance than the often-repeated story, that while at Yale he had been declared fit and likely to become some day President of the United States, is the unmistakable fact that his prolonged sojourn in New England exercised a marked influence upon the formation of the political opinions which he held in the beginning of his political career.

Having returned to Abbeville, he began to practise law; but it does not appear that the public were especially eager to avail themselves of his services as an attorney and counsellor, nor that he distinguished himself in any case of importance. A man of his general ability and uncommon logical acuteness could not have failed to acquire a prominent standing in this calling if he had devoted himself to it with his whole energy. Yet he would undoubtedly never have become a great lawyer, because he was not objective enough to examine his premises with sufficient care, while he built his argument upon them with undeviating and most incisive logic, thereby frequently arriving at most shocking conclusions with nothing to stand upon except a basis of false postulates. Moreover, such natures never attain greatness, unless they pursue an aim which fills the whole head and heart with the force of a burning passion, a frame of mind into which but few men can be put by the common law; and of these few Calhoun certainly was not one. He was a born leader of men, and nature had destined him for a political career. While at college the exciting questions of the day had engrossed his whole attention, and the intelligence and earnestness with which he discussed them proved that he would try to have a hand in shaping the events of the future. Sooner and in a higher degree than he himself had probably dared to anticipate, this wish was to be fulfilled.

He had barely had time to get again familiar with the surroundings of his youth, when he was sent by his district to the state Legislature. The stage was too small to draw the eyes of the nation upon the young man, but it was the right place to prove his fitness for a larger one. In 1811 he was elected a member of Congress, and in the same year he married his cousin, Floride Calhoun. She was possessed of a modest fortune, which enabled him to steer with all sails set into the open sea of politics. On November 4 he took his seat in the House of Representatives, having previously removed to **Bath on the Savannah.**

CHAPTER II.

HOUSE OF REPRESENTATIVES.

THE times were most favorable for a clever and ambitious young statesman to make a brilliant *début*. The policy of commercial restrictions, with which Jefferson and Madison had tried to force England and France to respect the rights of neutrals, had signally failed. The party in power had not the candor and moral courage to acknowledge that it had stumbled into grave mistakes, but it was apparent that it could no more, for any length of time, pursue its old course. If the great European war should last much longer — and there was no prospect of its speedy termination — the United States would evidently be forced to abandon all half-hearted and two-edged measures, and to adopt a clear and decisive policy. It was perhaps impossible to satisfy the commercial States; but thus much was certain, that their dissatisfaction was too great and too well-founded to permit an expectation that they would jog on with impunity in the old ruts. Nor would either the honor or the vital interests of the Union allow that it should bow its head in meekness, and receive with folded arms the stripes which the belligerent powers were pleased to lay on its back. Whatever might be resolved upon and done, it was sure to raise a great clamor among a considerable portion of the people; yet something must be done, and in such circumstances the race generally is to the swift and the battle to the strong.

It was a coincidence of the utmost importance that the ranks of the revolutionary patriots had, by this time, become so thinned that the representatives of a new generation could grasp the helm without having to encounter the opposition of long acknowledged authority. It so happened, also, that among these new-comers on the political stage there were some exceptionally young men, possessed of a much higher order of talent than most of their seniors. So the leadership of the nation in this great crisis fell into the hands of untried and inexperienced men, who had hardly reached maturity, yet were fully conscious of their own power and worth, and who were impelled by a high-toned pride and ardent patriotism, and urged on by the glowing visions of an unbounded ambition. It was therefore to be expected that, true to the nature of hot-blooded, daring, and self-relying youth, they would ad-vise the cutting of the Gordian knot which the silver-haired sages of the Revolution had vainly tried to disentangle. At which side of it, in their opinion, the stroke of the sword should be dealt, could not be doubtful from the first. In spite of Napoleon, the majority of the people had not yet entirely lost the enthusiastic sympathy awakened by the French Revolution, and the services rendered by France to the United States in the war of independence were still unforgotten. On the other hand, the old wounds which had been inflicted by the blows exchanged with England had not quite ceased to rankle; the emancipated daughter smarted under the overbearing haughtiness of the mother, whom she had once forced to submit to her just claims. Then, too, above all else, Napoleon's violent decrees against the rights of neutrals were to a considerable extent mere stage lightnings, while the English Orders in Council told with terrible effect upon the commerce and the general prosperity of the United States, and the pretended right of visitation, which was frequently exercised with studied insolence, cut the American pride to the quick. Prudential reasons of great weight might be urged against resenting all these injuries at this time with powder and lead, and personal interest as well as party spirit would surely put these reasons into the strongest light. But it was no less certain that the passionate and indignant appeals to the counter-reasons would awaken a loud echo in numberless bosoms, since every patriot had to confess to himself that they too had great weight.

The general elections for the Twelfth Congress had resulted in favor of the war party. It was principally due to his position towards this overshadowing question that Henry Clay owed his election to the speakership; and for the same reason the Speaker awarded the second place on the Committee on Foreign Relations to the new member from South Carolina. Mr. Crallé, the editor of Calhoun's works, assures us that at the first meeting of the members Calhoun was — on motion of Mr. Porter of Pennsylvania, to whom the Speaker had assigned the chairmanship — unanimously chosen to preside over their deliberations. So he held from the first the place which, next to the speakership, was the most important in the House of Representatives.

On November 29, 1811, the committee, to which that part of the President's message relating to foreign affairs had been referred, submitted its report. Although the report was presented by Mr. Porter, it seems likely that it was mainly written by Calhoun. The essence of it was contained in the following sentences:

"To wrongs so daring in their character, and so disgraceful in their execution, it is impossible that the people of the United States should remain indifferent. We must now tamely and quietly submit, or we must resist by those means which God has placed within our reach.

"Your committee will not cast a shade on the American name by the expression of a doubt which branch of this alternative will be embraced; . . . the period has arrived when, in the opinion of your committee, it is the sacred duty of Congress to call forth the patriotism and the resources of the country."

The report concluded with six resolutions, which were designed to give effect to this opinion.

So the first act of Calhoun on the national stage was to sound the war-trumpet. Henceforth incessant war, war to the bitter end, was to be his destiny to the last day of his life; though it was in later years to be waged not against a foreign aggressor, but against internal adversaries, against the peace of the Union, against the true welfare of his own section of the country.

On December 12 Calhoun delivered his first set speech in Congress, defending the resolutions and refuting the arguments of John Randolph, who was himself a member of the Committee on Foreign Relations. On a former

occasion Calhoun had addressed to the House
a few remarks on a question of little importance, which he had concluded with an allusion
to the diffidence and embarrassment which a
young man necessarily felt in speaking to the
assembled representatives of the nation. Now,
however, there was in his whole tone and manner no more the slightest trace of such a feeling. He did not speak with arrogance, and
still less was there anything personally offensive in what he said, or in the manner with
which he said it. From the beginning of his
public career he observed the parliamentary
proprieties with the rigor and naturalness of
the born gentleman. Often did he prove that
he could wield with equal force and dexterity
the trenchant sword and the massive club, but
he always attacked the argument of his adversary and not his person, and he was never
guilty of the hectoring and bullying tone in
which so many of the Southern politicians indulged with keen relish. From the first he
entered the lists with the proud conviction of
being fully the equal of any man, and he al
vays spoke in the weighty tone of authority.
Upon him the shaking of Randolph's long finger made no impression. With open visor he
met the much-dreaded antagonist, and though
he did not throw him to the ground, yet the

Virginian came out of the fight only second best. They exchanged many a tilt, and the ill-humor with which Randolph spoke of Calhoun in his private correspondence, shows how much he felt the wounds received from the lance of that adversary.

Calhoun began his speech with the open avowal "that the committee recommended the measures now before the House, as a preparation for war;" and he added, "such, in fact, was its express resolve, agreed to, I believe by every member, except that gentleman [Randolph]. . . . Indeed, the report could mean nothing but war or empty menace." With lofty indignation he repelled the insinuation that, though there was adequate cause for war, the people would not deem their violated interests and outraged rights of sufficient moment willingly to defray the costs of fighting for their vindication.

"But it may be, and I believe it was said, that the people will not pay taxes, because the rights violated are not worth defending; or that the defence will cost more than the gain. Sir, I here enter my solemn protest against this low and 'calculating avarice' entering this hall of legislation. It is only fit for shops and counting-houses; and ought not to disgrace the seat of power by its squalid aspect. Whenever it touches sovereign power, the nation is ruined. It is too short-sighted to defend itself. It is a compromising spirit, always ready to yield a part to save the residue. It is too timid to have in itself the laws of self-preservation. It is never safe but under the shield of honor. . . . Sir, I am not versed in this calculating policy; and will not, therefore, pretend to estimate in dollars and cents the value of national independence. I cannot measure in shillings and pence the misery, the stripes, and the slavery of our impressed seamen; nor even the value of our shipping, commercial, and agricultural losses under the Orders in Council and the British system of blockade."

With equal candor he answered Randolph's question, why then, if all this was so, war was not declared immediately: " Because," he said, " we are not yet prepared." That there was any danger in avowing this and, at the same time, using the threatening language employed by himself and those who shared his views, he denied; because, he said, England would never be provoked into beginning hostilities from a fear of uniting " all parties here."

After this speech the passing of the resolutions by the House could not be understood otherwise than as a formal announcement that war would be declared so soon as, in the opinion of the war party, the country should be sufficiently prepared. So far as it depended

upon the House, the great question was **virtu-**
ally decided, and the war party pushed **vigor-**
ously on towards the bloody goal. They needed
half a year more to reach it. President Madison was about the last man to long for the
laurels of "the conquering hero." His whole
character as well as his political **convictions**
made him exceedingly loath to gratify, **the**
wishes of the young Hotspurs, who nevertheless dragged him along by a strong rope. As
Jefferson's Secretary of State and as President
he had advocated and pursued a policy, the
legitimate consequence of which was war. He
could not now take a decided stand against the
war party without acknowledging that this policy had been, from beginning to end, a mistaken one, — an avowal which no statesman
will easily make, and which, on the part of
Madison, would have been a formal renuncia-
tion of his aspirations for a second term. That
was the vise in which he was held by the war
party, and mercilessly they screwed it tightei
and tighter. In vain he tried to conciliate
them by consenting to follow their lead ; they
.nsisted that he should assume the full responsibility, and they would be satisfied with nothing less.

On April 1 the President sent a message to
Congress, recommending an embargo. **Mr**

Grundy said that he understood it " as a war measure, and it was meant that it should directly lead to war," and Calhoun afterwards declared " its manifest propriety as a prelude to war." Without granting to the opposition the necessary time to develop their views, Congress, on April 4, passed the bill laying an embargo on all vessels. It was limited to sixty days solely because those who held the destiny of the country in their hands were fully resolved that it should not " be permitted to expire without any hostile measure being taken against Great Britain."

It was not due to the President that this announcement, indirectly made by Calhoun on May 6, was not fulfilled to the letter. Another message laid before Congress at length all the wrongs which the United States had suffered for so many years. " We behold," it said, " in fine, on the side of Great Britain a state of war against the United States, and on the side of the United States a state of peace towards Great Britain." Therefore it was now incumbent on Congress to decide whether force should be opposed to force. This was virtually a recommendation of war. In the name of the Committee on Foreign Relations, Calhoun presented a report to the House, advising " an immediate appeal to arms," and, at the same time, he moved that a formal declaration of war should be issued against Great Britain. On the following day the House passed this to the third reading, after Randolph's motion, renewed by Milnor, to open the doors, and Stow's request to postpone the final action to the next day, had both been rejected. Thus the majority crowned the high-handed recklessness with which, ever since the beginning of the session, they had bent the just claims of the minority under their imperious will. In later years Calhoun learned well enough to clamor for the rights of the minority, while he was but too apt to forget that the majority also had rights, and, above all others, the right to rule. Perhaps the time was not far distant when he and his associates would have reason to rue their present abuse of power, for the declaration of war received a majority of only thirty votes, although the Democratic majority in the full House was seventy.

In the Senate, the defection from the party even threatened to become fatal to the wishes of the war party. On motion of Mr. Gregg, of Pennsylvania, the bill providing for the declaration of war was recommitted by a majority of four. Not until June 17 did a sufficient number of reluctant Democrats yield to allow the amended bill to be passed to a third reading. The House agreed to the amendments on the following day.

A few days after the declaration of war, the House took up the question, whether and how far the restrictive policy concerning commerce should be abandoned. The Committee on Ways and Means reported a bill for the partial suspension of the Non-Importation Act. This was not deemed sufficient relief in the States on which the mistaken policy hitherto pursued had weighed most heavily. Mr. Richardson, of Massachusetts, moved the total repeal of the whole restrictive system. The motion was not agreed to ; but when it was renewed the following day in a modified form, rendering the proposition somewhat less sweeping, the casting vote of the Speaker was required to carry the day against the opposition. For two years more the pernicious policy was persisted in.

Calhoun had separated himself on this important question from the majority. He earnestly advocated the repeal of the Non-Importation Act. His obligations as a party man he satisfied by denying that Jefferson's and Madison's policy could be justly charged with pusillanimity, — a compliment the more empty, because the closing remarks of his speech proved that he himself was not convinced of the truth of the assertion. It was a question not of motives, but of policy, and as to that he said : " The restrictive system, as a mode of resistance, and a means of obtaining redress of our wrongs, has never been a favorite one with me." The reasons on which he supported his opinion were sound, and the whole manner in which he treated the subject was that of a statesman standing on sufficiently elevated ground to take in the whole view, and not to be misled by petty details. On the past he bestowed but a slight glance, very properly confining himself to the effect which the maintenance of the old policy would have under the altered circumstances. From this point of view, he condemned it without qualification in measured but severe terms. "With no small mortification," he asked those who had supported the war, and now thought its success dependent upon the continuation of the Non-Importation Act, whether the war was to be "an appendage only" of this act? "If so, I disclaim it. It is an alarming idea to be in a state of war, and not to rely on our courage or energy, but on a measure of peace." The assertion that, if the Non-Importation Act should be continued, a speedy restoration of peace might be relied upon, he declared to be delusive and a cause of alarm, for "it will debilitate the springs of war. . . . We have had a peace like a war. In the name of Heaven, let us not have the only thing that is worse, a war like a peace." This solemn warning was certainly not out of place, but if it was necessary to utter it within a week after the declaration of war, he ought to have pondered well ere he did his best to push tho country into a conflict which, whatever it might become in the course of time, was originally not a national but a party war, or rather a war of the party leaders.

This all-important point had not been soon enough taken into due consideration, either by him or his associates. This is the one great blame resting upon the war party, which even those cannot gainsay who otherwise fully approve of their course. The whole war was one uninterrupted struggle against the evil consequences of this fact. There was much truth in what Calhoun had asserted in his speech on May 6. It was, indeed, to a great extent, the second war for the liberty and independence of the United States, but it was irretrievably vitiated by its party origin. How the ambitious plans of the young leaders were dashed to pieces! Instead of Canada being conquered, the time came when Calhoun, with tears in his eyes, had to ask the assistance of Webster to pull the government out of its financial difficulties, which had come to such a climax that the worst might be apprehended. It was a deep humiliation. Yet where is the American patriot who would wish to erase these pages from the tablets of the history of the Union?   Much less could any one wish to miss them in the career of Calhoun, for in one respect, and that the most important one, they are the most attractive and satisfactory in the record of his life.   There is at this time nothing of sectional prejudice and narrowness in him.   He stands on the broadest national ground, and his political sins are mainly due to the impatient ardor and buoyancy of his patriotism.   Undoubtedly he pursues the aims of his personal ambition with full consciousness; he does not, however, seek its satisfaction at the expense of the Union, but by promoting what he is fully convinced that the interests and the honor of his country demand.   The word " nation," which Calhoun in later years struck from the political and constitutional dictionary of the United States as having no basis whatever to rest upon, either in fact or in law, is at this time frequently in his mouth.   How could it be otherwise, as the idea of it was deeply imbedded in his heart and constantly occupying his mind?   His solicitude for the *national* interests did not cease with the war, nor was it confined to objects immediately connected with the war or referring exclusively to the relations of the Union to foreign powers.

In a speech delivered January 31, 1816, on a motion to repeal the direct tax, he drew a sketch of his views concerning the lessons to be derived from the experiences of the war as to the policy which the United States ought to pursue in future. The starting-point of his argument was the assertion that "future wars with England are not only possible, but . . . highly probable,—nay, that they will certainly take place," because the United States would "have to encounter British jealousy and hostility in every shape; not immediately manifested by open force or violence, perhaps, but by indirect attempts to check your growth and prosperity." He therefore deemed it necessary gradually to prepare for this emergency, not only by increasing the military forces of the Union, but also by systematically developing those germs of giant strength which Providence had bestowed upon and intrusted to the American people. "As to the species of preparation, . . . the navy most certainly, in any point of view, occupies the first place. It is the most safe, most effectual, and cheapest mode of defence." The internal strife during the war would have lost much of its bitterness, if the majority had from the first understood this obvious truth, and acted accordingly. The violation of the rights and interests of the citizens

ɔf the States, as a seafaring people, had given
rise to the war, and yet the demand of the New
England States to wage it principally by sea
had remained unheeded, until experience forced
the majority to acknowledge, if not in words, at
least by deeds, that for once the opposition was
not prompted exclusively by local interests and
a factional spirit.   If the party had listened to
the advice of Calhoun with regard to the wishes
and complaints of the opposition, the animosity
of the Northeastern Federalists would never
have reached the pitch to which it finally came.
In the light of later events, it is one of the most
interesting facts in the life of Calhoun that, in
the course of the war, the question was for a
while seriously discussed in New England
whether the people of that section should not
try to form an alliance with South Carolina
against the narrow anti-commercial policy of
Virginia and her followers.

The above-mentioned speech also contains
the first declaration in favor of internal improvements. " Let us make great permanent
roads ; not, like the Romans, with views of sub
jecting and ruling provinces, but for the more
honorable purposes of defence, and of connect
ing more closely the interests of various sections
of this great country." It is true that Calhoun's immediate object in this is also the

safety of the country in future wars; but he is not only gratified that the building of roads will incidentally tend towards nationalizing the Union; he urges upon Congress the measure *because* it will have this effect. Always starting from the same point, he furthermore comes to the conclusion that the national government should bestow its protecting care upon the industrial interests of the country; and here, too, he expressly states that other reasons also should induce Congress to adopt this policy.

" In regard to the question how far manufactures ought to be fostered, it is the duty of this country, as a means of defence, to encourage its domestic industry, more especially that part of it which provides the necessary materials for clothing and defence. . . . The question relating to manufactures must not depend on the abstract principle that industry, left to pursue its own course, will find in its own interests all the encouragement that is necessary. Laying the claims of manufacturers entirely out of view, on general principles, without regard to their interests, a certain encouragement should be extended at least to our woolen and cotton manufactures."

It is remarkable that in the whole speech there is no mention whatever made of the Constitution. The thought does not enter his head that constitutional objections could possibly be raised. The reason of this is simply

that the statesman has not yet been transformed into the attorney of a special cause.
He proceeds, as a matter of course, from the
assumption that the first question a statesman
has to ask himself is not what is constitutional,
but what is wise and politic, unless it mani-
festly contravenes a provision of the Constitution, and to take it for granted that the constitutional power exists, until the contrary is
proved. As the people have not been created
for the sake of the Constitution, but the Constitution has been established by the people to
secure and further the welfare of the people,
this is the only rational course; and it is perfectly safe, since, as every measure is sure to
meet with some opposition, any constitutional
flaw with regard to the proposition will certainly be pointed out, if it can be discovered
without the aid of a microscope and hair-split-
ting sophistries of pettifogging lawyers. Only
when, instead of the national interests, the interests of the slave-holders had become the
glasses through which Calhoun viewed everything, he began to search the Constitution for
the power to do what he had once recommended
as prudent and even necessary, and then he
discovered things in it which he had never
dreamed of before; nay, its general spirit un
derwent a radical change in his eyes.

On January 8, 1816, Calhoun, as chairman of the Committee on National Currency, reported a bill " to incorporate the subscribers to the Bank of the United States." In a speech which he delivered on February 26, in support of the bill, he referred to the constitutional question, but merely in order to state that it "had been already so freely and frequently discussed, that all had made up their minds on it." So, according to his own statement, he had most deliberately come to the conclusion that Congress had the constitutional power to establish a national bank. Though this has necessarily to be inferred from the fact of his reporting the bill, it had to be expressly stated on account of his subsequent attempts to make himself and others believe that he had been compelled by the financial embarrassments of the government to waive the constitutional question. That these embarrassments exercised a powerful influence upon the formation of his opinions cannot be doubted, but even in regard to the expediency of the measure he was not solely controlled by them. "As to the question vhether a national bank would be favorable to tJe administration of the finances of the government, it was one on which there was so little doubt, that gentlemen would excuse him f he did not enter into it." He does not say

"now," or, "under the present circumstances,"
but makes a general statement without any re-
striction whatever. There is nothing astonish
ing in this, for the additional strength which it
was supposed that the national government
would derive from the bank was at this time
no cause of alarm to him; and as to the other
political and economical considerations involved
in the problem, he moved as yet in as thick a
fog as the whole people. The fact is, that with
regard to all the great economical problems,
which were soon to agitate the country so
deeply, Calhoun held exactly the opposite
ground to that which he afterwards occupied,
on the constitutional question as well as on that
of expediency. He and his partisans have done
their very best to invalidate the charge of inconsistency, but they have not been able to
succeed; for although an edition of his speeches
was published in which those earlier efforts
were omitted, the speeches themselves could
not be wiped from the records of Congress,
and, as was his wont, he had expressed himself too plainly and explicitly to render the art
of subsequent interpretation of any avail. One
would greatly wrong him by doubting whether
he was afterwards as sincere as now, but his
sincerity does not alter the fact that he completely reversed his position. His partisans

have paid him a bad compliment by asserting that his earlier utterances cannot with fairness be called upon to bear witness against his later doctrines, because they were but his first impressions, put before the public without due deliberation, in an unguarded manner, on the spur of some particular occasion. Had the House of Representatives sunk to such a bottomless depth that it followed the leadership of a young zealot who did not know how to bridle his tongue, but on the gravest questions of the day babbled out the first thoughts that happened to flit through his giddy brain? What, then, were the subjects which this chairman of most important committees seriously reflected upon, if not these, almost the only ones on which he deemed it worth his while to make long speeches? Moreover, this unpardonable levity and thoughtlessness must have lasted a long while, for he clung to these opinions for years, frequently repeating them and urging them upon Congress with increased energy.

His speech on the New Tariff Bill (April 6, 1816) was a long and carefully prepared argument in favor of the whole economical platform on which the Whig party stood to the last day of its existence. He started with the bold proposition that it was a matter of " vital impor tance, touching . . . the security and permanent prosperity of our country," to afford adequate protection to the cotton and woollen manufactures. Even Henry Clay and Horace Greeley have not been able to put their favorite doctrine into stronger language. Nor was he satisfied to have the fostering care of the government confined to these goods. His final aim was the industrial independence of the United States from Europe, and this, he thought, could be attained by protective duties. He bitterly complained of the unexpected "apathy and aversion" which manifested themselves on this subject. In his opinion the country was "prepared, even to maturity, for the introduction of manufactures." If he deemed it nevertheless necessary to assist them with protective duties, it was in order "to put them beyond the reach of contingency." There is not one word in the whole speech warranting the interpretation that he demands only momentary aid for the manufactures, which had been stimulated into existence by the war, and would now inevitably have to succumb to English competition, if they should not be propped up by artificial means. He advocated a " system," to which the only well-founded but not "decisive objection " was, "that capital employed in manufacturing produced a greater dependence on the part of the employed

than in commerce, navigation, or agriculture."
Though this was to be regretted, it was "more
than counterpoised" by other "incidental political advantages."

"It produced an interest strictly American, — as
much so as agriculture, in which it had the decided
advantage of commerce or navigation. . . . Again, it
is calculated to bind together more closely our widely-
spread republic. It will greatly increase our mutual
dependence and intercourse ; and will, as a necessary
consequence, excite an increased attention to internal improvements, a subject every way so inti-
mately connected with the ultimate attainment of
national strength and the perfection of our political
institutions."

He regarded the fact that it would "make
the parts adhere more closely ; that it would
form a new and most powerful cement, and out-
weigh any political objections that might be
urged against the system."

In a speech on February 4, 1817, on a bill to
set aside the bank dividends and bonus as a
permanent fund for the construction of roads
and canals, Calhoun, for the first time, entered
upon an extended argument on the constitutional question with regard to internal improvements. The objection that it is necessary to
secure the previous assent of the States, within
the limits of which the internal improvements

are to be made, he declared to be not " worth
the discussion, because the good sense of the
States may be relied on.   They will, in all
cases, readily yield their assent."   Also as to
the power of Congress he is so explicit that,
when he afterwards positively denied it, his
opponents need not have troubled themselves
about an argument of their own ; so far as he
was concerned it would have sufficed to read
some extracts from this speech : —

" It is mainly urged that the Congress can only apply the public money in execution of the enumerated
powers.   I am no advocate for refined arguments on
the Constitution.   The instrument was not intended
as a thesis for the logician to exercise his ingenuity on.
[If he had but followed the example of the Persian
king, and charged his body servant to repeat to him
these two sentences every morning!]   It ought to
be construed with plain good sense ; and what can
be more express than the Constitution on this point?
. . . If the framers had intended to limit the use of
the money to the powers afterwards enumerated and
defined, nothing could have been more easy than to
have expressed it plainly. . . . But suppose the Constitution to be silent, why should we be confined in
the application of moneys to the enumerated powers?
There is nothing in the reason of the thing, that I
can perceive, why it should be so restricted ; and the
habitual and uniform practice of the government
coincides with my opinion. .   . In reply to this uni

form course of legislation, I expect it will be said that our Constitution is founded on positive and written principles, and not on precedents. I do not deny the position; but I have introduced these instances to prove the uniform sense of Congress and the country (for they have not been objected to) as to our powers; and surely they furnish better evidence of the true interpretation of the Constitution than the most refined and subtle arguments. Let it not be argued that the construction for which I contend gives a dangerous extent to the powers of Congress. In this point of view I conceive it to be more safe than the opposite.. By giving a reasonable extent to the money power, it exempts us from the necessity of giving a strained and forced construction to the other enumerated powers."

Thus he was not only the champion of the constitutionality of internal improvements, but he boldly avowed latitudinarian principles with regard to the general construction of the Constitution. It was a rather remarkable coincidence that this was the last great speech which he delivered as a member of the House of Representatives. He was called to act on another stage, where less, or no, opportunity was offered to develop his views on these subjects before the whole people, but there is no proof lacking that he adhered to them for some time longer.

CHAPTER III.

SECRETARY OF WAR.

ALTHOUGH Calhoun, in a speech delivered on January 17, 1817, had deprecated the feeling which made " the very best talents of the House, men of the most aspiring character, anxious to fill the departments or foreign missions," he himself, less than two months afterwards, readily accepted a place in Mr. Monroe's cabinet as Secretary of War. The duties of his office stood in no direct relation to the economical policy of the federal government, but, as he was anxious to see his views adopted, he had no difficulty in laying them again before Congress. A resolution of the House of Representatives, of April 4, 1818, had called on him for " a plan for the application of such means as are within the power of Congress, for the purpose of opening and constructing such roads and canals as may deserve and require the aid of government, with a view to military operations in time of war." His report o' January 14, 1819, began by laying down the sound and broad principle that,

"a judicious system of roads and canals, constructed for the convenience of commerce and the
transportation of the mail only, without any reference to military operations, is itself among the most
efficient means for ' the more complete defence of the
United States.' Without adverting to the fact that
the roads and canals which such a system would require are, with few exceptions, precisely those which
would be required for the operation of war, such a
system, by consolidating our Union [!], and increasing our wealth and fiscal capacity, would add greatly
to our resources in war."

He then traced in general outlines a vast
plan of roads and canals, concluding his argument with the following significant remarks:—

" Many of the roads and canals which have been
suggested are no doubt of the first importance to the
commerce, the manufactures, the agriculture, and political prosperity of the country, but are not, for that
reason, less useful or necessary for military purposes.
It is, in fact, one of the great advantages of our
country, enjoying so many others, that whether we
regard its internal improvements in relation to military, civil, or political purposes, very nearly the same
system, in all its parts, is required. . . . If those
roads or canals had been pointed out which are necessary for military purposes, the list would have been
small indeed."

In a report of December 3, 1824, " on the
condition of the military establishment," etc.,

he recurred once more to the subject with the same explicitness and emphasis. There is therefore no reason to suppose Mr. Nathan Sargent guilty of exaggeration, when he writes that in June, 1824, " Mr. Calhoun spoke of his projected improvements and the great benefits that the country would derive from them with a warmth, earnestness, and enthusiasm which indicated that his whole soul was in ' the system ' he had projected." After he had exchanged the Secretaryship of War for the Vice-Presidency, at a public dinner given in his honor in the Pendleton District on April 26, 1825, the following toast was received with great enthusiasm : " Internal improvement : guided by the wisdom and energy of its able advocates, it cannot fail to strengthen and perpetuate our bond of union." Again, on May 27, 1825, at Abbeville, on a similar occasion, he himself said, " I gave my zealous efforts to all such measures : . . . a due protection of those manufactures of the country which had taken root during the period of war and restrictions ; and finally, a system of connecting the various portions of the country by a judicious system of internal improvement." With the approval of South Carolina, he still pointed with satisfaction and pride to his agency in promoting what she and he were soon so decisively to con

lemn as impolitic, unjust, dangerous to the independence of the States, and unconstitutional.

In later years, Calhoun would have given
much if he could have torn these leaves from
his book of record as a Representative and as
Secretary of War. Else these were the bright-
est and happiest years of his public life, though
the first premonitory gusts of the storms which
were to rage through all the rest of it began
while he held the latter office. Many of his
friends and admirers had with regret seen him
abandon his seat in the legislative hall for a
place in the President's council. They apprehended that he would, to a great extent, lose
the renown which he had gained as a member
of Congress, for they thought that the dialectic
turn of his mind rendered him unfit to become
a successful administrator. He undeceived
them in a manner which astonished even those
who had not shared these apprehensions. The
Department of War was in a state of really
astounding confusion when he assumed the
charge of it. Into this chaos he soon brought
order, and the whole service of the department
received an organization so simple and at the
same time so efficient that it has, in the main,
been adhered to by all his successors, and proved
itself capable of standing even the test of the
civil war. Niles's "Register" said on March
27, 1824 : —

"Judging from the various reports that all of us have seen from the War Department, the order and harmony, regularity and promptitude, punctuality and responsibility, introduced by Mr. Calhoun in every branch of the service, have never been rivalled, and perhaps cannot be excelled; and it must be recollected that he brought this system out of chaos. Never was the business of any department in such a state of *perfect confusion* as that now under his charge at the time when he was placed at the head of it. The open or unsettled accounts, of all sorts, must have amounted to nearly fifty millions of dollars. How great was the labor to cleanse this Augean stable! But, mightily supported by the acute and indefatigable Mr. Hagner, the old and filthy accounts are nearly disposed of."

Calhoun himself said, with just pride, in a report to the President, "The result has been that, of the *entire amount* of money drawn from the Treasury in the year 1822 for the military service, including the pensions, amounting to $4,571,961.94, although it passed through the hands of no less than two hundred and ninety-one disbursing agents, there has not been a single defalcation, nor the loss of a cent to the government." And the principal employees of the department, in taking leave of him in a short address (February 28, 1825), bore the following testimony to his administration

" The degree of perfection to which you have carried the several branches of this department is believed to be without parallel. . . . From these (your personal character and private virtues) have proceeded the harmonious interchanges which have made the burden of details with which the undersigned are charged comparatively light."

Neither, on the other hand, were severe criticisms lacking. John Quincy Adams writes in his Diary : —

" The truth is that of the reforms in the War Department while he [Calhoun] was at its head, the most important was the reduction of the army from ten thousand men to six thousand men, utterly against his will, against all the influence that he could exercise, and to his entire disapprobation ; and all the other changes of organization were upon plans furnished by Generals Brown and Scott, and carried through Congress chiefly by the agency of John Williams, of Tennessee. Mr. Calhoun had no more share of mind in them than I have in the acts of Congress to which I affix my signature of approbation."

Even the most thorough examination of the records of the War Department would probably not clearly show whether and how far the latter assertion is true. For argument's sake, however, it may be granted that it is true to the letter. Would that really deprive Calhoun of

all merit in the reforms? Is it not one of the
most indispensable qualities of a statesman to
know where to go for advice, and to follow wise
counsels?

Others were not satisfied with denying that
the reforms were due to the initiative of the
Secretary. We read in the same Diary, under
date of June 2, 1822, that General D. Parker
said to the writer, "The management of the
War Department had been inefficient and extravagant, which was very susceptible of demonstration." The reproach of extravagance was
not wholly without apparent foundation. Calhoun very properly considered himself in duty
bound to advocate and promote the interests
of the army in every way not incompatible
with the true interests of the United States,
and as to these he, with equal propriety, refused
to accept the amount of money to be spent as
constituting the principal consideration. The
best is the cheapest, though the first outlay is
larger. In private life this maxim is nowhere
better and more commonly understood than by
the people generally in the United States. The
American politicians, however, partly for demagogical purposes and partly from honest stupid-
ity, up to this day but too frequently consider
it an absurdity, though they are in other respects lavish to the verge of criminality with

the public money. Calhoun fully understood that with regard to great public interests the miser's policy is the worst extravagance. It was, perhaps, not quite so certain as Adams thought, that the reduction of the army was really a "reform," and the Secretary undoubtedly deserved much praise for taking a decided stand against those who wanted to screw down the rations and the wages of the privates, and to some extent even those of the officers, to the lowest possible point.

As to "abuses" in other respects, it is too much to say that Calhoun is absolutely blameless. In one important instance he has laid himself open to the charge of unfair dealing in the negotiation and conclusion of a treaty with an Indian tribe. Upon the whole, however, he advocated a policy towards these wards of the nation, which it would have been well for all the parties concerned to adopt and pursue with undeviating honesty. Even in our days his Indian reports might be profitably studied with regard as well to the cardinal mistakes committed in the Indian policy as to what ought to be done. To those who try to lift the responsibility for the hapless fate of the Indians from the shoulders of the American people, and allege a decree of Providence, the following testimony of Calhoun will be unsavory reading: —

" As far, however, as civilization may depend on education only, without taking into consideration the force of circumstances, it would seem that there is no insuperable difficulty in effecting the benevolent in tention of the government. It may be affirmed, almost without qualification, that all the tribes within our settlements and near our borders are even solicitous for the education of their children. With the exception of the Creeks, they have everywhere freely and cheerfully assented to the establishment of schools, to which, in some instances, they have contributed. The Choctaws, in this respect, have evinced the most liberal spirit, having set aside $6,000 of their amnesty in aid of the schools established among them. The reports of the teachers are almost uniformly favorable, both as to the capacity and docility of their youths. Their progress appears to be quite equal to that of white children of the same age, and they appear to be equally susceptible of acquiring habits of industry. At some of the establishments a considerable portion of the supplies are raised by the labor of the scholars and the teachers. With these indications, it would seem that there is little hazard in pronouncing that, with proper and vigorous efforts, they may receive an education equal to that of the laboring portion of our community."

Whether his theorizing propensities had anything to do with his taking such a favorable view of the capability and the desire of the Indians to raise themselves out of the darkness

and sloth of their savage state need not here
be inquired into. In judging this question Calhoun was, at all events, a sufficiently matter-of-
fact man to see that, in spite of this supposed
natural capability for becoming civilized, their
actual civilization was impossible so long as the
leading principle of the Indian policy hitherto
pursued was not abandoned :—

" The political relation which they bear to us is by
itself of sufficient magnitude, if not removed, to prevent so desirable a state from being attained. We
have always treated them as an independent people;
and however insignificant a tribe may become, and
however surrounded by a dense white population, so
long as there are any remains it continues independent of our laws and authority. To tribes thus surrounded, nothing can be conceived more opposed to
their happiness and civilization than this state of
nominal independence. It has not one of the advantages of real independence, while it has nearly all
the disadvantages of a state of complete subjugation.
The consequence is inevitable. They lose the lofty
spirit and heroic courage of the savage state, without
acquiring the virtues which belong to the civilized.
Depressed in spirit and debauched in morals, they
dwindle away through a wretched existence, a nui-
sance to the surrounding country. Unless some sys-
em can be devised gradually to change this relation,
and with the progress of education to extend over
them our laws and authority, it is feared that all of

forts to civilize them, whatever flattering appearances
they may for a time exhibit, must ultimately fail.
Tribe after tribe will sink, with the progress of our
settlements and the pressure of our population, into
wretchedness and oblivion. Such has been their past
history, and such, without this change of political relation, it must probably continue to be."

Who would to-day venture to deny that the
main error of the Americans in dealing with
the Indian problem is here pointed out with
the utmost clearness, and that subsequent history has fully borne out these assertions ? With
the same keen-sightedness with which Calhoun
discerned the causes of the evil, he also found
the means for its gradual cure : —

" Preparatory to so radical a change in our relation
towards them, the system of education which has been
adopted ought to be put into extensive and active
operation. This is the foundation of all other improvements [?]. It ought gradually to be followed
with a plain and simple system of laws and government, such as has been adopted by the Cherokees, a
proper compression of their settlements, and a division
of landed property. By introducing gradually and
judiciously these improvements, they will ultimately
attain such a state of intelligence, industry, and civilization as to prepare the way for a complete extension of our laws and authority over them."

It is not probable that Mr. Schurz has eve

read this long-forgotten report, but whoever has been acquainted with it, and has also paid some attention to the Indian policy of Mr. Hayes's Secretary of the Interior, must have been struck by the coincidence of the views of South Carolina's great doctrinarian and of the modern "theorist," who, sixty years later, has dealt more successfully with the Indian problem than perhaps any other man.

Of the other charges brought against the management of the War Department, but one more need be mentioned, and this one because it had a long history and made considerable noise at the time. We allude to the so-called Rip-Rap contract. A government contract for the delivery of a large quantity of stones at Old Point Comfort had been awarded to a certain Elijah Mix, a man of ruined commercial reputation. Calhoun was not aware of this fact concerning Mix, and he was satisfied that the conditions agreed upon were as favorable for the government as any that could be obtained at the time; but he had awarded the contract without publicly advertising it, as the law required. This fact became known when Mix failed to fulfil his obligations, and the House of Representatives prohibited any further disbursements from the appropriation made for this purpose. This untoward occurrence was

the more annoying because the chief clerk of
the department, a brother-in-law of Mix, had,
with the knowledge of the Secretary, afterwards
bought a part of the contract. Calhoun had not
approved of his doing so, warning him that he
would expose himself to disagreeable insinua-
tions; but neither, on the other hand, had he
forbidden it, since it was not "illegal." After
Calhoun had become Vice-President, this story
was revived by an application from Mix for another government contract. Although his bid
was the lowest, it was refused, because the history of the Rip-Rap contract proved him to be
an irresponsible person. In the course of these
transactions a private letter from Mix, in which
he charged Calhoun with having received a
share of the profits of the Rip-Rap job, found
its way into the press. Calhoun thereupon
(September 29, 1826) addressed a letter to the
House of Representatives, "claiming investigation by the House" "in its high character of
grand inquest of the nation," at the same time
announcing to the Senate that he would not preside over its deliberations until the vile calumny
had been duly disposed of, — two steps of doubtful propriety, and if not unconstitutional, at all
events extra-constitutional. The House of Representatives might easily find itself left with no
time at all for transacting its legitimate busi

ness, if it could be required to grant the claim of every government official of a certain rank for an investigation of charges privately[1] preferred by any private individual; and it would be strange indeed if a United States official had the right to refuse to attend to his constitutional duties, because somebody had been pleased to calumniate him. If the Vice-President might do so why not the President, the Justices of the Supreme Court, the President *pro tempore* of the Senate, the Speaker of the House,—nay, any member of Congress? Neither of these objections was entirely overlooked at the time, but the House nevertheless appointed a committee of investigation. Calhoun was far from being satisfied with its proceedings, although the report declared, "They are unanimously of the opinion that there are no facts which will authorize the belief, or even suspicion, that the Vice-President was ever interested, or that he participated, directly or indirectly, in the profits of any contract formed with the government through the Department of War."

No decent person had ever doubted that such was the case. The whole scandal was an empty

---

[1] Calhoun's assertion that the accusation had been accorded place in the official records of the Department of War was proved to be wholly unfounded.

bubble, but, like every scandal, it was filled with mal-odorous gases. Calhoun would have done well to treat it with silent contempt, instead of pricking it, for neither in Congress nor out of it was there a lack of persons who willingly used against him everything which they could lay their hands on, and the old truth *semper aliquid hæret* applied to him as well as to any other person. In spite of the praise bestowed upon his administration of the War Department by all impartial men, many members of Congress selected just this department as the principal butt of their ill-humor. John Quincy Adams writes on June 2, 1822, " The President had enough to do to support the Secretary of War. He had already brought himself into collision with both Houses of Congress by supporting him." Though these animadversions were, in the opinion of Adams, not wholly unfounded, yet he was far from thinking them quite justified. This latter fact is the more to be noticed, because Adams cannot be considered an entirely unprejudiced witness, though the stern old man was certainly most honestly convinced that he judged his colleague with the strictest impartiality and justice.

Adams leaves us in no doubt about the true cause of these attacks upon Calhoun : —

" There was a time during the last session of Con

gress when so large a proportion of members was enlisted for Calhoun that they had it in contemplation to hold a caucus formally to declare him a candidate [for the presidency]. But this prospect of success roused all Crawford's and Clay's partisans against him. The administration of his department was scrutinized with severity, sharpened by personal animosity and factious malice. Some abuses were discovered, and exposed with aggravations. Cavils were made against measures of that department in the execution of the laws, and brought the President in collision with both Houses of Congress. Crawford's newspapers commenced and have kept up a course of the most violent abuse and ribaldry against him."

The presidency was at the bottom of these acrimonious bickerings, and though Adams would never have committed the slightest conscious wrong in order to secure this prize, yet he coveted it too ardently to be favorably disposed toward a prominent rival.

The estrangement between Adams and Calhoun cannot be ascribed solely to this reason, but nobody who has the least knowledge of human nature will doubt that this must have had a great deal to do with it. When the two statesmen came into such close official relation by becoming members of Mr. Monroe's cabinet, Adams must be considered, if we take his usual austerity and chilliness into due consideration, to have spoken almost enthusiastically of his younger colleague. On January 6, 1818, he says, " Calhoun thinks for himself, independently of all the rest [namely, the other members of the cabinet], with sound judgment, quick discrimination, and keen observation. He supports his opinions, too, with powerful eloquence." For several years this good opinion grows ever stronger : —

" **Mr.** Calhoun is a man of fair and candid mind, of honorable principles, of clear and quick understanding, of cool self-possession, of enlarged philo· sophical views, and of ardent patriotism. He is above all sectional and factious prejudices more than any other ʀtatesman of this Union with whom I have ever acted. He is more sensitive to the transient manifestations of momentary public opinion, more afraid of the first impressions of the public opinion, than I am."

Thus Adams wrote on October 15, 1821; and again, only twenty-five months later, he says, " Calhoun, who in all his movements of every kind has an eye to himself; " and on the 2d of April, 1824, " Precedent and popularity, — this is the bent of his mind. The primary principles involved in any public question are the last to occur to him. What *has been done* and what *will be said* are the **Jachin** and Boaz of his argument." As Adams did not accuse Calhoun of any special dishonorable act, this change of opinion is certainly so great that the explanation for it must be partly sought in the last sentence of the following entry in his Diary (September 5, 1831): —

"Mr. Calhoun was a member of Mr. Monroe's administration, and during its early part pursued a course from which I anticipated that he would prove an ornament and a blessing to his country. I have been deeply disappointed in him, and now expect nothing from him but evil. His personal relations with me have been marked, on his part, with selfish and cold-blooded heartlessness."

It is well known how much inclined Adams was to charge with ingratitude and base intrigues those with whom his political life had brought him into close personal contact; and furthermore, that the real experiences which he actually encountered in this respect were bad enough to sour a less distrustful and sweeter temper than his. Calhoun, too, he did not blame without reason, and, so far as our present sources allow us to judge, by far the larger part of the responsibility for the unkind feeling between the two rested upon the Carolinian. Adams's well-founded complaints against Calhoun, however, chiefly arose after the presidential contest had been decided for this time. Calhoun professed to think that Monroe should

be succeeded by a Northern man, and declared
that, if such should be the case, his first choice
would be Adams. If he, nevertheless, vigor-
ously pushed his own candidacy, it was, as he
asserted, because he thought that of all the
prominent candidates Mr. Crawford, of Georgia,
had the best chance, and him he would oppose
to the utmost extent of his power, because he
not only had no high opinion of his talents, but
could not respect him as a man. So far as
Calhoun was concerned, the war was, indeed,
principally waged between his partisans and
those of Crawford. "As Calhoun stands most
in his [Crawford's] way," says Adams's Diary on May 2, 1822, " the great burden of his
exertions this session and the last has been
against the War Department; while Calhoun,
by his haste to get at the presidency, has made
a cabal in his favor in Congress to counteract
Crawford's cabal, and the session has been little
more than a violent struggle between them;
both, however, countenancing the insidious attacks upon the Secretary of State."

Calhoun was thrown in this tussle with his
crafty colleague of the Treasury. The same
authority, which is unimpeachable on this question, says, Calhoun's "projected nomination
for the presidency has met with hardly any
countenance throughout the Union. The prin

cipal effect of it has been to bring out Crawford's strength, and thus to promote the interest
of the very man whom alone he professes to oppose. Calhoun now feels his weakness, but is
not cured of his ambition." Crawford, however, was to be still more disappointed than
Calhoun, and so far as the struggle between
these two is concerned it was the former infinitely more than the latter who could, with justice, be accused of double-dealing and an unfair
underground warfare. Yet no sincere friend of
Calhoun can look quite undismayed upon this
chapter of his public life. The presidential
fever, that typical disease which has proved
fatal to the true glory of so many statesmen of
the United States, permeated the very marrow
of his bones. His ambition did not betray
him into any dishonorable act, but his eye became dimmed with regard to the public weal,
because, consciously or unconsciously, the fatal
consideration, what effect his course would
have upon his standing as a candidate, entered
more or less into every question. His blind
admirers, if there still be any left, will, of
course, not admit the truth of this assertion,
and will claim that to him, too, the celebrated
saying of Henry Clay applies, that he would
rather be right than be President. The cool,
unbiassed student will, indeed, probably come to

the conclusion that there was not much difference between the two in this respect; but if
there were nothing else to sustain the charge
against Calhoun, it would be sufficiently proved
by the influence which he allowed his presidential aspirations to exercise upon his personal relations. The lofty independence of mind and
truly chivalric spirit, which were his real nature, appear blunted. He stoops to cover with
an approving and admiring smile a resentment
which is lurking in a corner of his heart, and on
the other side to break off all social intercourse
with old and highly respected associates, merely
because others, whose good services he wishes
to secure, might not like these connections.
The champion of slavery, who, with head erect,
flashing eye, and the deep-toned voice of solemn
conviction and apostolic infallibility, dares the
whole civilized world, is every inch a *man*,
though a sadly mistaken one; but the politician, who is craving with thirst for the presidency, is like Ulysses before the suitors, still
a hero, but with the beggar's rags of human
frailty and weakness covering the " divine "
shoulders.

Calhoun's hopes rested mainly on his popu
larity in Pennsylvania, the grateful affection
of the army, and the admiration of the young
men. With them his comparative youth was

an additional claim on their support; for it was
or account of his age that his career seemed to
shine with uncommon lustre. With his elders,
however, this was one of the principal objec- .
tions against his being already put at the head
of the nation. Joseph Story wrote, on September 21, 1823, to the Hon. Ezekiel Bacon, " I
have great admiration for Mr. Calhoun, and
think few men have more enlarged and liberal
views of the true policy of the national government. But his age, or rather his youth, at the
present moment, is a formidable objection to
his elevation to the chair." But even if he had
stood in the beginning of the sixth instead of
the fifth decade of his life, his wishes would
probably not have been gratified. The whole
movement in his favor was premature, and had,
at this time, something artificial in it. There
was, after all, nothing in his career to stir up
a general enthusiasm, by means of which he
might have ridden on the crest of a great popular wave over the heads of all his competitors
into the White House. The mass of the people were in a sober mood, verging upon indifference. The election, therefore, turned much
'ess upon principles or great questions of policy
than upon personal predilections ; and this
being the case, it soon became evident tha'
Calhoun had no chance whatever. Even in

Pennsylvania, where he owed his popularity partly to the vigor with which, in 1816, he had advocated a protective tariff, he was dropped. The Harrisburg convention nominated Jackson, but gave to Calhoun the second place on the ticket as candidate for the vice-presidency. This was a solution of the question with which he could be well satisfied. If he had been from the first the weakest candidate for the presidency, he was undoubtedly the strongest for the vice-presidency; and as he had already been spoken of for the first place, his election to the second would, in the eyes of many people, give him a kind of equitable claim to be, in due time, elevated " to the chair." Niles's "Register" of November 6, 1824, said, "He is the only candidate in whose favor the *people* have moved, and the voice of the people should always be respected." Adams had already, in the preceding February, spoken of the " courtship of the New England Federalists by Mr. Calhoun," and of " the newspapers set up in Massachusetts to support Mr. Calhoun." Webster wrote to his brother Ezekiel, on March 14 of the same year, " I hope all New England will support Mr. Calhoun for the vice-presidency. If so, he will probably be chosen, and that will be a great thing. He is a true man, and will do good to the country in that situa tion." Webster's hopes were not disappointed. The Jackson and the Adams parties united on Calhoun. He received 182 of the 261 electoral votes, and among these were all the New England votes, with the exception of those from Connecticut and one from New Hampshire.

CHAPTER IV.

VICE-PRESIDENT.

As the presidential election turned out, the combination vote by which he had been chosen put Calhoun into an annoying and very embarrassing position with a view to his own presidential aspirations. Although Jackson had received a plurality of the electoral votes, Adams was elected by the House of Representatives. That the House was perfectly justified in doing this, not only by the letter, but also by the spirit of the Constitution, no person can deny who is possessed of common sense and is willing to use it. Article XII., section 1, of the Constitution would be an absurdity if the House were morally obliged to choose the person upon whom a plurality of the votes had been bestowed. Besides, to whom would the preference have to be accorded, if the person receiving the plurality of the electoral votes had not also received a plurality of the popular votes? The Jackson partisans, however, were determined to seal their ears and eyes hermetically against every suggestion of reason. They declared Adams's elec

tion to be an outrage, a rebellion of the ser-
vants against the masters, for no matter what
the Constitution said and required, the "*dcmos
krateo* principle," as Senator Benton expressed
it, with a somewhat sorry display of his knowledge of Greek, had been trampled under foot.
The nomination of Henry Clay, whose influence had given the decision in favor of Adams,
for Secretary of State filled the cup of their
wrath to overflowing. The cry of "bargain"
was raised, and though it was proved over and
over again to be a base calumny, it did not completely die out until long after Adams and Clay
were resting in their graves.

So the two camps, to whose union in his behalf Calhoun owed his elevation, stood arrayed
in deadly conflict against each other. To remain neutral between them was to put himself
between anvil and hammer. But with which
party was he to side? Justice pleaded for
Adams, ambition spoke eloquently for Jackson.
Can there be any doubt that this keenest logician, who had never been and never became a
fanatic of the "*demos krateo* principle" as it
was now understood by the Jackson party, took
a correct view of the constitutional question?
In 1837, in the debate on the bill for the admission of Michigan as a State into the Union, he
very emphatically reproved his adversaries for

an argument, according to which " the authority of numbers sets aside the authority of the
law and the Constitution."   And he added,
" Need I show that such a principle goes to the
entire overthrow of our constitutional government, and would subvert all social order?"
But from the beginning it was evident that the
majority of the people would declare for Jackson.   To support Adams was therefore to postpone to a remote future, if not to renounce altogether, the realization of his wishes.

The temptation proved too strong for Calhoun.   It is possible, and perhaps not unlikely,
that Adams judged him too harshly in attrib-
uting everything he did and left undone to
the wish of undermining the administration.
Thus, for instance, it seems hardly probable
that the reason for Calhoun's celebrated decision, which denied the right of the Vice-Pres-
'dent to call a Senator to order, was really, as
Adams believed, only unwillingness to check
Randolph's violent abuse of the administration.   There was more than enough of the doctrinarian in him to render it likely that he
honestly thought this power would be, or at
least could lead to, an abridgment of the liberty
of speech.   This much, however, is certain.
that the Vice-President was far from anxious
to sustain the political credit of the President

nay, though he knew how to maintain the decorum of his office, he was in fact one of the leaders of the opposition. Mr. Nathan Sargent relates that Calhoun had said to him in December, 1825, or January, 1826, " Such was the manner in which it [Adams's administration] came into power that *it must be defeated at all hazards, regardless of its measures.*" Charity bids us assume that he deceived himself at the time; but when, instead of ardent desire, bitter disappointment became his constant companion, whispering its suggestions into his ear, the man and the statesman would have been ashamed to have this sentiment recalled to his memory.

For a while it seemed as if Calhoun had not been betrayed by his ambition into a miscalculation. In the presidential election of 1828, Jackson carried everything before him, and Calhoun was reëlected Vice-President by 171 electoral votes. As it was understood that Jackson did not intend to be a candidate for reëlection, Calhoun was apparently more likely than ever to reach the goal of the White House But in fact, so far as this wish was concerned, his star had already passed its zenith. The personal relation between Jackson and Cal houn was no longer what it was supposed to be. On the surface the waters were still perfectly smooth, but .in the hidden deep they were agitated to a degree boding no good to either Calhoun or the country. In the formation of his cabinet Jackson had recognized the claims of Calhoun to his consideration by inviting Mr. Branch, of North Carolina, Mr. Berrien, of Georgia, and Mr. Ingham, of Pennsylvania, to seats in it. Calhoun, however, thought himself not well treated, because — with the exception, perhaps, of Ingham — these were not the men he had wished to see in the council of the President, though they were reputed to be his fast friends. Yet this was not a cause of the breach which was soon to occur between the two men, but merely a symptom of a certain coolness and an incipient mutual distrust, antedating the inauguration of Jackson, and originating in the leading political question of the day.

In 1824 the tariff question had deeply agitated the whole country. The protectionists had carried the day, but only by a slender majority, and the opposition, especially in the plantation States, had assumed a threatening aspect. Not only the expediency and justice of a protective tariff was violently contested, but also its constitutionality was most strenuously denied. The excitement reached such a height that the "Southron" and the Columbia "Telescope' advised the calling of a congress of the opposition States.

Calhoun did not approve of the passionate way in which the question was treated. Yet in the summer of 1825 he declared at a dinner given in his honor at Augusta, Georgia, that " No one would reprobate more pointedly than myself any concerted union between States for interested or sectional objects. I would consider all such concert as against the spirit of our Constitution." The national tendencies still prevailed with him, and, as has been proved before, he had not yet forsworn the economical tenets which he had so zealously defended for years. His faith in them had, however, begun to be strongly shaken, and after he had once entered upon their reëxamination he felt compelled to become their most irreconcilable enemy.

It was no whim or " gray theory " which caused the steadily progressing consolidation of the Southern States with regard to the economical questions. Slavery, in consequence of the enormous development of the cotton culture, had become the determining principle of the whole political, economical, and social life of the Southern States, and a protective tariff was absolutely incompatible with the interests of the slave-holders. Indolence and a certain slovenliness pervaded the whole life of the South, because some kinds of honest labor — all that the

South was pleased to call " menial services "—
were dishonored by slavery; and thereby all
work, except the " living by one's wits," had
come to be looked upon more or less as a dire
necessity, instead of the blissful destiny of man.
No white man could ever lose " caste." No
matter how lazy, poor, ignorant, and depraved
he might be, yet, by virtue of the color of his
skin, he was a born member of the aristocracy,
and absolutely nothing could deprive him of
his place in it; for the gulf which separated the
whites from the negroes could no more be
bridged over than that between heaven and hell.
As the human mind is constituted, no more
powerful incentive could be offered to the mass
of the population to sink deeper into nerveless
shiftlessness. The middle classes are the back-
bone of every civilized community, and slavery
prevented the formation of a well-to-do, intellectual, and progressive middle class more effectually than any express law could have done.
To work one's way up from the lower *strata* of
society into the real aristocracy of the great
land-owners, that is the great slave-holders, was
an enterprise beset with almost insuperable
difficulties, and the spirit of the community
did not encourage the undertaking of the arduous task. The greater the difference between
this real aristocracy and the bulk of the white

population actually was in every respect, the more the former was forced to affect absolute equality with the lowliest of their fellow-citizens. These had to be persuaded that their interests were identical with those of the rich planters ; and, as they had in fact more to suffer from the effects of slavery than the slaves themselves, this could only be accomplished by systematically instilling into them a dull self-conceit and suicidal arrogance, which mistook shreds and tatters for purple and ermine. They looked down upon every other form of civilization with an air of contemptuous superiority, which would have been exceedingly ludicrous, if it had not been infinitely sad. That was an education rendering those who were cursed with it eminently fit to listen to political discussions, and to retail the pretentious and vain political wisdom that had been showered upon them from the stump, in their idle neighborly chats, but making them bad farmers, while unfitting them for everything but farming. The population could never become dense, for the slave, who had to work without the spur of self-interest, tilled the soil, in spite of all overseers and whips, in a manner which, instead of improving it, exhausted it in the shortest possible time. Those who did the work could afford utterly to dispense with thinking, and the one head of the master could not supply this want, nor did he, in most cases, even try to do so. More and more it became the rule that the planter lived on credit, eating up his crop before it had been harvested; and if he was rich enough to grow richer, the surplus was almost invariably invested in more land and slaves. What did it matter if the rich soil was speedily turned into a barren waste! There were boundless tracts of land of still richer soil left for him to go to, with his " hands."

In a community thus constituted there is little need of artisans, and still less of efficient and skilful ones. " The upper ten thousand " had the means to supply their wants from any distance; with the mass of the people neither the means nor the wishes extended much beyond the necessaries of life; and, finally, the claims of the slaves upon life were confined to a hut, coarse raiment, coarse food, and the coarsest agricultural implements. The artisan, however, is the necessary precursor of the manufacturer. Where the standard of civilization is too low to require a numerous class of laborers skilled in all sorts of handiwork, manufacturing on a large scale is as impossible as the putting up of the roof before the building of the walls which are to support it. Moreover, the landed aristocracy which, under democratic forms, wielded the whole political and social power, could not but be averse to the development of a middle class such as the North and all Europe — with the exception of the southeastern parts and Russia — had to boast of. There was, in later years, much talking and passing of resolutions upon the duty and necessity of bringing about the industrial and commercial development to which the bounties of nature had evidently destined the South. At the same time, however, the spirit which animated those middle classes in the North and in Europe, and which alone made them what they were, was denounced and abused as a deadly poison, the introduction of which into the South was more to be feared than the plague. And these denunciations, dictated by the instinct of self-preservation, were but too well founded. With the building up of commerce and the industrial pursuits, that is, with the spreading of culture and prosperity, the delusion would inevitably vanish that the interests of the small slave-holders and the rest of the white population coincided with those of the great planters. These last would have planted abolitionism at the very doors of their mansions, and would have invited it to the seat of honor at their hearth-stones. Slavery doomed the South to be and to remain an almost exclusively agricultural country, and, at the same time, to use up at a steadily advancing rate the capital which Providence had bestowed upon her in the shape of a fertile soil and a genial climate. So long as slavery remained the dominant interest in the Southern States, they, for that very reason, had to be hostile to a home industry, if it needed to be artificially nursed into existence by high protective tariffs. Everything they needed of industrial products they were obliged to buy from elsewhere, and they of course wanted to buy where they could get the articles best and cheapest. But the protective tariffs forced them to buy inferior American goods at a higher price, or to pay for the European wares much more than their real value. We need not here inquire into the wisdom of this "American system" from a national point of view. Thus much was incontestable, that it ran counter to the immediate interest of the South, or, to speak more correctly, of the great slave-holders. Therefore, as the nature of things cannot be changed, this had to remain a "fixed fact" so long as the interests of the slave-holders held undisputed sway over the slave States. If, however, a government pursues an economical policy, which is permanently opposed to the immediate interests of a geographical section of the country, this section will never acknowledge that the policy is or can be compatible with the true national interests.

Thus far no statesman, either south or north of Mason and Dixon's line, had fully grasped the question. The plantation States felt the effect of the American system, but they did not understand the original cause of the irreconcilable conflict of interests between the two sections of the Union, nor was any one aware that the conflict was irreconcilable to the fullest extent of the word. This fact was the more obscured because some special interests, as those of the sugar and indigo planters, caused an alliance between a part of the extreme South and the protectionists ; and furthermore, because the border States, in consequence of their geographical situation and the contest between the slave-holding interest and the free-labor system, limped on both sides. Yet it was as certain as a proposition of Euclid that the conflict was irreconcilable, and therefore " irrepressible," because freedom and slavery are antagonistic ideas, acting with equal energy upon the intellectual, political, economical, social, and moral life of a people. It has been truly said that " compromise is the essence of politics ; " genuine compromises, however, can only be concluded with regard to *measures*, never between principles, that is, between intellectual and moral conceptions which.

In their very essence, are the opposite poles of an idea.

In relation to the concrete question, these plain truths were, at the time, as little understood by Calhoun as by any other statesman of the country. As he was not a member of Congress during the contest which terminated in the Missouri compromise, we know but little of his position towards the slavery question at this memorable period. Enough, however, is known of it to prove that he had not as yet deeply reflected upon it. Like all the other members of Mr. Monroe's cabinet, he admitted the constitutional right of Congress to prohibit slavery in the Territories. If he had perceived that this was the pivotal point on which the whole slavery question was ultimately to turn, and that upon its decision the existence of slavery depended, he certainly would not have done so. Not that he would have wittingly misinterpreted the Constitution, but he would have seen the whole instrument in a totally different light. Already the maintenance of slavery was, in his view, an incontestable right under the fundamental law of the land, and also it was an absolute necessity. Already it was a matter of course with him that everything else must yield to this consideration. Adams writes on Feruary 24, 1820, in his Diary : —

"I had some conversation with Calhoun on the slave question, pending in Congress. He said he did not think it would produce a dissolution of the Union, but if it should the South would be from necessity compelled to form an alliance, offensive and defensive, with Great Britain.

"I said that would be returning to the colonial state.

"He said, Yes, pretty much, but it would be forced upon them."

Ten years after Calhoun's death, the South tried the realization of this programme. Long before he had begun to concentrate the whole power of his intellect upon the examination of this problem, his unerring instinct unveiled the remote future. While the thinker and the practical statesman but just enter upon the task which was to constitute the dark glory of his life, the seer points to the end, which is to come after his own bones have been turned into dust.

It was not the territorial but the economical question which opened the eyes of Calhoun and pushed him with irresistible force into a new path, so that Adams said rather too little than too much when he declared that "his career as a statesman has been marked with a series of the most flagrant inconsistencies." But he wronged him grievously in asserting that "his

opinions are the sport of every popular blast,'
and that he " veers round in his politics, to be
always before the wind, and makes his intellect
the pander of his will."   If these reproaches
ever had any foundation, he mastered this weakness just *while* and *because* he abjured his former political faith.   Mr. Curtis most justly
says, in his " Life of Daniel Webster," " Mr.
Calhoun was a man of deep convictions."   His
veering round was gradual, because it was not
done to serve some impure personal end, but
was the result of an honest change in his opinions.   After it had once begun, it went steadily
on without pausing for a single moment, because he had taken his stand on a *principle*, and
followed up the consequences of it with masterly
logic and fatalistic sternness of purpose.

The tariff of 1828 gave birth to his first great
political manifesto, the so-called South Carolina
Exposition.   The document issued by the legis
lature of that State does not concern us here ;
we have only to deal with Calhoun's original
draft of it.   Nor is it now of any interest
whether his economical reasoning was correct
or fallacious ;   only the political conclusions
which he drew from his economical premises
are of historical importance.   The essential
point of these economical premises is that, according to him, there is a *permanent* conflict of

Interest with regard to the tariff policy between the " staple States " and the rest of the Union. The reason of this is simply that the staple States are exclusively devoted to agriculture, and will forever remain purely agricultural communities, because " our soil, climate, habits, and *peculiar labor* are adapted " to this " our ancient and favorite pursuit." This was the wizard's wand which worked such an astonishing metamorphosis in the mind of Calhoun that one is tempted to believe that a new man, whom we have never met before, has stepped upon the stage. In the beginning of his career we have heard him praised as absolutely free from sectional prejudices ; and we have seen that he, indeed, judged everything from a national point of view, hardly deigning to answer the objections which legal quibbles, party passion, and local interests raised against what the welfare and the honor of the " nation " demanded. But now he speaks of " our political system resting on the great principle involved in the recognized diversity of geographical interests in the community," and adopts this for the rest of his life as the basis of all his political reasoning and his whole political activity. The " Exposition " fills fifty-six printed pages, but it does not contain a single sentence bearing directly on the national interest. This point is only incidentally

mentioned, with the assertion that the pretended
unconstitutional usurpation of the federal government, which has called forth the " Exposition," seriously endangers the political morality
and the liberty of the republic.   The national
statesman is transformed into the champion of
the interests and the rights of the minority, and
the reason of the change is that the minority is
a geographical section with a " peculiar labor "
system, which creates a " recognized diversity "
of interests.   His first question is no more, What
ought the federal government to do, and what
has it the right to do ? but, What effect has the
policy of the federal government on the staple
States in their peculiar situation, and what constitutional means have they for counteracting
the pernicious effects of the federal policy ? The
corner-stone of the political edifice of the United
States is henceforth to him no more the principle that the majority is to rule, but that the
minority has the right and the power to check-
mate the majority, whenever it considers the
federal laws unconstitutional ; in other words,
whenever different views are entertained about
the powers conferred by the Constitution upon
the federal government, those of the minority
were to prevail, provided it was deemed worth
while to have recourse to the last " constitu
tional " resort.

The Articles of Confederation had been supplanted by the Constitution in order to render the Union "more perfect." If this purpose was to be fulfilled, the Union must continue to grow more perfect, for where life is there is also development. Either it was an illusion that the historical destiny of the North American continent could be fulfilled by welding it into one Union composed of many republican commonwealths, and then the Union would, sooner or later, fall to pieces, no matter what the Constitution said; or the authors of the Constitution had correctly understood the genius of the American people, and had skilfully adapted their work to the peculiar natural conditions of the country, and in that event the States would steadily go on growing together as the parts of an organic whole, no matter what this or that man, or even this or that section, might be pleased to proclaim as the correct interpretation of the Constitution. Calhoun had been so well aware of this fact that a favorite argument of his in support of the policy advocated by him had been the favorable effect it would have upon the "consolidation of the Union." Now there was in the whole political dictionary no term more abhorred by him than this. The sovereignty of the States, in the fullest sense of the term, is declared to be *the* essential principle of the Union ; and it is not only asserted as an incontestable right, but also claimed as an absolute political necessity in order to protect the minority against the majority. The authority quoted for this opinion is not any section of the Constitution, but the Virginia and Kentucky resolutions, with their doctrine, that the States have the right " to interpose " when the federal government is guilty of a usurpation, because, as there is no common judge over them, they, as the parties to the compact, have to determine for themselves whether it has been violated. This theory is brought by Calhoun into the more precise formula that each State has the right to " veto " a federal law which it deems unconstitutional. Whether such a veto is to be an injunction against the execution of the law throughout the Union, or only in the individual State, and, in the latter case, what is to become of the principle that different federal laws cannot prevail in different parts of the Union, we do not learn from the " Exposition." We are only told that the veto ought to be pronounced by a convention as representing the sovereignty of the State, but it is left undecided whether it might not also be done by the legislature.

Calhoun was very far from having completely killed the old national Adam in his bosom. He therefore could not entirely suppress the feeling that, if this theory were to be put into practice, it might lead after all to very strange consequences with regard to the legislative activity of the federal government; nay, with regard to the life of the Union itself. So he hastened to show that the veto was by no means so terrible a thing as it might appear at the first glance. In adopting the Constitution the States had so far abandoned their sovereignty that three fourths of them could change the compact as they pleased. If, therefore, it was desired that the federal government should have the contested power, it was only necessary that three fourths of the States should say so, and all the damage done would be that the exercising of the power had been postponed for a while. How was it that these penetrating eyes failed to see that the federal legislation might thereby be turned into a bulky machine, more fatal to healthy political life than Juggernaut's car to the fanatical worshippers? But leaving this practical objection aside, how was it that he failed to see that thereby one fourth of the States would get the power to change the Constitution at will? Suppose — and the case might certainly very easily happen — that the federal government exercises a power which has been actually granted to it by the Constitution, and that a State sees fit to veto the law, that the question, as must be the case, is submitted to all the States, and the objecting State is supported by one fourth of the whole number. Is any dialectician sharp enough to disprove the fact that, in such a case, the Constitution, though not a single letter is either added or erased, has been actually changed by one fourth of the States, though that instrument expressly requires the consent of at least three fourths to effect the slightest change? Working in defence of the peculiar interests of the slave-holders with the lever of the state sovereignty, Calhoun thus begins to subvert the foundation of the whole fabric of the Constitution.

The practical conclusion to which Calhoun came was, "that there exists a case which would justify the interposition of this State, in order to compel the general government to abandon an unconstitutional power, or to appeal to this high authority [the States] to confer it by express grant." He, however, deemed it "advisable" "to allow time for further consideration and reflection, in the hope that a returning sense of justice on the part of the majority, when they come to reflect on the wrongs which this and the other staple States have suffered, and are suffering, may repeal the obnoxious and unconstitutional acts, and thereby prevent the necessity of interposing the veto of the State."

Daniel Webster wrote on April 10, 1833, to Mr. Perry, " In December, 1828, I became thoroughly convinced that the plan of a Southern confederacy had been received with favor by a great many of the political men of the South." If this suspicion was well founded the above-quoted sentence of the Exposition proves that Calhoun, at all events, was not privy to such a plot. He not only had no desire to force a crisis upon the country, but he had strong hopes that it would be avoided, and he plainly stated his reasons for these hopes. He was " further induced, at this time, to recommend this course, under the hope that the great political revolution, which will displace from power on the 4th of March next those who have acquired authority by setting the will of the people at defiance, and which will bring in an eminent citizen, distinguished for his services to the country and his justice and patriotism, may be followed up, under his influence, with a complete restoration of the pure principles of our government." But it is to be noted that he meant exactly what he said, neither more nor less. He *hoped* that by the influence of Andrew Jackson the protectionists would be defeated, but ne did not feel quite

sure of it; and if his hopes should not be realized, he had explicitly stated what, in his opin
ion, ought to be done. In order to leave no
doubt whatever on this point, he followed up
the last-mentioned sentence with the declaration that, in thus recommending delay, he
wished it "to be distinctly understood that
neither doubts of the rightful power of the
State nor apprehension of consequences" constituted the smallest part of his motives.

Calhoun's reason for not trusting too implic-
itly in Jackson's influence to bring about a revolution in the economical policy of the federal government was the double programme
on which the general had been elected. In the
South he had been sustained as a friend of
'Southern interests," *i. e.*, as an anti-protec-
tionist; while in New York, Pennsylvania, and
the West he had been supported as the firm
friend of the tariff and of internal improvements. The inaugural address touched this
leading question of the day but very slightly,
and with such cautious vagueness that neither
party was satisfied, because neither knew what
it had to expect from the new President. The
first annual message, which had been looked for
with keen expectation, gave no more satisfaction to either. All that could be safely inferred
from it was that the President would gladly see

some duties reduced, but it contained nothing to justify the hope of the South that he would, on principle, throw his whole weight into the scales against the entire protective system. Calhoun even saw a direct bid for the favor of the protectionists in the proposal to divide the expected yearly surplus among the States for the execution of internal improvements. He began to look upon the President with a certain distrust, and this feeling was fully reciprocated by Jackson. Those who had no opportunity to observe the actors closely, while the curtain was down, did not, however, become aware of the fact that an ominous disturbance in the friendly relations between the two first officers of the government had occurred, until the society of the capital had begun to become convulsed by the tragi-comical intermezzo of the Mrs. Eaton affair.

No serious historian will be expected to enter upon the details of this once celebrated case of the American *chronique scandaleuse*. It is the less necessary to do so because it in fact only helped on and accelerated the important political events, of which it has frequently been said to have been the main cause. It suffices to recall to the memory of the reader that Mrs. Eaton was reported to have had before her second marriage illicit intercourse with her present

husband, the Secretary of War, and that therefore many ladies refused to admit her into their
company. Jackson, prompted partly by his
generous temper, and partly by the bitter recol-
lections of what had been said against his own
wife, exerted all his influence to break the social
ban under which the wife of his Secretary and
personal friend had been put. The ladies, however, were not to be dictated to, and they carried the day against the victor of New Orleans.
Against the wives of the members of his cabinet even the President's iron will was power-
less, and Calhoun, the Vice-President, according
to his own statement, considered it his duty
to take the lead in this determined opposition
against the attempt to force the suspected lady
upon society. Van Buren, on the contrary, who
was a widower and led a bachelor's life, even
surpassed his wonted politeness in his treatment
of Mrs. Eaton. Jackson, however, was utterly
unable to draw the correct line between private
and public affairs whenever his feelings were enlisted in a cause. Van Buren therefore greatly
ingratiated himself with the President by assid-
uously paying his court to Mrs. Eaton, while
Calhoun, by strictly adhering to the rigid
course of morality, which has always distinguished the family life of South Carolina, had
to pay for it by a corresponding decline in Jack

son's good will. Both Van Buren and Calhoun ardently wished to succeed the general in the presidency, and neither of them failed to see that Jackson's favor might go far towards deciding who should be the next occupant of the White House. Moreover, Calhoun was serving his second term as Vice-President. All the precedents were against his presenting himself once more as a candidate for reëlection, and he justly apprehended that to return for four years into private life might postpone the realization of his long-deferred hopes *ad calendas Græcas.* He was therefore most anxious that Jackson should serve but one term, while, for the same reason, Van Buren and his partisans were not less zealous advocates of Jackson's reëlection.

So, while everything was yet quiet and smooth on the surface, the mine was dug and charged; one spark sufficed to lead to a great catastrophe. Calhoun himself remained to the end of his life firmly convinced that Van Buren was the engineer who had constructed the ingenious battery for the explosion. Though there is no documentary proof for it, yet it can hardly be doubted that Van Buren did in fact take part in devising the scheme; but he was too wary and too cunning in such transactions ever to do himself what could be done as well, or even better, by some devoted friend. Adams, however, writes on January 30, 1831, "Wirt concurred entirely with me in opinion that this was a snare deliberately spread by Crawford to accomplish the utter ruin of Calhoun." The opportunities for these two men to be well informed were too good not to require that the greatest weight be accorded to their opinion. Besides, the powder for the petard was confessedly furnished by Crawford's guilty indiscretion. He divulged the secrets of certain of the cabinet meetings of Monroe's administration, which filled Jackson's mind with deep hatred and contempt against Calhoun. If we were writing the biography of Andrew Jackson, it would be necessary, in this connection, to review the whole controversy concerning the general's conduct in the Seminole war. But in a life of Calhoun we can with propriety dispense with that thankless task, confining our remarks to a single point in it, and even that may be treated with great brevity.

In the course of his operations against the Seminoles, General Jackson had not only crossed the Florida boundary, as he was authorized to do in case the object of the campaign could not otherwise be attained, but he had forcibly taken possession of the Spanish forts at St. Mark's and Pensacola. In July, 1818, the question as

to whether and how far these high-handed proceedings should be sustained by the administration formed the subject of long and earnest
discussions by Mr. Monroe and his cabinet.
The general had acted in good faith. A letter
to the President, in which he communicated his
intentions, having accidentally remained unanswered, he mistook the silence for tacit consent,
and afterwards, without regard to dates, even
adduced a subsequent letter of the Secretary of
War to a third person as proof that the government had given him full discretion. This was
by no means the view which Mr. Monroe and
his cabinet took of the matter. Even Adams,
who went farthest in supporting the general's
course, did not undertake to justify it wholly by
rules of international law, but deemed it necessary to adduce considerations of high policy for
his opinion. Calhoun, as Adams states in his
Diary, "principally bore the argument against
me, insisting that the capture of Pensacola was
not necessary upon principles of self-defence,
and therefore was both an act of war against
Spain and a violation of the Constitution ; that
the administration, by approving it, would take
all the blame of it upon themselves ; that by
leaving it upon his responsibility they would
take away from Spain all pretext for war and
'or resorting to the aid of other European pow-

ers, — they would also be free from all reproach
of having violated the Constitution   that it was
not the menace of the Governor of Pensacola
that had determined Jackson to take that
place ; that he had really resolved to take it
before ; that he had violated his orders, and
upon his own arbitrary will set all authority at
defiance." He therefore demanded an investigation of the general's conduct ; but although
"all the members of the cabinet, except myself
[Adams] are of opinion that Jackson acted not
only without, but against, his instructions," and
" that he has committed war upon Spain," a
middle course was finally adopted, which, without directly and formally disavowing the general, satisfied Spain.

Jackson knew that his conduct had not met
with the approval of the administration, but he
had heretofore believed that the contemplated
proceedings against him had been principally
urged by Crawford, and that, on the other
hand, Calhoun had exerted himself in his defence. Now, however, a letter from Crawford
to Senator Forsyth (April 30, 1830), which had
been written for this purpose, was put into his
hands, and undeceived him on the latter point,
at the same time giving a false and malicious
coloring to the whole transaction. If any member of the administration had been animated

by a really *hostile* spirit against the general, it had been Crawford; yet Crawford now pretended that, upon learning all the attending circumstances, he had become satisfied that Jackson was fully excused, if not justified. And the weight which he thus shook from his own shoulders he shifted upon the back of Calhoun, by the bold exaggeration that the latter had persistently demanded the *punishment* of the general.

These revelations threw Jackson into a towering passion. On May 13 he sent Crawford's letter with a curt note to Calhoun, demanding "to learn of you whether it be possible that the information given is correct." Calhoun might have declined to answer the interrogatory, because nobody had a right to demand from him a confession concerning what had passed in the cabinet meetings of the administration, of which he had been a member. He, however, replied with a long statement and elaborate argument, which had too much the character of a justification of his conduct and of an impeachment of Crawford's behavior and motives. Though he proved that Jackson could and ought to have known that the proceedings in Florida were, at the time, considered by him (Calhoun) transgressions of the orders issued from his department, and that he had, without any personal hostility, acted according to his convictions of duty, for which he owed no account to the general either then or now, all such arguments did not avail him anything, and his dignity would have been better served by taking higher ground. Most truly did he say, "It was an affair of mere official duty, involving no question of private enmity or friendship;" but that was a view which Andrew Jackson was absolutely unable to understand. In theory he may have admitted the possibility of an honest difference of opinion, but whatever related to himself he could only see in an eminently personal light; and if any one whom he deemed his friend had the misfortune and audacity to differ with him, the brand of Cain was indelibly stamped on that man's forehead. All Calhoun got for his pains was violent, impudent, and absurd abuse, mingled with ludicrous pathos. He was charged with "secretly endeavoring to destroy my reputation," while the poor victim "had too exalted an opinion of your honor and frankness to believe for one moment that you could be capable of such deception. . . . I repeat, I had a right to believe that you were my sincere friend, and, until now, never expected to have occasion to say of you, in the language of Cæsar, *Et tu, Brute!*"

The reproach of a lack of frankness was

nowever, not quite unfounded, but it was *now*, rather than heretofore, that Calhoun was guilty of it. He declared in his reply of May 29, " I neither questioned your patriotism nor your motives." Adams's Diary, that invaluable source of historical information, furnishes the proof that this was not strictly true. On July 14, 1818, Adams gives it as his impression that "Calhoun, the Secretary of War, generally of sound, judicious, and comprehensive mind, seems in this case to be personally offended with the idea that Jackson has set at naught the instructions of the department." Again, in a short synopsis of a conversation between himself and Calhoun, on March 2, 1831, two weeks after the publication of the correspondence with Jackson, Adams writes, —

" He said, too, that his remark in the cabinet meeting, in reply to my argument that Jackson's taking the Spanish forts had been defensive, to meet the threats of Masot, namely, that Jackson had determined to take the province before, was not with allusion to the letter of January 6, 1818,[1] but to a rumor that Jackson had been personally interested in a previous land speculation at Pensacola."

This breach witn Jackson was the death-blcw to the presidential aspirations of Calhoun.

[1] Jackson's letter to the President, before alluded to, which had accidentally remained unanswered.

Mr. Wirt thought " that he had blasted his prospects of future advancement forever," and Adams called him " a drowning man," at the same time, however, asserting that he " nevertheless entertains very sanguine hopes." Perhaps this expression was a little too strong, but at all events Calhoun maintained his candidacy a while longer, although he not only had to encounter the enmity of Jackson's partisans, but could also no longer count upon the support of New England, which had become ill-disposed towards him by reason of the political course of his friends in Congress. It was rumored that Clay's Western friends were inclined to take him up, in case they should find the chances of their own champion desperate, and Calhoun himself seems to have thought it possible that, if he should conclude to run against Jackson, the election might revert once more to the House of Representatives. But the drift of public opinion was too strong not to destroy these illusions very speedily. Calhoun's disappointment was, undoubtedly, very bitter; but those strangely misjudged the man who attributed to it the terrible energy with which he nenceforth pursued the course upon which he had entered with the South Carolina Exposition. He was not driven by disappointed am bition into a sectional policy with a view to wards tearing the Union asunder, in order to become the chief of one half, because he could not be the chief of the whole. Slavery *had* split the Union into two geographical sections, and, in spite of everything man could do, the rent widened into a chasm, and the chasm into an abyss. That was not the work of Calhoun, but the unavoidable consequence of the fact that the Union was composed of free and slaveholding States. He could not have done it if he had wanted to, and he was as far as any man from wanting to do it. The only effect of the disappointment of his ambition was the quick dispersion of the mist which had hitherto been lying over his eyes as over those of the whole people. The shackles of minor considerations and personal interests began to fall from his limbs. Embittered but free, he henceforth pursued his course, forming alliances without heeding the claims of old or new party connections, and not afraid to encounter the enmity of any one; never ceasing to love and cherish the Union, but learning to love slavery better and better. He was not a demi-god, but a man, having his full share of human weakness and ittleness. But nature had not only endowed him with a powerful brain; the marrow of his oones and the core of his heart were sound. Not for the world would he have betrayed his country, and even slavery could not turn him into a dark conspirator. Yet it has been pretended that he was guilty of such betrayal and conspiracy merely in order to see the title President prefixed to his name. Those who, like Senator Benton, honestly believed this, stumbled into an egregious blunder, because, in spite of all their keen-sightedness, they remained blind to the fact that the wedlock between slavery and freedom could not be a lasting one. What they attributed to the traitorous machinations of his disappointed ambition would have happened, even though out of every fibre of John C. Calhoun a Henry Clay, a Daniel Webster, and a Thomas Benton had been made. It was not a crime, but it was his misfortune, that he saw everything relating to slavery with such appalling clearness, discerning, with unerring eye, the last consequences at the first glance.

As soon as all hope had to be given up that the protective system could be destroyed with Jackson's help in the regular parliamentary way, Calhoun resumed the contest at the point where he had left it with the South Carolina Exposition. His second manifesto — " Address to the People of South Carolina," dated Fort Hill, July 26, 1831 — was published in the " Pendleton Messenger." The whole question of the relation which the States and the general govern

ment bear to each other, *i. e.*, of state sovereignty, was reargued. The key-note of his
whole argument and of his whole subsequent
political life is the assertion, "The great dis-
similarity and, as I must add, as truth compels
me to do, contrariety of interests in our country
. . . are so great that they cannot be subjected
to the unchecked will of a majority of the whole
without defeating the great end of government,
without which it is a curse, — justice." This
is the real broad foundation of his doctrine that
the Union could never have a safe foundation
upon any other legal basis save state sovereignty, which enables the minority to defend
themselves against usurpations. No new argument is adduced either on the constitutional or
on the economical question, but the whole reasoning is closer and the language is more direct
and bolder. The federal government has dwindled down to a mere " agent " of the " sovereign States," and the veto power of these is
termed " nullification."

Calhoun had, of course, not expected to convince his adversaries. What he wanted was to
mark off the old, widely trodden road with the
utmost precision, so that in future no gap could
be reasoned into it, and to consolidate his own
party, and to inspire it with resolution to live
up to its profession of faith. The apprehen

sion that this would be done was great enough to dampen the ardor of the protectionists when the tariff question came again before Congress. The duties were considerably reduced, but the plantation States were not satisfied either with the amount or with the manner in which the reduction was effected. South Carolina received the new tariff as a declaration that the protect've system was " the settled policy of the country," and on August 28, 1832, Calhoun issued his third manifesto, determined to have the die cast without further delay. This letter to Governor Hamilton of South Carolina is the final and classical exposition of the theory of state sovereignty. Nothing new has ever been added to it. All the later discussions of it have but varied the expressions and amplified the argument on particular points. Thirty years later the programme laid down in it was carried out by the South piece by piece, and the justification of the Southern course was based, point by point, upon this argument.

The late champion of a *national* policy and of *consolidating* measures now takes for his starting-point the assertion that, " so far from the Constitution being the work of the American people collectively, no such political body, either now or ever, did exist." The historical review by which he tried to prove this assertion con tains two seemingly slight, but in fact very important, errors. The colonies did not " by name and enumeration " declare themselves free and independent States, nor is the Constitution declared " to be *binding* between the States so ratifying," but Article VII. of the Constitution reads, " The ratification of the conventions of nine States shall be sufficient for the *establishment* of this Constitution between the States so ratifying." From these historic " facts " he draws the conclusion " that there is no direct and immediate connection between the individual citizens of a State and the general government." Strange indeed! for the authors and the advocates of the Constitution thought that the most important change effected in the political structure of the Union, by substituting the Constitution for the Articles of Confederation, was exactly the establishment of direct and immediate connections between the individual citizens and the federal government; and not a single day passed in which a great number of citizens were not actually brought into contact with the federal government, in the courts, in the custom-houses, in the departments, etc., without being reminded in any way whatever that they were citizens of this or that particular State. If the relation between the individual citizen and the federal government

were, in fact, exclusively through the State,
then, indeed, it might have been true that
" it belongs to the State as a member of the
Union, in her sovereign capacity in convention,
to determine definitely, as far as her citizens
are concerned, the extent of the obligation
which she has contracted ; and if, in her opinion,
the act exercising the power [in dispute] be unconstitutional, to declare it null and void, which
declaration would be obligatory on her citizens."
The federal government is floating in the air
without a straw of its own to rest upon, the
sport of the sovereign fancies of the States.
" Not a provision can be found in the Constitution authorizing the general government to
exercise any control whatever over a State by
force, by veto, by judicial process, or in any
other form, — a most important omission, designed, and not accidental." And the actual
state of the case corresponds with the right,
for " it would be impossible for the general
government, within the limits of the States, to
execute, legally, the act nullified, while, on the
other hand, the State would be able to enforce,
legally and peaceably, its declaration of nullification." Yet nullification is declared to be
" the great conservative principle " of the Union.

Undoubtedly, there is method in this madness,
but madness it is nevertheless ; for the whole

theory is neither more nor less than the systematization of anarchy. The Union is constructed
upon the principle that the essence of the idea
State, the supremacy of the will which has to
act for the whole, — that is, in a free State, the
government of the laws, — is by principle excluded from its structure. If there ever was an
illustration of the "tragedy of Hamlet with the
part of Hamlet left out," here it is. This vast
republic, to which the future belonged more
than to any other state of the globe, was to be
a shooting star, a political monster without a
supreme will, because this could be lodged nowhere with safety. The resort to force—
"should folly or madness ever make the attempt" — would be utterly vain, if at all possible, for " it would be . . . a conflict of moral,
not physical, force." This moral force, however, was also but a rope of sand, if a sovereign
State should so will it. Even a decision by
three fourths of the States would by no means be
unconditionally binding upon all the members
of the Union. " Should the other members undertake to grant the power nullified, and should
the nature of the power be such as to defeat
the object of the association or union, at least
as far as the member nullifying is concerned.
t would then become an abuse of power on
the part of the principals, and thus present a

case where secession would apply." The Union was to have laws only so long and just so far as *every* constituent member of it was pleased to submit to them. In his great political testament, the " Disquisition on Government," Calhoun directly says, " Nothing short of a negative, absolute or in effect, on the part of the government [!] of a State can possibly protect it against the encroachments of the united government of the States, whenever [!] their powers come in conflict." And as even this might prove not to be a sufficient protection, each State was to have, in the form of the right of secession, a most absolute veto against all its co-States. What a nice checker-board the United States might become, if the exercise of this right should get to be the political fashion ! Suppose the States at the mouths of the great streams, and four or five others commanding a part of their navigable waters, should secede, what a pretty picture the map of the United States would present ! Why, the German *Bund* of by-gone days would have had a most formidable rival. Calhoun himself would have turned with disgust and contempt from the idea of thus bridging over the craggy actualities of life with the cobwebs of an over-subtle logic, .f he had conceived the possibility of his theory being ever put into practice in *this* manner. I seemed to him so plausible *only* because he was fully conscious of the fact that, if it were ever put to the test, the Union would split into *two solid geographical sections.* Never would he have stultified his intellect by this ingenious systematization of anarchy, if he could not have written, —

" Who, of any party, with the least pretension to candor, can deny that on all these points [the great questions of trade, of taxation, of disbursement and appropriation, and the nature, character, and power of the general government] se deeply important, no two distinct nations can be more opposed than this [the staple States] and the other sections ? "

CHAPTER V.

ON November 24 the South Carolina convention passed the nullification ordinance, which was to take effect on February 1, 1833. Calhoun at once resigned the vice-presidency, in order to take the seat in the United States Senate, vacated by General Hayne, who had been elected Governor of South Carolina. Hundreds of eyes closely scrutinized the face of the "great nullifier" as he took the oath to support the Constitution, but the firm repose of his countenance dispelled all doubts of his sincerity. His personal courage, however, was seriously questioned by many. Benton and others assure us that he finally yielded, because he had been informed that Jackson had threatened to hang him as high as Haman. This dramatic anecdote has been repeated so often that the mass of the American people have come to believe it as an undoubted historic fact. That Jackson may have uttered some such threat is probable enough, but Calhoun never betrayed such a weakness of nerves as to justify a suspicion that an empty threat could wipe from his brains all remembrance of the Constitution. And an empty threat this most certainly was, if it was ever made. Jackson was not now the general commanding in the wilds of Florida, but President of the United States; and Calhoun was not an Arbuthnot or Ambrister, but a senator of the United States. The section of the Constitution, however, has yet to be written which empowers the President to hang any man, and especially a United States senator. The hanging story may have been good enough at the time for political purposes, but it deserves no place in history. Yet Calhoun knew well enough that not only he personally, but also his State, was playing a high game, in which eventually powder and lead, and perhaps even the hangman, upon the requisition of the courts or of a court-martial, might speak the last word. He therefore did yield, but only because Congress and Jackson — notwithstanding the justly celebrated " proclamation " — yielded still more. The explanations with which Calhoun accompanied his affirmative vote on a certain provision of the tariff bill, after he had declared it unconstitutional, were vain talk ; he bent his proud neck, because Mr. Clayton had left him no alternative except to submit, or to let the whole compromise fail. On the other hand, however, the new tariff conceded in the main the demands of South Carolina, and the so-called Force Bill, which gave the President the means to subdue by force of arms any resistance to the laws of the Union, was only passed after the passage of the tariff bill had been fully secured. Congress, with the reluctant approval of the President, bought the acquiescence of South Carolina, and then the daring little State was told that she would have been crushed had she persisted in her mad course. A dread — honorable and patriotic indeed, but on the part of the federal government much to be regretted — of the consequences had forced both parties from their original stand-point. The principle was purposely left undecided, and, as to the immediate practical questions, a compromise was effected; but if either party had a right to claim the victory, it was certainly not Jackson and the majority of Congress, but Calhoun and South Carolina.

Another, and perhaps the best, proof that apprehensions for his personal safety, on account of Jackson's reported threats, had nothing to do with the course pursued by Calhoun, is the calmness with which he reviewed the field after the contest was over. There was not a single man in either camp who judged the results of it more correctly than he. Whenever a suitable opportunity was offered, he claimed, in a calm and dignified but very decided manner, that the overthrow of the protective. system was due to the resistance offered by South Carolina, and that the conservative and beneficial character of nullification had been proved by experience. At the same time, however, he never failed to acknowledge that the doctrine of states-rights had suffered a defeat by the passage of the Force Bill. He even laid greater stress upon this fact, and exaggerated its significance. On April 9, 1834, he delivered a speech in support of a bill, which he had introduced, to repeal the obnoxious act, although by its own limitation the power conferred by it on the President was to expire at the termination of this session. Those who charged him with doing so only in order to appear consistent, greatly deceived themselves. From the moment that he had assumed the leadership of the states-rights party the *principiis obsta* was always present to his mind, and the unswerving rigor with which he applied it goes far to explain why he held such a unique position among the Southern statesmen in the slavery conflict. " The precedent, unless the act be expunged from the statute book, will live forever, ready, on any pretext of future danger, to be quoted as an authority to confer on the chief magistrate similar or even more

dangerous powers, if more dangerous can be devised."   Therefore he declared it "subversive
of our political institutions, and fatal to the liberty and happiness of the country," although,
as to the immediate object for which it pur-
ported to be passed, the compromise tariff had
rendered it a piece of waste paper ere it had
been inscribed on the statute book.   He was
not lulled into the sleep of false security by the
calm after the first blast of the storm.   Already in the so-called Edgefield letter of March
27, 1833, declining an invitation to a public
dinner, he had written, "The struggle to preserve the liberty and Constitution of the country, and to arrest the corrupt and dangerous
tendency of the government, so far from being
over, is not more than fairly commenced. . . .
Let us not deceive ourselves by supposing that
the danger is past.   We have but checked the
disease.   If one evil has been remedied, another
has succeeded."

As he declined all public demonstrations proposed to be given in acknowledgment of the
stand he had taken against the federal government, because he did not want to carry fuel to
the fire of his calumniators, who attributed his
course solely to impure personal motives, so also
he abstained from currying the favor of his own
party by shouting triumph and flattering them

with pæans. To sound the tocsin was the ungrateful task of the rest of his life, and the greater the success of the slave power the harder he pulled the rope. In August, 1833, he wrote to the citizens of Newton County, who had tendered him a public dinner, —

"I utter it under a painful but a solemn conviction of its truth that we are no longer a free people, — a people living under a Constitution, as the guardian of their rights ; but under the absolute rule of an unchecked majority, which has usurped the power to do as it pleases, and to enforce its pleasure at the point of the bayonet. . . . This condition we had been long approaching ; and to it we are now absolutely reduced by the proclamation and force act. . . . So long, then, as the act of blood stains our statute book, and the sovereignty of the States is practically denied by the government, so long will be the duration of our political bondage."

This is the *ceterum censeo*, which recurs in all his speeches during the next years. In his first great speech after the nullification session, he declared, —

"I stand wholly disconnected with the two great parties now contending for ascendency. My political connections are with that small and denounced party which has voluntarily retired from the party strifes of the day, with a view of saving, if possible, the liberty and the Constitution of the country in this great crisis of our affairs."

He had not become a Whig, nor had he ceased to be a Democrat, but he was one of the most uncompromising adversaries of Jacksonism. In all the leading questions of these years, so full of bitter strife, he stands in the front rank of the opposition, but he has no more in common with Clay and Webster than before. He and they fought side by side *against* a common enemy, but he did not fight with them *for* a common cause. In their defensive warfare against the removal of the government deposits from the United States Bank, these three occupied the same ground; but when it came to the question of renewing the charter of the bank, or to the general problem of the currency, their ways separated, though they did not diverge so much as one would suppose from Calhoun's subsequent course.

With regard to the bank, he sat as yet, so to say, on the fence. He did not conceal the lively distrust and grave apprehensions with which he viewed the close connection of the government with a privileged moneyed corporation of such enormous means, but the reasons of expediency still prevailed over the objections which would have been decisive with him, if he had felt free to follow his inclination and general principles. He himself even reminded the Senate of the fact that the bank would probably not have been established, if it had not been for his exertions. His argumentation was as clear and logical as usual and it led him to definite practical propositions; and yet his speeches leave the impression upon the reader's mind that he himself did not know exactly what to think and what to will. Like the country, he was in a state of transition with regard to this perplexing problem, and it is a curious fact that so early as 1834 he pointed out the ultimate solution of it; but he did it in such a way that it would be absurd to claim for him the honor of the discovery. In his speech of January 13, on the removal of the deposits, he said, —

" So long as the question is one between a Bank of the United States, incorporated by Congress, and that system of banks which has been created by the will of the Executive, it is an insult to the understanding to discourse on the pernicious tendency and unconstitutionality of the Bank of the United States. To bring up that question fairly and legitimately, you must go one step farther : you must *divorce* the government and the banking system. You must refuse all connection with banks. You must neither receive nor pay away bank-notes; you must go back to the old system of the strong-box, and of gold and silver. . . I repeat, you must *divorce* the government entirely from the banking system ; or, if not, you are bound to incorporate a bank as the only safe and efficient means of giving stability and uniformity to the currency."

Calhoun was not a " statesman " of the type which, at this time, began to become only too common in the United States. He did not owe his position to the grace of King Caucus and the favor of his grandees, the washed and unwashed patriots of the primary meetings. He therefore did not know and understand everything by intuition, as this privileged class of mortals do, but he was obliged to study and reflect upon the subjects with which he had to deal as a legislator. As a seat in the legislative hall was in his opinion as well the most responsible as the most honorable post in which a man can be put by the confidence of his fellow-citizens, he applied himself to this task with all the thorough-going earnestness of his nature. It is therefore a matter of course that his speeches never lacked a positive element of more or less, and not unfrequently of considerable, merit. Yet ever since the Southern Samson has put his head into the lap of the Delilah of state sovereignty, his strength is on the wane whenever he returns to his old place among the builders of his country's greatness and happiness. Critically to dissect the arguments of others and to expose the weak points of their devices, to denounce their inconsistencies and mercilessly to lash the moral shortcomings of their policy, and, above all, to point out the breakers ahead of the ship of state, — these are the things in which he excels.

Jackson's administration offered a wide field for the vigorous application of all these peculiar qualities, and it was but human that Calhoun should avail himself the more willingly of the opportunity on account of his personal relations with the President. His speeches on the removal of the deposits and on Jackson's protest against the resolution of the Senate, denouncing it as an unwarrantable assumption of power, exposed the President's high-handed way of dealing with the Constitution and the laws, also the gross fallacies and inconsistencies of his reasoning, in a truly masterly way, and were not less admirable defences of the constitutional rights and privileges of the legislative branch of the government. He did not spare the President, but neither his personal grievances nor the intensity of his political anger and disgust carried him beyond the line which respect for the office ought to draw whenever the chief magistrate of the republic is spoken of ; and his most vigorous thrusts were not aimed against the person, but against the system which had been inaugurated by Jackson.

If the high-toned moral severity of the above-mentioned speeches was seasoned now and then with cutting irony and haughty defiance, Cal houn's remarks on the wholesale dismissal of federal office-holders without cause betray patriotic sadness and deep anxiety for the future of his country. The subject was of too serious a nature to permit him to indulge in personal animosities or party bickerings. The removal of the deposits, the protest, the whole bank question, though all of great import, were after all but questions of the day, which would soon be dead issues, of no interest to anybody except the student of history. But would not the very life-blood of the body politic be poisoned if the government should fall into the hands of mercenaries, with whom politics constituted only a trade, to which they devoted themselves for the sake of the " spoils " of office? Was not the love of country in danger of being drowned in the whirlpools of party strife, if the official spokesmen of the national parties should be men who owed their position to the dexterity with which they gathered followers around their standards by means of the spoils? Would not the politics of the republic degenerate more and more from a contest about great public measures, principles, and ideas, into a mean scuffle about the husks, if it should become an acknowledged principle that " to the victor be-

long the spoils "? Would not every party be
forced to follow suit if the example should be
once successfully set, — for what party could
hope to vanquish with untrained volunteers the
skilled bands of lansquenets fighting for booty?
Would not the management of the public affairs rapidly sink until it became a by-word, if,
instead of fitness for the office, the services rendered to the party, or rather to the chiefs of the
party, should become the criterion for all the
appointments, and if the federal offices should
come to be filled with those who had not succeeded in private life; for would not the others
at best consider the federal offices but momentary make-shifts, if ability and faithfulness
could no longer secure their tenure? Last, but
not least, would not the people begin to turn
with disgust from politics when they saw the
statesmen more and more ousted by mere bread-
and-butter politicians? And what is the life of
a democratic republic worth if the people accus-
tom themselves to consider politics the monopoly of a set of men whom they do not respect?

In his speech on the removal of the deposits,
Calhoun had said, with burning indignation:—

" Can he [Secretary Taney] be ignorant that the
whole power of the government has been perverted
into a great political machine, with a view of cor
rupting and controlling the country? Can he be

ignorant that the avowed and open policy of the
government is to reward political friends and punish
political enemies? . . . With money we will get partisans, with partisans votes, and with votes money, is
the maxim of our public pilferers. . . . With money
and corrupt partisans a great effort is now making to
choke and stifle the voice of American liberty through
all its constitutional and legal organs by pensioning
the press; by overawing the other departments; and
finally by setting up a new organ, composed of office-
holders and partisans, under the name of a National
Convention, which, counterfeiting the voice of the
people, will, if not resisted, in their name dictate the
succession."

In a speech of February 13, 1835, he summed
up the ultimate results of the spoils system in
the following words: —

" When it comes to be once understood that politics are a game; that those who are engaged in it but
act a part; that they make this or that profession not
from honest conviction or an intent to fulfil them, but
as the means of deluding the people, and through
that delusion to acquire power, — when such profes-
sions are to be entirely forgotten, the people will lose
all confidence in public men; all will be regarded as
mere jugglers, — the honest and the patriotic as well
as the cunning and the profligate; and the people will
become indifferent and passive to the grossest abuses
of power on the ground that those whom they may
elevate, under whatever pledges, instead of reforming

will but imitate the example of those whom they have expelled."

Does not this passage read like a cutting from an editorial of the last number of an "independent" newspaper of the present day, advocating civil service reform? But though he foresaw with astonishing perspicacity what this mischievous innovation must inevitably lead to, the root of the evil and the remedy for it he discovered no more than did any of his contemporaries. The uniform practice of the preceding administrations concerning dismissal from office — even Jefferson's hardly forming an exception, although the loud complaints of the opposition had not been wholly unfounded — made him believe that nothing more was needed than to deprive the President of the power which, as he contended, had been conferred upon him under a mistaken construction of the Constitution. He himself, as he openly avowed, had formerly held the opposite opinion, and the argument with which he supported the assertion that the power of appointing did not imply that of dismissing was more ingenious than profound and sound. But whatever the true answer to the constitutional question be, the great mistake lay in the supposition that the evil could be cured by putting the power of dismissal from office under the direct control of

Congress or the Senate. Experience has proved
that Congress was more to be feared than the
President ; for, in spite of the clear provision of
the Constitution, even the power of appointment has in the main virtually passed from the
hands of the President into those of the members of Congress ; and the civil service reform-
ers of our days usually consider this the worst
feature of the actual system. Calhoun, like the
whole Whig opposition, mistook a mere symptom for the cause of the disease. Because
Jackson's administration assumed more and
more the character of the reign of an autocrat,
they apprehended that the encroachments of
the Executive upon the domain of the other
departments of the government, and more especially the legislative, would continue to un-
dermine the Constitution until the whole fabric
of republican liberty should be in danger of top-
pling to the ground. The above-quoted de-
nunciation of the National Convention, "composed of office-holders and partisans," which
was to "dictate the succession," closed with the
following words : "When the deed shall have
been done, the revolution completed, and all
the powers of our republic, in like manner, consolidated in the Executive and perpetuated by
his dictation." Calhoun and the Whigs failed
to see that, whosoever might become President

ıt could not possibly be an Andrew Jackson II.
Jackson might be powerful enough virtually to
nominate his *successor*, but to appoint an *heir*
was beyond his power. The presidential office
was only the means of exercising this extraordinary power; but the source of it was the
peculiar disposition of the majority of the people towards him, and this peculiar disposition
was a thing which he could not bequeath to
anybody. Van Buren knew this so well that
in his letter accepting the nomination by the
Baltimore Convention he humbly declared, "As
well from inclination as from duty, I shall, if
honored with the choice of the American people, endeavor to tread generally in the foot-
steps of President Jackson." He was Jackson's
choice, but the heirs of the general were the
politicians, and Van Buren would never have
occupied the White House if he had not been
one of the master minds of the politicians. If
he had ever presumed to speak in Jackson's
tone and to act in his autocratic spirit, the
"Sage of Kinderhook" would have been considered by his own party to be out of his senses.

March 4, 1837, did not inaugurate a second
"era of good feeling. The opposition remained loud and passionate, but the melodies
of their war-songs were changed, or they were
at least sung in another key. To pretend that

Martin Van Buren would "name " his successor, and that there was still immediate danger of the liberties of the country being crushed by the consolidation of all powers in the Executive, would have been simply ridiculous. The fears entertained on this head during the administration of Jackson had certainly not been fictitious, though they had been generally very highly colored for the sake of effect. The best proof of their serious character was furnished by a movement for an amendment to the Constitution, abolishing the veto power of the President. Calhoun, however, had not so far lost the sobriety of his judgment as to approve of this idea. He declared the veto "indispensable," because without it "the independence of the President," so far as concerned Congress, would be destroyed. He shared for the moment the erroneous views of the Whigs as to the future, but as to the past, *i. e.*, the origin of the evil, he went farther back than they. The encroachments of the Executive upon the legislative and judicial department of the government were with him "the *second* stage of the revolution;" but it had begun " many years ago, with the commencement of the restrictive system, and terminated its first stage with the passage of the Force Bill of the last session, which absorbed all the rights and sovereignty of the States, and consolidated them in this government." Thus his argument returned to its starting - point. The only way to secure "the preservation of our institutions" was to adopt the doctrine of state sovereignty with all its consequences; and the last cause of all the evils complained of, by which the liberty of the country, and perhaps even the existence of the republic, were put in jeopardy, was the violation of this fundamental principle by the federal government.

From this time forward, every speech of Calhoun which is not strictly confined to some special subject, contains a repetition of these two assertions in some form or other, and his inclination is constantly growing to make the range for his observations, on all subjects whatsoever, wide enough to permit some remarks on these topics, or at least a passing allusion to them. The wiseacres, who laughed all the warnings of the alarmists to scorn, began to consider him a kind of monomaniac on this head. Yet it was they whose minds wandered through the dales and o'er the hills of cloud-land, while his feet remained firmly planted on the rock of actualities. Every day the slavery question became more exclusively the needle which determined the course of the politics of the country, and if safety for the interests of the slave-holders could be obtained at all in the Union, it was only through the doctrine of state sovereignty No one understood so well as Calhoun that the appearance of the abolitionists had laid the axe to the root of slavery, though they were but a handful of men and women, with neither fame, social position, office, money, nor the general approbation of the public mind to make them formidable adversaries; and therefore as yet no one fully understood how terribly in earnest he was and how correctly he read the future, when he declared at every opportunity that the minority, that is the South, was doomed, if state sovereignty was not recognized as the central pillar on which the dome of the Constitution rested.

In January, 1831, William Lloyd Garrison had established in Boston "The Liberator," with the programme of "immediate and unconditional emancipation," and in December, 1833, the American Anti-Slavery Society had put forth its "declaration of principles," declaring against slavery a war which excluded the possibility of peace. The slave States were thrown into a wild excitement by the proceedings of the enthusiastic little band, and in the North the mob, very generally countenanced by public opinion and even by the authorities, had begun to hunt the agitators down as criminals who like Western horse-thieves, were of too **danger** ous a character to be admitted within the pale of the law. Some time, however, was yet to elapse, ere the question came directly before Congress. An occasional remark on "the fanatics and madmen of the North, who are waging war against the domestic institutions of the South, under the plea of promoting the general welfare," is therefore about all we hear from Calhoun on this subject, during the first years. But when at last the discussion made its way into the halls of legislation he at once took part in it in a manner which proved that for a long time all his faculties had been concentrated upon the topic; for he, and he alone, fully mastered it.

CHAPTER VI.

SLAVERY.

In the Senate the flood-gates of debate were opened by Calhoun's motion (January 7, 1836) not to receive two petitions for the abolition of slavery in the District of Columbia. The war of words, in which nearly one half of all the senators took part, lasted until March 11. Even by his Southern colleagues Calhoun was severely reproved for opening this box of Pandora. They accused him of going on a quixotic expedition in search of abstract political principles, because he himself declared that the abolitionists could not possibly " entertain the slightest hope that Congress would pass a law, at this time, to abolish slavery in this District, . . . and that seriously to attempt it would be fatal to their cause." Was it not a frivolous playing with fire and powder to force the discussion of this question upon Congress, since the material rights and interests of the South were abso-lutely secured by the perfect unanimity of Congress, most energetically backed by public opinion in all the Northern States ? Would not this uncalled-for debate do more to promote the cause of abolitionism than all the pamphlets and emissaries of the abolitionists had been able to do? For whether his consti tutional argument was sound or not, it was an incontestable fact that his motion was considered by the North a wanton attack upon the right of petition.

There was undoubtedly a good deal of truth in all these objections to the course pursued by Calhoun. Yet the charge was wholly unfounded that he was endeavoring intentionally to incense the North and the South against each other, in order to promote the purposes of his party. He spoke the simple truth when he asserted, in his speech of March 9, 1836, that, "however calumniated and slandered," he had "ever been devotedly attached" to the Union and the institutions of the country, and that he was "anxious to perpetuate them to the latest generation." He acted under the firm conviction of an imperious duty towards the South and towards the Union, and his assertion was but too well founded that these petitions for the abolition of slavery in the District of Columbia were blows on the wedge, which would ultimately break the Union asunder.

That the attack of the abolition petitions was not directed against slavery in the States, but merely against slavery in the District, was, though not from the legal point of view, yet as to the ultimate practical result, matter of absolute indifference. If, as all the petitions asserted, the nature of slavery made its existence in the District a national disgrace and a national sin, the same disgrace and the same sin weighed down every Southern State. Calhoun's assertion, therefore, could not be refuted, that "the petitions were in themselves a foul slander on nearly one half of the States of the Union." If the national legislature now, in any way, offered its assistance to brand the peculiar institution of one half of the constituent members of the Union, it certainly violated the spirit of the Constitution; for the Constitution, as everybody admitted, not only tacitly recognized slavery as a fact which the States exclusively had power to deal with, but moreover served in many essential respects as its direct support and protection. Calhoun was therefore unquestionably right when he said that, unless an undoubted provision of the Constitution compelled them to receive such petitions, it was their duty to reject them at the very threshold; and he proved that there was no such absolute compulsion by an undoubted constitutional provision. On the other hand, however, inasmuch as some obligations were imposed upon the whole Union with re gard to slavery, the existence of slavery in some of the States was actually and legally also a concern of those States in which it did not exist. And in respect to whatever actually and legally concerned the people, they had a constitutional right to demand that their representatives should listen to their wishes and grievances presented in the form of petitions. Besides, no ingenuity could reason out of the Constitution the power of Congress over slavery in the District; for somewhere the power had to be lodged, and the legislative power of Congress over the District was expressly declared to be "*exclusive* in all cases whatsoever." To lay down the principle that Congress was in duty bound to shut its door against all anti-slavery petitions was therefore most certainly an abridgment of the right of petition. The opponents of Calhoun were, in fact, no less right than he. Not their arguments, but the facts, and the Constitution, which had been framed according to the facts, were at fault. The founders of the republic had been under the necessity of admitting slavery into the Constitution, and the inevitable consequence was that conclusions which were diametrically opposed to each other could be logically deduced from it by starting the argument *first* from the fact that slavery was an acknowledged and protected institution which, so far as the States were concerned, was out of the pale of the federal jurisdiction ; and *then* from the no less incontestable fact that the determining principle of the Constitution was liberty, and that the spirit and the whole life of the American people fully accorded with the Constitution in this respect.

The flaw in all the reasoning of Calhoun on the slavery question was, that he took no account whatever of the latter fact. The logical consequence of this was that his constitutional theories were of a nature which rendered the acquiescence of the North in them an utter impossibility. He never became fully conscious of this fact, which rendered all his exertions to obtain absolute safety for slavery *in the Union* as vain as the pouring of water into a cask without a bottom. His reasoning on the dangers which threatened slavery in the actual Union, under the actual Constitution, was, however, not in the least affected by it. From the first he saw them with such an appalling clearness that his predictions could not but seem hallucinations of a diseased mind so long as the people, both at the North and at the South, had not been taught by bitter experience that the conflict was irrepressible, because a compromise between antagonistic principles is *ab initio* an impossibility. From the first he saw, predicted

and proved that, unless his constitutional doctrines were accepted, slavery could not be safe
in the Union, and that therefore the slave States
would have to cut the ties which bound them
to the North.

"Our true position," he declared in the above
mentioned speech, "that which is indispensable to
our defence *here*, is, that Congress has no legitimate
jurisdiction over the subject of slavery either here or
elsewhere. The reception of this petition surrenders
this commanding position; yields the question of jurisdiction, so important to the cause of abolition and
so injurious to us; compels us to sit in silence to witness the assault on our character and institutions, or
to engage in an endless contest in their defence. Such
a contest is beyond mortal endurance. We must in
the end be humbled, degraded, broken down, and
worn out.

" The senators from the slave-holding States, who,
most unfortunately, have committed themselves to
vote for receiving these incendiary petitions, tell us
that whenever the attempt shall be made to abolish
slavery they will join with us to repel it. . . . But I
announce to them that they are now called on to re-
deem their pledge. *The attempt is* NOW *being made.*
The work is going on daily and hourly. The war is
waged not only in the most dangerous manner, but
in the only manner that it can be waged. Do they
expect that the abolitionists will resort to arms, and
commence a crusade to liberate our slaves by force?

9

Is this what they mean when they speak of the attempt to abolish slavery? If so, let me tell our
friends of the South who differ from us that the war
which the abolitionists wage against us is of a very
different character, and far more effective. It is a
war of religious and political fanaticism, mingled, on
the part of the leaders, with ambition and the love
of notoriety, and waged not against our lives, but our
character. The object is to humble and debase us
in our own estimation, and that of the world in general; to blast our reputation, while they overthrow
our domestic institutions. This is the mode in which
they are attempting abolition, with such ample means
and untiring industry; and *now is the time* for all
who are opposed to them to meet the attack. How
can it be successfully met? This is the important
question. There is but one way: we must meet the
enemy on the frontier, — on the question of receiving; we must secure that important pass, — it is our
Thermopylæ. The power of resistance, by an universal law of nature, is on the exterior. Break
through the shell, penetrate the crust, and there is
no resistance within. In the present contest, the
question on receiving constitutes our frontier. It is
the first, the exterior question, that covers and pro-
tects all others. Let it be penetrated by receiving
this petition, and not a point of resistance can be
found within, as far as this government is concerned
If we cannot maintain ourselves there, we cannot on
any interior position. . . . . There is no middle ground
that is tenable."

Has not the history of the slavery conflict fully borne out every one of these assertions? Calhoun reads the future as if the book of fate were lying wide open before him. Only as to the means by which he proposed to avert the impending dangers he was as blind as all the rest of the people. If the enlistment of the moral and religious sentiment of the world against slavery was a war, in which the South must ultimately break down, what was the use of hermetically closing the Capitol at Washington against all the manifestations of the spirit of abolitionism? Since when did the civilized world or even the American people wait for the gracious permission of Congress, ere they dared to form their religious opinions or moral convictions? And if the religious, moral, and political convictions of Congress and of the people did not agree, which of the two would finally have to yield, Congress or the people? Even if it had been but a political question, the attempt would have been simply absurd to decree it out of existence by a resolution of the legislature not to listen to what the people had to say about it. But if it was also a moral and religious question — which most certainly it was — the attempt was doubly ab surd. There is no "frontier" which can be successfully defended against ideas, and ne

' shell " is so hard that such ideas cannot penetrate it. The confession that, if the shell were broken through, there was no resistance within, amounted therefore to a confession that slavery would at last succumb, if the slave-holding States remained in the Union.

From all sides Calhoun was accused of stirring up sectional animosity and strife in a most unwarrantable manner, by exciting the South with his wild talk about awful dangers, which had nowhere any existence except in his own feverish brain. The truth, however, was that he did not see spectres in broad daylight, but that he took too hopeful a view of the future. What in his opinion was but a dire eventuality, which could be easily averted, was, by his own showing, the inevitable end of the slavery conflict. Abolitionism tolled the death-bell of slavery *in the Union*, and dearly have the American people had to pay for it, that they ever doubted Calhoun's declaration that, whenever the slave-holding States had to choose between the Union and slavery, they would not hesitate for a moment to decide in favor of slavery.

" We love and cherish the Union ; we remember with the kindest feelings our common origin, with pride our common achievements, and fondly anticipate the common greatness and glory that seem to await us: but origin, achievements, and anticipation

of common greatness are to us as nothing, com
pared with this question. It is to us a vital question. It involves not only our liberty, but, what is
greater (if to freemen anything can be), existence
itself. The relation which now exists between the
two races in the slave-holding States has existed for
two centuries. It has grown with our growth, and
strengthened with our strength. It has entered into
and modified all our institutions, civil and political.
None other can be substituted. We will not, cannot,
permit it to be destroyed. . . . Come what will, should
it cost every drop of blood and every cent of property, we must defend ourselves; and if compelled,
we would stand justified by all laws, human and divine; . . . we would act under an imperious necessity. There would be to us but one alternative, — to
triumph or perish as a people. . . . I ask neither sym
pathy nor compassion for the slave-holding States.
We can take care of ourselves. It is not we, but the
Union, which is in danger. . . . We cannot remain
here in an endless struggle in defence of our character, our property and institutions."

Calhoun spoke to deaf ears. The petition
was received, but the prayer of the petitioners
was rejected by an overwhelming majority after
a short and unimportant debate, in which the
South was repeatedly and emphatically assured
that thus a precedent was to be established for
the rejection of all similar petitions, without
any discussion, directly after their reception.

James Buchanan was the father of the great device of thus, with an obliging compliment to both sides, slipping through between the hammer and the anvil. It was a new trial of the old art of cloaking by empty formulas the contradiction of principles and the collision of facts. The petitioners did not see any material difference between a refusal to receive and a rejection on principle without any discussion ; and the principle, on the unconditional maintenance of which alone, in Calhoun's opinion, the safety of slavery depended, was surrendered. Ill-will against the South had nothing whatever to do with that. Though slavery was not liked in the Northern States, they were as yet but too willing to satisfy the demands of the South. They shunned the agitation of the slavery question more than did the South, and they were most willing to suppress abolitionism. The trouble only was that there was no way of doing it. It is hardly to be supposed that the more intelligent and educated Southerners can have deemed it possible for the North to adopt the means which the Southern radicals proposed, with insulting imperiousness ; and yet there was a goodly number of Northern politicians who readily consented to decree even the impossible.

President Jackson's message of December 2 1835, had invited Congress to pass a law pro

hibiting, " under severe penalties, the circulation in the Southern States, through the mail,
of incendiary publications intended to instigate
slaves to insurrection." In point of fact, no
such publication had ever been issued by any
American press; but what the President really
wanted was, of course, clear enough: the mails
should be closed to all publications tainted with
the spirit of abolitionism. On Calhoun's motion, this part of the message was referred to a
special committee, which, on February 4, 1836,
introduced a bill, accompanied by a report.
Calhoun, who was the author of the bill and of
the report, defended them on April 12, 1836,
in one of the most remarkable speeches ever
delivered either by him or by anybody else in
Congress. The recommendation of the President was rejected, because a law " discrimi-
nating, in reference to character, what publications shall not be transmitted by the mail,"
would be an abridgment of the liberty of the
press. Moreover, and above all, the principle
upon which such a law would have rested delivered the South, bound hand and foot, to the
discretion of the federal government. If Con
gress had the right to determine what publications were incendiary and to forbid their transmission through the mail, it evidently had also
the right to decide what publications were not

incendiary and to enforce their transmission through the mail. Both objections were unquestionably well founded, and an unsophisticated mind would have naturally expected to see the conclusion drawn from them that the publications of the abolitionists could not be legally excluded from the mail. The bill, however, prohibited "deputy-postmasters from receiving and transmitting through the mail, to any State, Territory, or District, certain papers therein mentioned, the circulation of which is prohibited by the laws of said State, Territory, or District." Calhoun, in fact, demanded it least as emphatically as Jackson the exclusion of abolition publications from the mail, and even the means by which he proposed to attain his end were virtually the same, though they appeared under a different nomenclature. The only real difference between the President and the senator was the constitutional doctrine on which they based their respective demands; but that was indeed a difference of the last importance. Jackson's idea was simply that, as slavery was an institution recognized by the Constitution, the federal government could not allow itself to be used for undermining it, but was obliged to protect it against attacks which were not only "unconstitutional," but "repugnant to the principles of our national compact and to the dictates of humanity and religion." Calhoun, on the other hand, took exactly the opposite view. According to him, the federal government had no right to meddle in any way whatever with this question; all it could do, and what at the same time was bound to do, was to enjoin upon its officers to conform themselves strictly to the laws of the State in which they happened to be employed.

" The internal peace and security of the States are under the protection of the States themselves, to the entire exclusion of all authority and control on the part of Congress. It belongs to them, and not to Congress, to determine what is or is not calculated to disturb their peace and security. . . . In the execution of the measures which may be adopted by the States for this purpose [to prohibit the circulation of any publication or any intercourse calculated to disturb or destroy the relation between master and slave], the powers of Congress over the mail, and of regulating commerce with foreign nations and between the States, may require coöperation on the part of the general government; and it is bound, in conformity with the principle established, to respect the laws of the State in their exercise, and so to modify its acts as not only not to violate those of the States, but, as far as practicable, to coöperate in their execution."

Calhoun's bill therefore provided that postmasters who " knowingly " transmitted or delivered any " paper " treating of slavery in a way contrary to the laws of the State should be punished by fine and imprisonment. Which clause of the Constitution conferred upon Congress the power to enact national laws for furthering the execution of the state laws, this strictest of the strict constructionists forgot to tell. Like a noble steed on the race-course he did not look to the right nor to the left, his course leading in a straight line to the goal. If he had but once cast a passing glance on either side, he could hardly have helped being himself amused at the strange consequences of his theory, if nature had not denied him all sense of humor so far as politics were concerned. The laws of the States on the incriminated publications might be as different as the glass splinters and the little pebbles in a kaleidoscope vary in shape and color. The federal law, therefore, would enjoin upon the postmasters to obey and execute some dozen different and perhaps even contradictory laws relating to the same subject, — a law which would at all events have the merit of novelty in the history of legislation. A postmaster in Massachusetts imprisoned for omitting to do a certain thing, and a postmaster in South Carolina imprisoned for doing this very thing, both punished in pursuance of the same federal law, — these two gentlemen, if no one else, would certainly not be convinced of the soundness of Calhoun's theory.

The United States statutes were not disfigured by such a monstrous law. The blot is sufficiently ugly that it received in the Senate nineteen votes, four of which were cast by Northern senators. Calhoun himself had probably not expected a more favorable result, for even of the four Southern members of the committee only Mason, of North Carolina, besides himself, had given the report and the bill an unqualified approval. The whole speech of April 12, 1836, gives the impression that its real purpose was not so much to convince the Senate of the necessity or propriety of passing this particular bill as to get the argument before the country as a new manifesto, or rather *pronunciamento*, of the slave power. At all events, it is only from this point of view that it is of great importance.

Calhoun had taken a great step beyond the stand-point which he had occupied during the nullification controversy. Then he had said that the federal government and the States were parties to a compact having no common judge, and therefore each was entitled to decide for itself as to the extent of its obligations under the compact, as to the violations of the same by the other party, and as to the means and the measure of the remedy. Only at this subsequent stage, and in evident contradiction of the alleged "party" relation, was the national government made to assume the position of an "agent" of the States. Now we hear nothing more of a compact; the federal government stands no more on an equal footing with the States; it appears only in the character of their agent, and a most humble, nay, a pitiful and despicable agent it is, for it is bound to do the bidding of every one of its constituent members, no matter how contradictory, how absurd, how outrageous their behests may be. Yet Calhoun has not changed his general constitutional theory concerning the relation between the federal government and the States. It appears in a modified light only because he does not confine his reasoning to the constitutional question. The history of the slavery question has forced him boldly to step beyond it, and plant his foot on the higher and firmer ground of the unalterable facts. He holds fast to the Constitution, for he shares the almost idolatrous veneration of the whole people for it; he knows how to find in it what he needs, and he is fully conscious that he would be a general without a single soldier in his army from the moment when his theories and his practical demands should avowedly come into conflict with its provisions. But the

leading idea of his whole argument is the too
well founded conviction that, whether in conformity with the Constitution or not, the issue
would be decided according to the facts. Slavery is, in his opinion, not only a fact, but an
immutable fact, because it is the direct outgrowth of the natural relation between the white
and the black races.

" To destroy the existing relations would be to destroy this prosperity [of the Southern States], and to
place the two races in a state of conflict, which must
end in the expulsion or extirpation of one or the
other. No other can be substituted compatible with
their peace or security. The difficulty is in the diversity of the races. So strongly drawn is the line
between the two in consequence, and so strengthened
by the force of habit and education, that it is impossible for them to exist together in the community, where
their numbers are so nearly equal as in the slave-holding States, under any other relation than that which
now exists. Social and political equality between
them is impossible. No power on earth can overcome the difficulty. The causes lie too deep in the
principles of our nature to be surmounted. But, without such equality, to change the present condition of
the African race, were it possible, would be but to
change the form of slavery."

When the Republicans, many years later,
made the political and social equality of the

freedmen one of the principal planks of their
party platform, they never, to the knowledge
of the author, quoted this declaration of Calhoun, though a higher authority than the foremost representative of the slave-holders could, of
course, not be adduced for the necessity of such
a radical change in the relation of the two races.
This is the best proof that, although, or perhaps
precisely *because*, Calhoun was the fanatical
champion of the ideas of the Middle Ages with
regard to *slavery*, he was so far in advance of his
times with regard to the *slavery question*, that
his prophetic warnings could not possibly be of
any use to the country. They were always at-
tentively listened to, here with patriotic anger,
there with scorn and disdain, and by some with
an involuntary shudder; but nobody really
brought them home to his understanding, and
therefore they were too soon forgotten, to be
transmitted as a portentous bequest to the generation which was to work out their fulfilment
in wading through an ocean of blood. Many
suspected him of treason, while he performed
only with a sorrowing heart the office of a Cas-
sandra ; they accused him cf planning the destruction of the Union, while he heaped one ir-
refutable argument upon another, proving the
impossibility of the maintenance of slavery in
the Union ; and when the very " dough-faces '

began to see that their clamoring for peace was as the whistling of a boy against the storm, they charged him with being the principal author of the catastrophe, because he had foretold it. His claim to a place among the first men who have acted a part on the political stage of the United States has never been contested, and yet he has been handed down to posterity a mere distorted shadow of the real man, because his incessant cries of " Beware ! " and " Woe to you !" remained fresh in the memory of the people, while the reasoning of which these warnings had been but the last conclusion, was forgotten or misconstrued. Yet in spite of all this, he and those to whom his memory has been dear have had no right to complain, because, though he was no traitor, but honestly and earnestly wished to see the Union preserved, still the Union and all that made it valuable and dear to him were "*as nothing*" to him compared with slavery.

This being the case in the fullest sense of the .erm, and slavery being an immutable fact, the word *compromise* is not to be found in his political vocabulary with regard to the slavery question. In a second speech on abolition petitions (February 6, 1837), be declares, "I hold concession or compromise to be fatal. If we con cede an inch, concession would follow conces-

sion, compromise would follow compromise, until
our ranks would be so broken that effectual resistance would be impossible." So as every
agitation of the slavery question in a hostile
spirit *eo ipso* touches the vitals of the " peculiar
institution," it must be suppressed, if the Union
is to be preserved. In the discussion of the
abolition petitions, his love of the Union had betrayed this slave of his own implacable logic
into the gross mistake of regarding the exclusion of the slavery question from the halls of
Congress as substantially identical with a total and permanent extinction of its agitation
everywhere and in every form. He clung to
this fallacy, because to renounce it was to acknowledge that, if the rest of his argumentation
was correct, his attempts to save slavery *and*
the Union were *ab initio* absolutely idle. Now,
however, he did not recur to this point, but
drew directly from his premises the conclusion
that the federal government was bound to effect the suppression of the agitation without
meddling in any way whatever with the "peculiar institution; " that is, that within the
sphere of its legitimate action, and to the fullest extent of its constitutional powers, it was
bound to do what the States demanded. No
justification for refusing to do so did or ever
would exist. Even the exercise of an unques

tioned constitutional power was no valid excuse.
The discretion of Congress had its limit in the
notion of every single State as to what its individual security demanded. A constitutional
federal law would instantly lose its validity and
constitutionality, if a State should see fit, under
the plea of securing its peace, to pass a conflicting law : —

"The low must yield to the high ; the convenient
to the necessary ; mere accommodation to safety and
security. This is the universal principle which governs in all analogous cases, both in our social and political relations. Whenever the means of enjoying or
securing rights come into conflict, — rights themselves
never can, — this universal and fundamental principle
is the one which, by consent of mankind, governs in
all such cases. Apply it to the case under consideration, and need I ask which ought to yield? Will
any rational being say that the laws of eleven States
of the Union which are necessary to their peace, security, and very existence ought to yield to the laws
of the general government regulating the post-office,
which at the best is a mere accommodation and convenience, — and this when the government was formed
by the States, mainly with a view to secure more perfectly their peace and safety? But one answer can
be given. All must feel that it would be improper
for the laws of the States, in such case, to yield to
those of the general government, and of course that
the latter ought to yield to the former. When I say

ought, I do not mean on the principle of concession. I take higher ground : I mean under the obligation of the Constitution itself."

This obligation he found in the clause which empowers Congress " to make all laws which shall be necessary and proper for carrying into execution " the powers vested by the Constitution in the government of the United States, whence he drew the seemingly so simple and unanswerable conclusion that no law, relating to a mere accommodation and convenience, could be proper, if it endangered the peace, security, and very existence of any one of the States.   Each State being the exclusive judge of what its peace and security demanded, the direct consequence was that each State had to decide upon the necessity and propriety of the federal laws.   Thus the final result of Calhoun's reasoning is again a systematization of anarchy, but it is an anarchy of a higher order than that which he had arrived at in the tariff controversy.   Then he had claimed for each State the right to nullify, so far as itself was concerned, a federal law which it deemed unconstitutional, and now he attributed to each State the right to invalidate a constitutional federal law, and to render it unconstitutional by passing a conflicting law.   Whether the law was to be invalidated only as to the particular State, or for the whole Union, we are not told. According to the theory, it ought to have been the former; but then the old difficulty arose, that there was a federal law which was a law but for a part of the Union, while, if it was invalidated for the whole Union, twenty-three sovereign States, which took no exception to what their senators and representatives in Congress had seen fit to do, had to submit to the will of one sovereign State.

We are not informed which horn of the dilemma Calhoun preferred; but in either case the absurdity was so glaring that he again could not have failed to see it, if, in the particular matter on which he reasoned, there had not been a solidarity of interests of all the slave-holding States. This is the more evident as, throughout the report and the speech, *each State* and *the slave-holding States* are interchangeably used as equivalent terms with regard to the question in hand. The constitutional question is argued in such a manner that the right and the power claimed belong to each State individually; and whenever he came to speak of the facts, that is to say, whenever he applied the theory to the legislative problem before the Senate, he said *the South, the eleven slave-holding States*, etc. In the report, too, as well as in the speech, the consideration of the fact predominates in a very remarkable degree over the constitutional argument: —

" He must be blind, indeed, who does not perceive
that the subversion of a relation which must be followed with such disastrous consequences can only be
effected by convulsions that would devastate the country, burst asunder the bonds of the Union, and engulf,
in a sea of blood, the institutions of the country.   It
is madness to suppose that the slave-holding States
would quietly submit to be sacrificed.   Every consideration — interest, duty, and humanity, the love of
country, the sense of wrong, hatred of oppressors, and
treacherous and faithless confederates, and, finally,
despair — would impel them to the most daring and
desperate resistance in defence of property, family,
country, liberty, and existence."

Yes, it is madness to suppose that the slave-
holding States would quietly submit to be sacrificed, — *that* is the pivot on which the report,
the speech, and the bill turn, and not on any
clause of the Constitution.   If "existence " was
at stake and " despair " sat at the council table,
then, indeed, it was a matter of course that not
only the Union, but also the whole Constitution,
was "as nothing."   Therefore, also, the speech
did not conclude with a maxim or rule of constitutional law, but with the announcement of
a fact : —

" I must tell the Senate, be your decision what it
may, the South will never abandon the principles of
this bill.   If you refuse coöperation with our laws

and conflict should ensue between yours and ours, the Southern States will never yield to the superiority of yours. . . . Let it be fixed, let it be riveted in every Southern mind that the laws of the slave-holding States for the protection of their domestic institutions are paramount to the laws of the general government in regulations of commerce and the mail; that the latter must yield to the former in the event of conflict."

In the opinion of those who neither saw nor thought beyond the immediate future, this announcement proved to be less than an empty threat. Not only was Calhoun's bill rejected, but in the same year another bill was passed by both Houses of Congress, and approved by the President, prohibiting postmasters, under severe penalty, from " unlawfully " detaining in their offices "any letter, package, pamphlet, or newspaper with intent to prevent the arrival and delivery of the same." Nowhere was the nullification of this law spoken of, and never again was an attempt made by federal legislation thus indirectly to abridge the liberty of the press. Yet Calhoun was right in the most essential point. The South never did abandon the principle of this bill; that is to say, the principle that slavery had to be protected and defended at all hazards, — with and under the Constitution, if possible, but protected and defended it must and should be, under all circum-

stances and by any necessary means. Calhoun
knew that well enough, and he therefore did
not wear the dismayed mien of a defeated man
With the same tone of deep, immutable conviction he repeated at every opportunity the
declaration that the South would never yield
in the slavery question, because it *could* not do
it. He did not live to see the day when this
declaration was put to its final test; but the delay was so long only because, through all these
gloomy years, the resistance of the North invariably broke down before the attacks of the
solid phalanx of the slave power. Calhoun had
been defeated in the question of the abolition
petitions and in that of the incendiary publications, because the South had not come up to the
mark ; but the inglorious victories of the North
augured nothing but ignominious defeats for
the future, while Calhoun could anticipate brilliant — but alas ! how terribly disastrous — victories, for he was sure that the South would
steadily advance towards the mark which he
had drawn for it. Therefore it would have
been a most egregious mistake to judge the situation by the immediate result of his movement in those two questions. The defeated
" doctrinaire " was not " shelved ; " on the con
trary, his influence was on the increase, though
he dared once more to throw the gauntlet into
the face of public opinion.

Nearly a year passed ere Calhoun addressed the Senate again on the slavery question. The old economical questions pushed themselves once more into the foreground. In spite of the compromise tariff, the revenues of the government increased at such a rate that the apprehension arose anew of seeing a vast surplus accumulate. The various propositions for averting that "calamity" or employing the superfluous money do not concern us here. It need only be mentioned that Calhoun considered it a serious danger, and as, in his opinion, the accumulation of the surplus could not be prevented, he earnestly advocated that it should be "deposited" in the treasuries of the States, according to their federal representation.

It is a very curious and even important fact, which, so far as our knowledge goes, has thus far been entirely overlooked, that Calhoun, besides his general reasons, had a special purpose in proposing such a disposal of the surplus revenue. In a letter to some citizens of Athens, Georgia (August 5, 1836), he writes: —

"Instead of being cut off from the vast commerce of the West, as had been supposed, we find, to our surprise, that it is in our power, with proper exertions, to turn its copious stream to our own ports. Just at this important moment, when this new and brilliant prospect is unfolding to our view, the Deposit Bill is

about to place under the control of the States interested ample means of accomplishing, on the most ex
tended and durable scale, a system of railroad com
munication that, if effected, must change the social,
political, and commercial relations of the whole country vastly to our benefit, but without injuring other
sections."

The federal government dares not do indirectly what it has no right to do directly — how
often had he declared this to be a fundamental
principle of constitutional law! And yet what
was this proposed distribution if not " internal
improvements" by indirection? True enough,
not internal improvements which Congress
deemed of national importance, but under the
exclusive control of the separate States, and intended, in the first place, to serve state interests. But it is not because the consistency of
Calhoun might be called into question that this
idea deserves more attention than it has hitherto received from historians. The arch-doc-
trinaire was in the South one of the first to see
that with the railroads a force had been introduced which was to exert a most powerful influence in shaping the destinies of the country, not
only in general, but also with regard to the relation of the two geographical sections lying re-
spectively north and south of Mason and Dixon's line. He himself proposed a certain route

through the Alleghanies, spending eight days on his exploring expedition, and walking over a considerable part of the ground. The interest which he manifested in this problem was so great that the Southern papers spoke of him as the fittest man to be made the president of the great Southern and Western Railroad Company. He was fully awake to the importance of the fact that the difference in the wealth of the two sections increased every year in favor of the North; and he saw that, as the general economical development would go on at an unparalleled rate in consequence of communication by steam, this difference would necessarily increase at the same ratio if the South should lag behind the North in realizing the possibilities created by the new invention. Yet his last conclusion could not have been more wrong, if every one of his premises had been erroneous. Not Congress and its tariff laws, as he supposed, but slavery was the cause of the remarkable phenomenon which justly rendered him so uneasy; and therefore the new invention, which was a blessing to all mankind, was sure to prove a curse to the slave-holders. As early as 1817 a representative of Louisiana had declared in Congress, "We need no roads·" and a country which needs no roads cannot have railroads. The will of the South was as nothing in this question. The principal cities might indeed be connected by rail, and it was done in the course of time ; but there were, so to speak, no brooks and rivers to feed the main streams, and, whatever the South might do, it could not create them. The idea of Calhoun, to make up for lost time and overtake the North by means of railroads, was a more preposterous delusion than any he had indulged in heretofore. No power on earth could spur the South into a livelier pace, because it is the very nature of the "peculiar institution " to move in a jog trot. The railroads only served to put this fact into a more glaring light ; while in the North they accelerated the economical development more than the wildest imagination could have anticipated at that time.

It was neither all nor the worst that Calhoun's hopes were to be wholly disappointed, and that a new impetus was to be given in the direction in which the economical development of the country had been moving ever since the adoption of the Constitution. He was undoubtedly right in doing his best for an extensive railroad system, for the less the South kept up in this respect with the North the more unfavorably would it compare in every respect with the non-slave-holding States. But every spike which fastened a rail in Southern soil was a nail driven into the coffin of slavery; for every engine, nay, every traveller and every bale of goods, came impregnated with the spirit of the times, which would not and could not brook slavery. The South had no choice; Calhoun was right in believing that self-preservation bade the South to grasp even more eagerly than the North at the cup which was to mankind what the alchemists had vainly tried to find for the individual, — an elixir of life; but slavery turned it into poison. The irrepressible conflict between North and South was to end with the disruption of the Union; but another and more intense irrepressible conflict gnawed the intestines of the South, and it was this that rendered the doom of slavery inevitable. Whatever the merits or demerits of the deposit scheme were from a general point of view, if the Southern States should invest their share in railroads, it would certainly have been the best use they could make of the money, and yet it would have been better for them to throw all the surplus into the sea.

The adoption of Calhoun's device led to one of the most curious episodes in the financial history of the United States, which abounds with strange incidents. But whatever may be thought of the remedy, it will not be denied that Calhoun was right in asserting that the govern ment ought not to take more out of the pockets of the citizens than it really needed for its legitimate purposes, and that a chronically plethoric treasury might have grave consequences. Calhoun chiefly apprehended that such a constantly overflowing purse would be a powerful means to corrupt the whole government machinery still more than heretofore, by leading to a further increase of the vast patronage of the federal government, and by enlisting all the federal officers still more exclusively in the party service, and that the independence and sovereignty of the States would thereby be still more endangered.

It had evidently become with him a matter of course that every legislative problem of a general character must, in some way or other, stand in close connection with these two questions. The alarming increase of the revenues was partly due to the enormous sales of the public lands, which were, to a great extent, bought on speculation. Here was certainly a problem of the first magnitude and beset with extraordinary difficulties; but it is, to say the least, rather surprising to see the greatest stress laid on the dangers which were to arise in those two respects from this source. This is not the place to discuss the great land question, and we will therefore not inquire into the merits or de merits of Calhoun's general opinions concerning it. The reason for his proposition (February, 1837) to cede the public lands to the new States, namely, " to place the senators and representatives from the new States on an equality with those from the old, by withdrawing our local control, and breaking the *vassalage* under which they are now placed," would, however, hardly admit of a serious criticism.

A less far-fetched opportunity was offered him to discuss state sovereignty, from a new point of view and in a thorough manner, in the debate on the question of admitting Michigan as a State. Congress had made the admission dependent upon the condition that Michigan should agree to a certain boundary line. This agreement had been made, but opinions differed as to whether it had been made in a legal or illegal manner. As to the concrete question, it suffices to say that Calhoun was of the latter opinion. We have to look somewhat more closely only at the general theory, which he proclaimed on this occasion.

Calhoun asserted that the condition concerning the boundary attached "simply to her *admission* into the Union," and did not affect in the least either the acceptance of her constitution by Congress or " the declaration that she is a State." There was no difference of opinion as to the first part of the assertion, but it was contended on the other side that Michigan was not and could not be a State before her admission into the Union. Calhoun proved that this assertion was incompatible with the act of Congress imposing the boundary condition. That, however, could not be decisive as to the main question. Contests upon great constitutional principles cannot be decided by appealing to the wording of a statute, because this might be grossly inaccurate and careless; besides, the Constitution would then be but a piece of wax in the hands of Congress, for Congress might at first pass a law to suit itself, and then declare the correct reading of the Constitution to be thus and thus, since this law says so and so. But Calhoun did not rest his case solely upon this act of Congress. He said : —

" I now go farther, and assert that it [the position of the friends of the bill before the Senate] is in direct opposition to plain and unquestionable matter of fact. There is no fact more certain than that Michigan is a State. She is in full exercise of sovereign authority, with a legislature and a chief magistrate. She passes laws; she executes them; she regulates titles, and even takes away life, — all on her own authority. Ours has entirely ceased over her; and yet there are those who can deny, with all these facts before them, that she is a State. They might as well deny the existence of this hall ! "

If Calhoun had been able under any circumstances to consider a question of this nature with a judicial mind, instead of entering upon its examination with the foregone conclusions of a passionate partisan, he would have perceived at the first glance that the case was far from being so plain as he made it out. Michigan was unquestionably no longer a Territory, and she did — and she did *of right* — all that he had mentioned. The most appropriate — or it is perhaps more correct to say the least inappropriate — name to be found in the insufficient nomenclature of political science for the commonwealth, therefore, was possibly a "State." That, however, was of very little consequence with regard to the point made by Calhoun. Everything depended upon the answer to the question what *kind* of a State it was, or, in other words, what the term "State" signified in this particular case. That Michigan was not *at this moment* a State in the most general acceptation of the term, even Calhoun would hardly have ventured to deny. Would he have dared to assert that, while the question of her admission into the Union was pending, she would have the right to declare war against some other sovereign power, to conclude treaties, to coin money, to grant letters of mark and reprisal, etc. ? Undeniably she lacked many of the most essen

tial powers inherent to sovereignty, and, in
consequence, she evidently was not a State as
that phrase is most frequently used.   Just as
evidently she was not a State of the Union
in the sense of the Constitution, for the question under consideration was her admission into
the Union. Yet no one pretended that she was
out of the Union. Whatever her legal relation towards the federal government might be,
she certainly was a part of the great commonwealth known by the name of the United States
of America. Calhoun could the less contest
this fact, because another proof which he adduced for his assertion was that Michigan had
elected senators, and, according to the Constitution, only States elect senators. This argument clearly went too far the other way. In
correct language, Michigan had not elected
senators of the United States, but she had
elected two men, who were to be her senators
in Congress after she had been admitted into
the Union. Also, since Michigan was a part of
the republic, the authority of Congress over
her had incontestably not "*entirely* ceased,"
for there is and can be no part of the republic
over which Congress has not some authority.
Whether this authority went so far as to give
Congress the right to remand Michigan into
her former territorial status, if she refused to

comply with the conditions imposed upon her admission into the Union, need not here be inquired into. Calhoun's argument is like a sword without a blade, if it be proved that Michigan was but a State in an inchoate condition, which could be perfected only by the act of Congress admitting her into the Union.

Calhoun did, of course, not contest that an act of Congress was needed to make Michigan a State of the Union, but he did not assent any further to the proposition just stated.

"I am told, if this be so, if a Territory must become a State before it can be admitted, it would follow that she might refuse to enter the Union after she had acquired the right of acting for herself. Certainly she may. A State cannot *be forced* into the Union. She must come in *by her own free assent,* given in her highest sovereign capacity through a convention of the people of the State. Such is the constitutional provision ; and those who make the objection must overlook both the Constitution and the elementary principles of our government, of which the right of *self-government is the first,* — the right of every people to form their own government, and to determine their political condition."

The right here claimed is not the right of secession. If secession, not as an eventually justifiable revolutionary act, but as a constitutional right, is a monstrous political absurdity, this right thus asserted concerning Michigan is an absurdity in comparison with which the right of secession is the soundest political conception, and even, like nullification, "a conservative principle." Calhoun now and afterwards maintained that a so-called enabling act of Congress was required to give a Territory the right to erect itself into a State. But if any political proposition can be called self-evident, it is certainly this: that an enabling act can only give permission to a Territory to erect itself into a State *of the Union.* Even if Congress could ever be so regardless of duty, and so mad as to give a Territory permission simultaneously with adopting a state constitution to will itself out of the Union, in which clause of the Constitution did this strict constructionist find the power granted to Congress to commit such a suicidal act? The Constitution, which Calhoun proclaimed the grandest embodiment of political wisdom thus far seen by the world, would have been the greatest monstrosity ever conceived by the human mind, if the Union could constitutionally lose all its territorial possessions, merely because the inhabitants of the Territories were pleased to bow themselves out of it, by way of acknowledging the privilege accorded them to become full members of the Union. That "so long as these sound principles are ob-

served " no State would ever " reject this hig
privilege," or would " ever refuse to enter this
Union," but rather would " rush into your em-
brace, so long as your institutions are worth
preserving," was an assertion of no consequence
whatever. The possibility stamps the theory
as such an infinite absurdity that it would be
an insult to the reader to discuss it at all, if
John C. Calhoun had not been its advocate.
But one month later he very correctly spoke
of " the public domain " as being " the property
of the whole people of the United States." So
an insignificant minority — the inhabitants of
the Territories — had the right to deprive the
whole people of this inestimable property, and
appropriate it exclusively to themselves, and,
with the indirect sanction of Congress, given
by the permission to adopt state constitutions,
set up in business for themselves, without perhaps even deigning to say good-by to this
Union, which improved so wonderfully upon
the example of King Lear. But enough, and
more than enough, of this doctrine, which every
school-boy will pronounce to be utter nonsense.
Yet one of the most acute political reasoners
produced by America honestly believed it, because it was a logical outgrowth of the doctrine
of state sovereignty and because the doctrine
of state sovereignty was the sheet-anchor which

held the worm-eaten bark of slavery to her moorings.

Poor man! Adams wrote some months later "Calhoun looks like a man racked with furious passions and stung with disappointed ambition, as he is." Certainly, Calhoun had not forgotten his bitter disappointments, nor had he ceased to hope that he would, after all, some time reach the goal of his wishes; but his personal ambition had long ago become wholly subordinate to the passions which the slavery conflict had awakened in his bosom. The encroachments of the slave power upon the domain of liberty went on at an alarming rate · but Calhoun derived no satisfaction from any success, because every advance disclosed to his mind more clearly the immensity of the space still to be traversed, ere the slave-holders could say to themselves: Put out the watch-fires, let us rest and enjoy the fruits of our toils, for there is nothing more to be apprehended. In his second speech on the admission of Michigan, he had thus very correctly characterized himself: —

"It has perhaps been too much my habit to look more to the future and less to the present than is wise; but such is the constitution of my mind that when 1 see before me the indications of causes cd. .ulated to effect important changes in our politica,

:ondition, I am led irresistibly to trace them to their sources, and follow them out in their consequences."

His name would appear in smaller letters in the history of the United States, but his happiness as a man would have been greater, if it had been otherwise. What wonder that passion raked its deep furrows into the face of a man who fought with all the fervor of his hot blood and all the energy of his iron will for a cause, and yet perceived that every victory gained increased the number and determination of its enemies, and rendered their ultimate triumph more probable, if not certain! If he had still been open to arguments on this head, this condition of the struggle would have necessarily awakened doubts in his mind concerning the justice of his cause; but as his stand had been irrevocably taken, the remarkable phenomenon had just the opposite effect. The denunciations of slavery by the abolitionists incited him to extol it in unmeasured terms.

In a brief but most important speech (February 6, 1837) the question of receiving the abolition petitions was taken up by him once more. It was not done with a view to a reconsideration of the memorable decision of the Senate, though he tried to prove that his opinion had been fully borne out by the course of

events.   He saw his prophecies about to be fulfilled, and his object was to warn the Senate
once more to arrest its fatal course down the inclined plane, which terminated in an abyss.

" I then said that the next step would be to refer
the petition to a committee, and I already see indications that such is now the intention. . . . We are
now told that the most effectual mode of arresting the
progress of abolition is to reason it down ; and with
this view it is urged that the petitions ought to be referred to a committee. That is the very ground
which was taken at the last session in the other
House ; but instead of arresting its progress, it has
since advanced more rapidly than ever. The most
unquestionable right may be rendered doubtful if
once admitted to be a subject of controversy, and that
would be the case in the present instance."

This was all very true, but Calhoun was
mistaken in supposing that it could be helped.
In this very speech, he himself furnished the
best proof that nothing, which either the Senate or any other earthly power could do, would
alter any of these facts in the least. True
enough, the attempt of the House of Representatives to reason abolitionism down had
oeen worse than futile. The antislavery spirit
could not be reasoned down; and yet Calhoun's
whole speech was nothing but an attempt to do
this very thing, and to do it with argument,

which unanswerably proved the truth of his
first assertion, that it could *not* be done.

" They who imagine that the spirit now abroad in
the North will die away of itself, without a shock or
convulsion, have formed a very inadequate conception of its real character ; it will continue to rise and
spread, unless prompt and efficient measures to stay
its progress be adopted. Already it has taken possession of the pulpit, of the schools, and, to a considerable extent, of the press, — those great instruments by which the mind of the rising generation will
be formed.

" However sound the great body of the non-slave-
holding States are at present, in the course of a few
years they will be succeeded by those who will have
been taught to hate the people and institutions of
nearly one half of this Union with a hatred more
deadly than one hostile nation ever entertained towards another. It is easy to see the end. By the
necessary course of events, if left to themselves, we
must become, finally, two peoples. It is impossible,
under the deadly hatred which must spring up between the two great sections, if the present causes
are permitted to operate unchecked, that we should
continue under the same political system. The conflicting elements would burst the Union asunder,
powerful as are the links which hold it together.
Abolition and the Union cannot coexist. As the
friend of the Union, I openly proclaim it, and the
sooner it is known the better. The former may now

be controlled, but in a short time it will be beyond the power of man to arrest the course of events."

What a bewildering tangle of contradictions! If the antislavery spirit, left unchecked, was sure to spread, and if it had already taken possession of the pulpit, of the schools, and of a considerable part of the press, — that is to say, of the three great formative agencies of public opinion, — who and what should then check it? Besides public opinion, there was no other power except the public authorities. In a democratic republic, however, the public authorities are the creatures of public opinion, and not its masters. And what did Calhoun want the public authorities to do? They were not to reason with the antislavery spirit, for to argue the case at all was to render the unquestionable right doubtful, and, as experience had taught, only served the cause which was to be put down. Was Congress to pass penal laws against the manifestation of the antislavery spirit in the pulpits, in the schools, and in the press? Would not the mere suggestion of such a law raise a storm of passionate debate, such as had never before swept through the halls of Congress? And if such laws could be passed in the face of the express provisions of the Constitution and against public opinion, how long could they remain in the statute book? But if Congress should not reason with the antislavery spirit, and could not pass penal laws against it, what could it do but maintain an indignant silence ? Yet that would have been the policy of the ostrich. The danger does not disappear because we shut our eyes against it. Nobody knew this better than Calhoun, and so he spoke in tones which would have chilled the blood in the veins of his audience if they had had the faintest idea in what an awful manner every word of his predictions would be fulfilled in due time. Therefore it was, by his own showing, a delusion, without the smallest particle of firm ground to rest upon, that the antislavery spirit could yet be controlled. It was the natural offspring of the moral convictions and the political sentiments of the times ; and, in consequence, every attempt to fetter it necessarily acted upon it as a spur. Calhoun could not have failed to understand that he had knocked the last vestige of his argument from under his feet, if it had not been so true that he spoke as a friend of the Union. Slavery had to be maintained though the skies should fall, yet that the days of the Union were numbered he would not believe until it was actually rent in twain. But abolition and this Union could not coexist; therefore there *had* to be some means of crushing abolitionism. though he

himself had been forced to demonstrate that
there was and could be none.

A man of so lucid a mind as Calhoun, and so
incapable of consciously shutting his eyes to
any truth because he did not like it, could not
rest satisfied with being snugly spun into such
a Gordian knot of contradictions. If it could
not be unravelled, perhaps it might be cut by
a bold stroke. The sword must, of course, be
taken from the armory of reason. Did not the
assertion that the antislavery spirit could not
be reasoned down admit of a restrictive qualification? Denunciations, constitutional arguments, warnings, and threats were alike power-
less. But could not the flood be stemmed, if
the antislavery spirit were proved to be an
egregious mistake and a gross blunder? This
it was that he now undertook to do.

The Philadelphia Convention had nearly de-
spaired of overcoming the difficulties thrown by
slavery in the way of a " better Constitution,"
although the moral view taken of slavery by the
North and the South differed at that time comparatively little. The more exacting the Southern States were with regard to slavery, the more
readily did they admit that it was a moral,
political, and economical evil. There was no
hypocrisy in these declarations, though unquestionably the intensity of conviction did not

generally correspond with the emphasis of lan
guage. The confessions would have been much
more guarded if it had been apprehended that
they might lead to disadvantageous consequences.
Why should slavery not be called a mildew and
a curse, since the North had no objection to having the whole responsibility for the existence
of the evil thrown upon England, and since it
was honestly believed that the prohibition of
the foreign slave-trade would cause its gradual
extinction? Was it not rather to be supposed
that the resistance of the North against the
demands of the South would be weakened by
an appeal to the sympathy of Northerners with
the unfortunate condition of their Southern
brethren, and by strengthening the hope that
the Southern States, prompted by their moral
convictions and by what they considered their
true interest, would make all possible exertions
to render the constitutional compromises in favor of slavery only temporary make-shifts? The
more these hopes proved to be vain delusions,
the more it became the settled policy of the
South to season its exactions with a strong
dose of sound moral sentiments. The South
nad begun with honest self-deception, and it
gradually sunk into conscious deception of others; hollow declamations took the place of true
and more or less deep sentiments. Now and

then a voice was heard energetically disclaim-
ing the least hostility against negro slavery
from any point of view. These bold confessions were, however, hardly noticed amid the
din of general protestations against " slavery in
the abstract," and though they were ominous
signs of the times, they were, in fact, of themselves of no great importance, because they
were after all but personal opinions. Only
when placed on the basis of a general principle
did they become a vital force, which pushed the
slavery conflict into a new phase of development. Calhoun now took this decisive step,
with full consciousness of its significance. He
not only denied that slavery " in the abstract "
was an evil, but he emphatically proclaimed
negro slavery to be a good.

" But let me not be understood as admitting, even
by implication, that the existing relations between
the two races in the slave-holding States is an evil:
far otherwise, I hold it to be a good, as it has thus
far proved itself to be to both, and will continue to
prove so if not disturbed by the fell spirit of abolition.
. . . The relation now existing in the slave-holding
States between the two [races] is, instead of an evil,
a good, — a positive good."

The argument that the negroes were greatly
benefited by slavery, because physically, intellectually, and morally their actual condition was

infinitely better than it would have been in
the wilds of Africa, was very old, and one still
meets with it occasionally. Was it not, then,
cruel and unchristian to declare the African
slave-trade piracy, and thereby deprive the poor
benighted Africans of every chance of under-
going this blissful change? But, however that
might be, why was it a blessing for native-born
Americans of the negro race to be kept in slavery, because it had been a blessing to their an-
cestors, two or more generations back, to be
transported from Africa to America, though
they were sold into slavery? But we need not
dwell upon the threadbare sophistry of the argument, because Calhoun only repeated what
had been said a thousand times before.

Of much more importance was his "appeal
to facts" to support the other assertion: That
slavery was also "a positive good" for the other
race. "In the mean time," he said, "the white
or European race has not degenerated. It has
kept pace with its brethren in other sections of
the Union, where slavery does not exist. It is
odious to make comparisons; but I appeal to all
sides whether the South is not equal in virtue,
intelligence, patriotism, courage, disinterestedness, and all the high qualities which adorn our
nature." Inefficient and unreliable as were the
statistics of the United States at that time, they

were full and accurate enough to tell a strange
story about how the South had kept pace with
the North with regard to intelligence, so far as
intelligence depends upon school instruction and
upon the whole character of the life of the community in which an individual happens to live.
The history of the slavery conflict and of the
questions which stood in close connection with
it furnished an odd commentary on the peculiar disinterestedness of the South. Some parts
of the local news and the advertising columns
of the Southern papers concerning slaves were
strange reading for one wanting to inform himself about certain virtues and high qualities
which adorn our nature. Yet Calhoun spoke
in good faith, — only he had "the upper ten
thousand" in mind, while he spoke of the white
race. Every year it became more evident that
the curse of slavery weighed upon the white
race as heavily as upon the negroes, if not even
more so. Only in one thing did Calhoun admit
the inferiority of the South, — in "the arts of
gain:" a most important thing, indeed, since
the arts of gain are the most powerful agencies of civilization. But the South was not responsible for this one weak point in its case, for
he traced it "mainly to the fiscal action of this
government." Adam was more successful in
covering his nudity with a fig-leaf than the

South in the attempt to account for its unsat·
isfactory economical condition by this charge
against the economical policy of the federal
government. Whether good or bad, that policy
had been the same for the whole country, and
the North had advanced with giant strides, while
the South, in spite of its natural advantages, its
cotton monopoly and the unparalleled increase
of the cotton culture, complained that "the fox
dwelt amid the hearth-stones of once blooming
plantations." There was no other essential difference in the condition of the two sections than
slavery and what had resulted from it, and to
slavery, therefore, the inferiority in the arts of
gain had ultimately to be traced.

This "appeal to facts" more than sufficed
to prove that heavy clouds, laden with storm
and lightning, overhung the sky of the sunny
South, if it adopted this doctrine of the positive
good of slavery to both races. For then it had
sealed with its own hands the decree of fate,
that it had steadily to go on from bad to worse.
But all this was as nothing compared with the
general principle, upon which Calhoun rested
his assertion: "I take higher ground. . . . I
hold, then, that there never has yet existed a
wealthy and civilized society in which one portion of the community did not, in point of fact,
live on the labor of the other." Almost in-

numerable have been the devices — "from the brute force and gross superstition of ancient times, to the subtle and artful fiscal contrivances of modern " — by which so small a share of the wealth of all civilized communities has been allotted to those by whose labor it was produced, and so large a share given to the non-producing classes.

"I might well challenge a comparison between them and the more direct, simple, and patriarchal mode by which the labor of the African race is, among us, commanded by the European. I may say with truth that in few countries so much is left to the share of the laborer, and so little exacted from him. . . . But I will not dwell on this aspect of the question; I turn to the political, and here I fearlessly assert that the existing relation between the two races in the South, against which these blind fanatics are waging war, forms the most solid and durable foundation on which to rear free and stable political institutions. It is useless to disguise the fact. There is and always has been, in an advanced stage of wealth and civilization, a conflict between labor and capital. The condition of society in the South exempts us from the disorders and dangers resulting from this conflict; and explains why it is that the condition of the slave-holding States has been so much more stable and quiet than that of the North. The advantages of the former, in this respect, will become more and more manifest if left

undisturbed by interference from without, as the
country advances in wealth and numbers. We have,
in fact, but just entered that condition of society
where the strength and durability of our political institutions are to be tested; and I venture nothing in
predicting that the experience of the next generation
will fully test how vastly more favorable our condition of society is than that of other sections for free
and stable institutions, provided we are not disturbed
by the interference of others, or shall have sufficient
intelligence and spirit to resist promptly and successfully such interference."

This was a manifesto of infinitely more import than all his writings and speeches on nullification. His warfare against the antislavery
spirit had been in the beginning strictly defensive. Because the broad shield of the Constitution completely covered the "peculiar institution" of the South against all legislative
interference by the federal government, therefore he had thought that it must also prove impenetrable to the arrows of abolitionism; and
with the doctrine of state sovereignty he had
built the citadel of nullification, which would in
all emergencies furnish a last unconquerable ref-
uge. Strong as this position was, he soon became convinced that it was not strong enough.
Without abandoning it, he now warned the
North that the permanent and absolute security

of slavery was a question of life and death with
the South, and that this plain fact would determine its action, if the antislavery spirit was not
promptly and forever crushed out.   A constant
warfare, calculated morally to ruin the slave-
holding States in their own eyes and in the
eyes of the civilized world, would not and could
not be endured by them.   Now he himself chal-
lenged not only the abolitionists, but the whole
North and the whole civilized world, to a decisive combat with those moral and intellectual
arms from which, according to his own statement, the slave-holding States alone had anything to apprehend, — a most audacious but unavoidable step.   If a successful defence was at
all possible, the attack had to be met with the
same weapons with which it was made.   As long
as the South apologized for slavery as a dire necessity, a vast majority of the Northern people
would insist upon having the constitutional obligations scrupulously fulfilled by the federal
government.   But they would do it less and less
willingly, because the antislavery spirit, which
was the spirit of the times, could not be checked
by the Constitution ; for the Constitution was a
rule of *action*, but not a law for the thoughts
and sentiments of the people.   If the hostile
feeling against slavery was to be conquered, the
people had to be convinced that it was mistaken

and wrong. And as slavery could not be an indifferent thing, if its maintenance was a question of life and death with the South, it must necessarily be a blessing. Thus the necessities of defence imperatively demanded the transformation of slavery from a curse into a most enviable institution, for moral and political reasons.

That there was some truth in Calhoun's assertions could not be gainsaid. The conflict between labor and capital constituted the significance of the times in the western world, and the slave-holding States knew nothing of it, because labor was owned by capital, and therefore capital arranged the relation in every respect wholly to suit itself. So long as labor did not appeal to brute force, the South was, in consequence, exempt from the dangers and disorders which result from this conflict in communities where labor, too, has its rights and is in a condition to defend its interests; there it was navigation on a pond, here on a never motion-ess and sometimes tempestuous sea; but there the sun bred poisonous miasmas in the stagnant waters, and the navigator was in danger of suffocating in the mire if the boat capsized by some accident, while here were the dangers, but also the vigor and all the resources, of real, ever-progressing life. Had Calhoun so entirely forgotten all that he had seen during his college years in New England that this difference really escaped his keen eye?　Had he grown to be so impreg·nated with the spirit of slavery that the spirit of the people of the free States had become to him a book closed with seven seals?　Could they ever be made to believe that slavery was "a positive good"?　And if this declaration would always have the sound of a blasphemy in their ears, what would he have gained for the security of slavery in the Union, even if his assertion were true?　The hatred of slavery in the North was as yet very far from being so deadly as he expected it to become in a little while; but still slavery was hated upon political, moral, and religious principles.　Principles, however, are vital forces in the history of mankind, and what a man believes to be a principle works with him as such.　Therefore, even if Calhoun were right, his declaration could only fan the flames of the conflict between South and North.　It was the formal announcement that this conflict never could terminate in a peace, nor even be interrupted by an honest truce.

All the free States were genuine democracies, and therefore the assertion that slavery is the most solid and durable foundation upon which to rear free institutions was in their eyes simply a *contradictio in adjecto*.　Whether the institu tions which the South reared on this base were good or bad, they were confessedly the products of a different civilization, — of a civilization differing from that of the North not only in details, but in the formative principle. It is, however, self-evident that two civilizations, with antagonistic formative principles, cannot permanently coexist in one political organism, because they move in opposite directions. Instead of reconciling the North and the civilized world to the existence of slavery, Calhoun's new gospel of slavery was a declaration of aggressive war. But one step more could be taken in this direction : the deeds could be made to conform to the theory, the conversion of the heathen to the new gospel could be undertaken ; the logical consequence of the doctrine of the " positive good " was the propagandism of slavery.

The time was not far off when the South, with Calhoun as its foremost leader, was to take this last step, which proved to be the beginning of the end. . For a while, however, the attention of the country was diverted from the slavery conflict by financial and other economical questions, which pressed themselves into the foreground in a most unpleasant manner.

We have seen how many wise heads in the Capitol at Washington, and among them that of Calhoun, were troubled by the fear that the

United States government stood in danger of
something like the fate of King Midas. But
instead of having to deal with an overflowing
treasury, they had to struggle with the disastrous consequences of the crash of 1837, the
worst economical crisis the country had as yet
experienced since the war of independence. Calhoun took a prominent but not a leading part
in all the questions mediately and immediately
connected with this catastrophe. To present
the reader with an intelligent synopsis of his
views would require a discourse on the general
history of the times, which cannot be com-
pressed within the small frame of this biography. It appears, however, the less necessary to
enlarge upon them, because no new principles
were involved in the discussion, and the stand
taken by Calhoun did not mark a new epoch in
his general career. From the personal point of
view it is almost of more interest that, in February, 1837, he had a last direct encounter with
General Jackson, who had taken him to task
for some remarks supposed to have been made
by Calhoun in a speech on the land question
As the hot-tempered President had based his
grossly abusive letter on an inaccurate report,
Calhoun had no difficulty in chastising him severely for this attempt " upon the privileges of
a United States senator ; " this time, however

himself overstepping the limits which the official station of his adversary should have imposed upon him.

Perhaps this incident influenced to some extent his language in the speech which he delivered a few days later on the relations of the United States to France;-but it would be ridiculous to suppose that personal hostility to Jackson was the reason of his opposition to the policy of the President in the indemnity question. He proved beyond contradiction that the untoward turn which this affair had taken was mainly due to the false steps of the administration, and he conclusively showed that in a war between the United States and France the former would have infinitely more to suffer, while neither could derive any advantage from it. The national pride was flattered to hear the victor of New Orleans blow the war trumpet so lustily and defiantly ; but the sober second thought of the people entirely agreed with Calhoun, that it would be madness, on a mere question of " etiquette," to provoke a war with the oldest ally of the United States, who had rendered them such signal services in their hour of need.

CHAPTER VII.

Much time was to elapse ere justice was rendered Calhoun with regard to the course he saw fit to pursue upon the leading question of the day, — President Van Buren's sub-treasury scheme, which was to sever entirely and forever the connection between the government and banks of every description. It was but natural that the Whigs were deeply chagrined to see Calhoun part company with them in the moment when, as he himself freely admitted, the continuation of the alliance would have led to the overthrow of the administration party; but they had no right to expect anything else from him. He was not guilty of any treachery, nor could he be justly charged with inconsistency, though in 1835, when the sub-treasury scheme was first introduced by General Gordon, he had declared it " premature," and in 1836, when the proposition was renewed by Benton, " impracticable at the time;" nay, even though he had himself proposed the establishment of a United States Bank for twelve years " as a better and more practical plan to unbank the banks." It accorded strictly with the facts when he declared, "We joined our old opponents on the tariff question, but under our own flag and without merging in their ranks." Nobody had ever pretended that he had become a Whig; he had concluded an alliance with the Whigs for the specific purpose of opposing the encroachments of the executive upon the domain of the other departments of government, and of counteracting all the dangerous tendencies of Jackson's unscrupulous autocratic rule. From Martin Van Buren, however, nothing was to be apprehended. "Executive usurpation had been arrested. The Treasury was empty, and the administration had scarcely a majority in either House or in the Union." The object of the alliance had been accomplished. The questions which were now the order of the day left the two great national parties intact, but Calhoun was free to join either side, because he belonged to neither. "He was master of his own move, and acknowledged connection with no party but the state-rights party, — the small band of nullifiers, — and acted either with or against the administration or the national party, just as it was calculated to further the principles and policy which we, of that party, regarded as essential to the liberty and institutions of the country." Viewing the general situation of the country in the manner he did, it was therefore a matter of course that he pitched his solitary tent for the present next the camp-fires of the administration party.

" We have, Mr. President, arrived at a remarkable era in our political history. The days of legislative and executive encroachments, of tariffs and surpluses, of bank and public debt and extravagant expenditure, are past for the present. The government stands in a position disentangled from the past, and freer to choose its future course than it has ever been since its commencement. We are about to take a fresh start. I move off under the states-rights banner, and go in the direction in which I have been so long moving. I seize the opportunity thoroughly to reform the government; to bring it back to its original principles; to retrench and economize; and rigidly to enforce accountability. I shall oppose strenuously all attempts to originate a new debt; to create a national bank; to reunite the political and money powers (more dangerous than church and state) in any form or shape; to prevent the disturbances of the compromise, which is gradually removing the last vestige of the tariff system. And, mainly, I shall use my best efforts to give an ascendency to the great conservative principle of state sovereignty over the dangerous and despotic doctrine of consolidation."

Had the Whigs, then, quite overlooked that although he had fought with them against

Jackson, it was an utter impossibility that he should ever exert himself for their ascendency? That the man who declared that he " wished to be considered nothing more than a plain and an honest *nullifier*," should " join the friends of the tariff, of a national bank, and the whole system of congressional usurpations, and utterly break down his old friends of 1827, who had taken shelter under his position, and thus give a complete and final victory to his old opponents of that period, and with it a permanent ascendency to them and their principles and policy, which, he honestly believed, could not but end in consolidation, with the loss of our liberty and institutions," — this, indeed, was a most preposterous idea. Calhoun, however, was mistaken in one point, and that the most material. The victory of the administration could never turn to the advantage of the states-rights party. The independent Treasury gave the administration of the finances a really political character for the first time, and it therefore necessarily contributed to the growing together of the "sovereign" States into a national Union.

Our sources do not inform us whether Calhoun ever became aware of this fact. His first great movement to bring the government " back to its original principles " looks less like the hope-

ful beginning of a thorough reform than like the
desperate effort of a man who is in danger of
being swallowed up by the surging waves, to pile
up dike upon dike till he has a wall so broad
and high that he can laugh the most furious
storms to scorn. Vain exertions, for his dikes
are not constructed of earth, stone, and mortar,
but of mere assertions. The most strenuous
efforts of the North to put down abolitionism by
public opinion had been met by the South with
the contemptuous remark that all the satisfaction the South got for its just complaints was
" words, mere words; " and now the great
leader of the slave power had nothing more
substantial to throw into the way of the antislavery spirit than " words, mere words." The
last aim and end of the bringing back of the
government to its original principles was the
security of slavery; and this was to be obtained
not by legislation, but by *resolving* this and that
with regard to the constitutional and political
aspect of the slavery question. Did these long
strings of resolutions, by being spread over the
journal of the Senate, acquire any secret virtue
which made them a wall of adamant, against
which all the arms of the antislavery spirit
would splinter like glass ? Whom did they
bind ? Not even the Senate itself, and yet
infinitely less the other departments of the

government or even the people. They had no
legal authority whatever, and though they
might be of great moral weight with many
persons, what effect was to be expected from
the mere opinion of the temporary majority
of the Senate, which might be changed at any
moment, if all the bulwarks of the Constitution were no longer deemed in themselves sufficient protection for the peculiar institution?
Surely, the resolution mania, which from this
time possessed Calhoun, is alone ample proof
how justly he was charged with being a doctrinaire.

But it was a great mistake to suppose that all
the weeks which the haughty planter forced the
Senate, at the expense of its legitimate legislative business, to pass in debate on his constitutional opinions were spent to no purpose. It
has been said before that, with regard to the
slavery question, this doctrinaire was the only
one who moved on at even pace with the events,
and he knew now as well as ever what he was
about. So far as he expected anything from his
resolutions for the greater security of slavery
he was not only disappointed, but he did in fact,
as he was charged on all sides with doing, pour
oil upon the flames. But the resolutions were
not only designed to serve as additional guards
for the "positive good" of the South · they

were besides a programme for the future, and as such they were a political event of the first magnitude.

The central idea of the resolutions of December 27, 1837, was, of course, that the safety of the South depended entirely upon the doctrine of state sovereignty, and their immediate purpose was to get the Senate formally pledged to this principle in its direct bearings on the slavery question. Hence the series was very logically opened by stating how the Union *came into existence* under the Constitution. It is declared that every State " *entered* into the Union " by its own voluntary act. The old Union under the Articles of Confederation, therefore, evidently had ceased to exist some time before; when and how, Calhoun unfortunately forgot to say. The Senate, however, with thirty-one against thirteen votes, assented to this bold falsification of a plain historical fact.

This premise once secured, Calhoun had won the game. From the purely Confederate nature of the Union the second resolution was deduced : that the intermeddling of States or of a " combination of their citizens with the domestic institutions or police of the others, on any ground, or under any pretext whatever, political, moral or religious, with a view to their alteration or subversion," is "not warranted by the Constitution." Pompous and positive as this resolution sounded, it was of so gelatinous a character that, while the political agitator could do anything he pleased with it, the constitutional jurist could not keep the smallest particle of it firmly between his fingers. Who was able to enumerate "the domestic institutions" to which the doctrine of the resolution could be rightfully applied? Webster showed conclusively that slavery, for one, did not belong to them. Where, too, was the master mind which could give a serviceable definition of "intermeddling," or of "with a view to their alteration," or of "not warranted by the Constitution"? If all this was to have so precise a meaning that the doctrines of rights should and could be fixed in laws, and their observance secured by compulsory legal measures, — and it was, obviously, only on this supposition that they could serve the purpose intended, — then everything which had relation to the domestic institutions of other States would become a punishable violation of the Constitution. The existence of slavery had to vanish from the consciousness of the free States; for until this happened their thoughts must be in some degree occupied with it; the thoughts must manifest themselves, and every manifestation of the thoughts

had, in and of itself, a tendency to operate an
"alteration" of the existing state of things. Yet
the resolution served well enough Calhoun's
main purpose. What this was, he plainly told
in his rejoinder to the suggestion to strike out
the word " religious," — that " the whole spirit
of the resolution hinged on that word." The
Senate was to declare that the anathema of the
Constitution rested on the heads of the fanatics
who presumed to question the rightfulness of
negro slavery on moral and religious grounds;
and the Senate complied with the demand ; only
fourteen out of forty-five votes being recorded
in favor of striking out the words " moral " and
" religious." But what had Calhoun gained
by that, even supposing that his interpretation
of the spirit of the Constitution was correct?
Would the religious convictions of the people
be subverted by the Constitution, or would the
latter become a dead letter from the moment
when it stood in acknowledged antagonism to
the former? Always there was the same fundamental error in all his reckoning. He clearly
perceives that the whole slavery question hinges
upon the political, economical, and moral antagonism between slavery and liberty, tries to
suppress some *manifestations* of it, and draws
from that suppression conclusions, as if it were
identical with the suppression of the antago

nism itself. But the futility of his efforts has pressed him another step forward : instead of merely forbidding the agitation to enter the Capitol, he now bids Congress declare that the Constitution wants to see every door in the free States hermetically closed against it.

To understand the whole import of the second resolution it is, however, necessary to read it in connection with the third, which indirectly overthrew the demand of the former, but of course in favor of slavery. This third resolution declared it to be the duty of the federal government to use its powers in such a manner as "to give . . . increased stability and security to the domestic institutions of the States that compose the Union." The people of the free States were to have no political, moral, or religious thoughts on slavery, or at least not to manifest them in any way whatever disagreeable to the slave-holding States; but they were bound, through the federal government, actively to exert themselves in its favor. It is not said in what manner and to what extent this was to be done; but did not the very generality of the terms used imply that it had to be done in *any* manner and to *any* extent declared necessary by the slave-holding States? For they alone had the right to judge what the stability and security of their peculiar institution demanded. There was not a trace of doctrinarian spirit in *this* resolution. It was a positive programme, big with consequences which would have curdled the blood in the veins of Calhoun himself, if he had foreseen them *all.* It was the first step towards deriving the practical results of the doctrine of the " positive good ; " the first step towards securing the services of the federal government for the glorious work of slavery propagandism.

The fourth resolution applied the foregoing doctrines by name to slavery, declaring all attacks on it " a manifest breach of faith, and a violation of the most solemn obligations, moral and religious." The Senate called upon to instruct the people in this spirit about their religious obligations ; abolition, according to Calhoun, in possession of the pulpits, the schools, and the press; the abolitionists declaring slav ery " the sum of all villainies," — was anything more needed to prove that two antagonistic principles were here in deadly conflict ? With this one line Calhoun had irrefutably demonstrated the vanity of all his efforts to save slavery and the Union.

The next resolution read, —

" Resolved, That the intermeddling of any State or States, or their citizens, to abolish slavery in this District, or in any of the Territories, on the ground

or under the pretext, that it is immoral or sinful, or
the passage of any act or measure of Congress with
that view, would be a direct and dangerous attack on
the institutions of all the slave-holding States."

If all that had been asserted in the preceding
resolutions was correct, this one was certainly
incontrovertible ; therefore it was all the more
significant that Calhoun refrained from declaring the abolition of slavery in the District of
Columbia unconstitutional, although he expressly stated this to be his opinion.   But while he
thus politely and obligingly bowed to the constitutional doctrines of the North, its moral and
religious convictions were once more imperiously bidden to leave this question alone. "The
deluded agitators must be plainly told that it is
no concern of theirs what is the character of
our institutions." Not a finger was to be raised
against slavery " under the pretext " of its im-
morality or sinfulness, not only where it actually existed, but also, added the sixth and last
resolution, where it *might* exist in future.

" To refuse to extend to the Southern and Western
States, any advantage which would tend to strengthen
or render them more secure, — or to increase their
limits or population by the annexation of new territory or states, on the assumption or under the pretext that the institution of slavery, as it exists among
them, is immoral or sinful, or otherwise obnoxious,

would be contrary to that equality of rights and ad
vantages which the Constitution was intended to secure alike to all the members of the Union."

One great merit this last resolution had : its
language was so plain that no child could mis-
understand it. The principle of slavery propagandism was proclaimed with the utmost boldness, and the federal government was absolutely
denied the right to interfere with it on any
ground or pretext connected in any way whatever with slavery. Not to interfere was, however, in this case, identical with an obligation to
lend a helping hand, for " the annexation of new
territory or states " could be effected only by the
Union. And why should the Union not exult-
ingly march on under the black flag of slavery
as far as the South was good enough to lead it ?
It is true, " many in the South once believed that
it was a moral and political evil," but " that folly
and delusion are gone. We see it now in its
true light, and regard it as the most safe and
stable basis for free institutions in the world.
. . . The blessing of this state of things extends beyond the limits of the South. It makes
that section the balance of the system ; the
great conservative power, which prevents other
portions, less fortunately constituted [!], from
rushing into conflict." Verily, here is a doctrinaire with a positiveness in his doctrine

powerful enough to grind into dust the columns of the most gigantic political edifice. Not long ago Calhoun had declared that nothing was needed to render the South perfectly safe save concert of will and action. Now, Providence had thrown ample opportunities into the way of the Union to test whether that was sufficient to cajole and whip the North into obedience, and to force upon it this programme of the slave power, which, by the very consciousness of its hopeless weakness, was under the imperious necessity of rendering itself the despotic master of the Union, in order to save itself.

After this great sally, several years passed ere Calhoun thought it opportune to make the next decisive move in the cause of self-government and republican liberty on the basis of slavery. The waves of party strife rolled high during all these years, and Calhoun was far from being an unconcerned and idle spectator. His speeches of this period fill a stately volume, and are fully on a level with his other parliamentary efforts on general legislative topics. Yet the biographer, who confines himself to what is really characteristic of the man or to what has exerted a determining influence on the history of his country, can pass them over with a few general remarks. What he himself said of the extraordinary session of Congress in 1841 applies, so far as he is concerned, to this whole time. " What are we doing, and what engrosses all our attention from morn to noon, and from week to week, ever since our arrival here at the commencement of this extraordinary session, and will continue till its end? What but banks, loans, stocks, tariffs, distribution, and supplies?" The old economical controversies, more or less altered by circumstances, are the battle-ground of the parties, fighting with undiminished ardor and varying success. The old arguments are repeated *ad nauseam.*   Though all the questions were of the highest importance, and much erudition, ingenuity, eloquence, and passion were displayed on both sides, the continuous reading of the debates is simply treadmill work. Calhoun's speeches, too, abound with repetitions. The statistical data, the illustrations, the arrangement of the thoughts, change; but he fights for his old doctrines with the old reasons: independent treasury, no bank, no internal improvements, no protective tariff, no distribution of the proceeds of the sale of the public lands, cession of the public lands to the States in which they are situated, no loans, etc. A good deal of sound reasoning, a good deal of bold and sometimes reckless generalizing, now and then exaggerated into a downright absurdity, may be found in all his

speeches on these interesting subjects. The
thorough student of the general history of the
United States cannot dispense with perusing
them all carefully, but they do not show either
the man or the statesman in a new light. From
the personal point of view, they are the most
interesting on account of some sharp encounters
which he had with Clay and Webster. Each
of the three great senators tried to demonstrate
his own consistency throughout his political career, and the inconsistency which had marked
that of his adversary; and each of them was perfectly successful as to the latter task, and, in
spite of infinite ingenuity and eloquence, sadly
failed as to the former. With the change of
conditions, their political convictions had
changed, and, by changing these, they had
learned to read the Constitution in a different
way. Neither of them lost anything in the estimation of the people by this fact, because it
was an honest change of opinion, and since their
constituents had gone through the same process
they might have had the manliness and candor
to avow it unreservedly. But perhaps the reproach that not one of them ventured upon a
stand-point of such moral elevation rests more
upon the general tendency of American politics
than upon them personally. Once, indeed, Calhoun openly confessed that ne had been orig

inally inclined to take a latitudinarian and
national view of the powers of the federal government; but when he spoke in the deep and
incisive tones of an authority, — and that became more and more his habitual way of speaking, — or when an opponent had nettled his self-
love, he was but too easily betrayed into wast-
ing his time and his ability in vain attempts to
knead his earlier sayings and political acts into
the mould of his present convictions.

Some of the speeches of this period require
particular notice, but they are precisely those
which were only remotely or not at all connected with the party issues.

The illegitimate connection of the civil service with party politics had become such a cry-
ing evil that another effort was made to strike
it at the root; but again the would-be reform-
ers sought the root where it did not lie. A bill
was introduced and debated upon, which, as
Calhoun expressed it, proposed " to inflict the
penalty of dismission on a large class of the officers of this government, who shall electioneer,
or attempt to control or influence the election
of public functionaries either of the general or
state governments, without distinguishing between their official and individual character as
citizens." Calhoun, who spoke on the bill on
February 22, 1839, declared it for this reason

unconstitutional. We need not inquire whether this charge was well founded, or whether he made good his case as to the constitutional question. Supposing that he was right, this defect of the bill could have been easily mended; but he very justly asserted that such a law would "prove either useless, or worse than useless."

"But suppose the immediate object of the bill accomplished, and the office-holders rendered perfectly silent and passive, it might even then be doubted whether it would cause any diminution in the influence of patronage over elections. It would indeed greatly reduce the influence of the office-holders. They would become the most insignificant portion of the community, as far as elections were concerned. But just in the same proportion as they might sink, the no less formidable corps of the office-seekers would rise in importance. The struggle for power between the *ins* and the *outs* would not abate in the least, in violence or intensity, by the silence or inactivity of the office-holders, as the amount of patronage, the stake contended for, would remain undiminished. Both sides, those in and those out of power, would turn from the passive and silent body of the incumbents, and court the favor of the active corps, that panted to supplant them; and the result would be an annual sweep of the former, after every election, to make room to reward the latter,—and this on whichever side the scale of victory might turn. The consequence would be rotation with a vengeance. The wheel would turn round with such velocity that anything like a stable system of policy would be impossible. Each temporary occupant, who might be thrown into office by the whirl, would seize the moment to make the most of his good fortune, before he might be displaced by his successor, and a system (if such it might be called) would follow, not less corrupting than unstable."

That was all true enough, but what had he to propose instead? "Place the office-holders, with their yearly salaries, beyond the reach of the executive power, and they would in a short time be as mute and inactive as this bill proposes to make them. Their voice, I promise, would then be scarcely raised at elections, or their persons be found at the polls." If he had changed but one word, — if he had said *party in power* instead of *executive power*, — this advice would, indeed, have been the egg of Columbus. The context hardly allows a doubt that he now, as before, only wished to assign a controlling influence over the removals to Congress or the Senate; and if that was to be the whole reform, his law, like the bill under discussion, would have been "useless, or worse than useless." As concerning the slavery conflict, so also in this question, he foresaw and foretold the impending dangers and inevitable evil consequences, and

he showed great ability in criticising the opinions of the other political physicians; but his
own prescriptions were poisonous drugs.

In respect to the civil service, this is not
very surprising, because, though Calhoun saw
clearer than most of his contemporaries, he had
after all not made a serious effort to push his
examination beyond the surface of the question; another generation was to grapple with
this problem, for it had to grow infinitely worse
ere the necessity of getting at the bottom of
it could be fully realized. But of the slavery
conflict he had a better right than anybody to
say, as he frequently did, that he had thoroughly examined it in all its bearings, and that
he understood it. Therefore the apodeictic manner in which he promised a radical cure, if but
the application of his remedies would be consented to, exposes him to the charge of having
been a dishonest quack, if he is not admitted to
have been an honest fanatic, who, like all fanatics, viewed his subject but from one fixed point
and under one unchangeable visual angle.

This deep conviction of his own infallibility
in relation to everything concerning slavery
rendered it a very significant fact that he once
was compelled to admit that he was at his wits'
end, and had no advice to offer. Of course
neither pride nor policy allowed the very words

to fall from his lips, but the folded arms and knitted brow with which, after reiterated loud complaints, he suffered the government to remain in the embarrassing situation, into which it had been thrown by trying to serve the interests of the slave-holders, spoke with a most impressive eloquence.

Two American vessels with negroes on board, the Comet and the Encomium, had been stranded, in 1830 and 1834, on the false keys of the Bahama Islands, and the local authorities of Nassau, New Providence, had refused to recognize the negroes as slaves and deliver them up to their owners. In 1835 a very similar case occurred. The brig Enterprise was forced by stress of weather into Port Hamilton, Bermuda, and the local authorities detained the slaves, pretending that they had become freemen by coming within English jurisdiction. The United States government took up all three cases in behalf of the owners, and claimed a fair compensation. England at last yielded as to the first two, but persisted in her refusal as to the last, and, at the same time, declared that no such claim would ever again be allowed. This distinction was based upon the fact " that before the Enterprise arrived at Bermuda slavery had been abolished in the British Empire.'

On March 4, 1840, Calhoun introduced in

the Senate a set of resolutions declaratory of what he conceived to be the principles of the law of nations applying to the case, and severely condemning the course of the English authorities. Some days later he delivered a long speech in support of the resolutions, and had the satisfaction of seeing them unanimously adopted. The South liked to dwell upon this fact as a striking proof of the justice of its claims. The unanimity of the Senate was, however, only apparent. Of fifty-two senators, only thirty-three voted; nineteen were evidently not satisfied that Calhoun had made good his case, but for reasons best known to themselves they preferred not to say so. The "unanimous" vote of the Senate was, in fact, a proof of the awe in which almost all the Northern politicians stood of the slave power, but there was very little reason to draw from it the conclusion that the doctrine propounded in the resolutions could not be called into question. Adams, who certainly knew as much of the law of nations as any member of Congress, wrote concerning the Enterprise resolutions, " Calhoun crows about his success in imposing his own bastard law of nations upon the Senate by his preposterous resolutions, and chuckles at Webster's appealing to those resolutions now, after dodging from the duty of refuting and confounding them then."

The essential point of Calhoun's doctrine was that he denied the right of England, with regard to citizens of foreign countries, to make any difference between slaves and other property, if by some unavoidable cause the slaves should momentarily come within the limits of her jurisdiction. This opinion was based upon the assertion that slavery was fully recognized by the law of nations. England did not directly and in so many words assert the contrary, but she proved by her acts that, at least so far as any positive obligations could be deduced from this principle, she refused to acknowledge its existence or its binding force upon her. This fact was in itself proof absolute that Calhoun's assertion could at best be true only with a most important qualification. He overlooked the fact that the law of nations is not immutable, but constantly changing and developing with the general development of civilization. The very fact that England assumed the position she did sufficiently proved that this law was in a state of transition as to the principle in question. The law of nations rests upon the free consent of the civilized peoples. If, therefore, the greatest maritime power of the world, with most extensive possessions adjacent to the sea or surrounded by it in all parts of the globe, withdrew its assent to a principle of which the practica application was confined to the sea-coast, it could no longer be maintained. That this was so with regard to the case in hand was the more evident, because none of the other European powers of any consequence had a practical interest in the question, and the hostility of public opinion all over the civilized world against slavery was constantly and rapidly increasing. Calhoun's resolutions, therefore, were neither more nor less than a vain protest against the onward course of civilization, and the Senate, by "unanimously" adopting them, announced to the world that the most democratic and most progressive state of the universe was bound to cry Halt ! and pull back the wheel of time whenever and wherever the interests of the slave-holders were in danger of being crushed by it.

To oblige the slave power, the Senate had made an ugly blot on the record of the United States, and the slave power did not derive the least advantage from it, nay, it even sustained positive damage. England did not change her course by a single point on account of the resolutions, and the attention of the world had again been called in the most pointed manner to the allegation that slavery was indeed a "positive good" and the best foundation of liberty. That was a positive damage, and no small one, for

every syllable of what Calhoun had said years
ago, with such impressive emphasis about the
part played by the moral convictions in the
tragedy of this conflict, was true. Every such
manifestation of the slave power caused its opponents to write with larger letters on their
own banner the device under which the slavocracy had been sailing ever since the adoption
of the Constitution : Let us alone! Slavery is a
state institution with which the federal government has no concern. Let us alone! To be
left alone in this sense was, however, to be
delivered over to destruction by the moral and
economical agencies which rule the world. The
'Let us alone" of the slave-holders meant,
You have not only to shut your eyes and ears,
but also to lock up your thoughts and your consciences, whenever our interests require you to
do so; for slavery is a domestic institution of
the sovereign States; but it is your duty to
throw the whole weight of the Union for us
into the scales, whenever we tell you that our
safety demands it, for the Constitution recog-
nizes and " guarantees " slavery. How long
would the North submit to such a bargain?
That question nobody could answer as yet; but
two things were certain : every time that the
federal government submitted to its enforce-
ment, the number of those in the North who

grew restive under it increased; and every time
that the slave-holders had succeeded in enforc-
ing it, they were compelled to push *both* sides
of their claim a long step farther. Calhoun,
understanding the nature of the slavery question better than any other Southern man, had
to march far ahead on both diverging lines, and
therefore, while no other single man has done
so much to erect the temple of the slave power,
also no other single man has done so much to
render its sudden downfall inevitable and to
hasten the catastrophe. So it was in this case.
What a triumph that not a single senator dared
to raise his voice against the "bastard law of
nations," and what a portentous humiliation to
have nothing but "words, words, and again
words" to oppose to England's "outrageous
course"! The South pocketed at the same time
the glorious impotent resolutions and a signal
defeat.

There is no question that Calhoun very
keenly felt the defeat, for he had declared that
a "vital principle" was involved for the South,
and that England "interdicted nearly as effectually the intercourse by sea between one half
of this Union and the other, as to the greatest
and most valuable portion of the property of
the South, as if she was to send out cruisers
against it." Yet he soon scrupulously avoided

touching upon the question even in private con
versation. But he deemed the success which
he had obtained over the North of more import,
for the obvious reason that the fate of the slave
power depended not upon the international, but
upon the national, standing of slavery. In November, 1841, the English authorities of Nassau dared to repeat their former offence under
most aggravating circumstances, for the brig
Creole was brought into the harbor by the very
slaves, who had successfully revolted and killed
one of the slave-holders in the struggle. Yet
Calhoun did not deem it necessary to hurl a new
set of resolutions against England; nay, he even
refrained from venting his wrath in a speech;
but he did not omit to commend very heart-
ily the remonstrance of Webster, as Secretary
of State, which was, indeed, based entirely on
the resolutions of March 4, 1840. "The letter
which had been read," he said, " was drawn up
with great ability, and covered the ground which
had been assumed on this subject by all parties
in the Senate." He hoped that it would " have
a beneficial effect, not only upon the United
States, but Great Britain. Coming from the
quarter it did, this document would do more
good than in coming from any other quarter."

Was it not an ominous sign of the times tha.
much praise, in such an affair, was bestowed

upon Daniel Webster from these lips? Further, the great statesman of Massachusetts could boast of having won the approval of the great Carolinian in another question relating to slavery. To the surprise of most people, as well in the North as in the South, Calhoun was in favor of the ratification of the treaty concluded at Washington, on August 9, 1842, in which the high contracting powers, England and the United States, obligated themselves to maintain a squadron of a certain strength on the African coast for the purpose of suppressing the slave-trade. It seems hardly necessary to state that Calhoun was not pleased with the agreement; very far from it, indeed. He premised his affirmative vote by the declaration "that there were several circumstances which caused no small repugnance on his part to any stipulations whatever with Great Britain on the subject of those articles; and he would add that he would have been gratified if they and all other stipulations on the subject could have been entirely omitted; but he must, at the same time, say he did not see how it was possible to avoid entering into some arrangement on the subject," and, considering all the circumstances of the case, he did not think this agreement bad enough to justify the rejection of the whole treaty, while it was better than to maintain the dangerous *status quo.* If Calhoun thought thus, it is not astonishing that Adams declared "the negotiation itself a *Scapinade;* a struggle be· tween the plenipotentiaries to outwit each other, and to circumvent both countries by a slippery compromise between freedom and slav- ery." But Calhoun was certainly no friend of slippery compromises. Was it then really only the embarrassing situation of the United States which caused him to consent to this? Adams thought not. He writes, " There is a temper- ance in his [Calhoun's] manner, obviously aim- ing to conciliate the Northern political sopranos, who abhor slavery, and help to forge fetters for the slave." But what reason did he have to wish just now to conciliate this numerous fam- ily of the species " dough-face " ?

The ambitious wish which had so long and so violently agitated Calhoun's life while he stood in his prime had once more taken hold of his mind, now that he had entered upon the years in which all that this earth has to be- stow begins to lose its charm and gloss, because the twilight has set in and the evening shades are darkening. The deep animosity which the nullification conflict had excited against him throughout the North had so far subsided that South Carolina ventured to urge upon her sister States his claims on the presidency. She is

tended no empty compliment. Her own admiration for her favorite son did not so entirely
becloud her judgment that she flattered herself and him with the anticipation of certain
success; but she deemed it so far possible that
she entered his name upon the list of candidates with all the hot and overbearing impetu-
osity with which she was wont to take up every
important question. Calhoun, too, indulged in
the hope that the dream of his earlier manhood
might at last be realized. At the end of 1842
he resigned his seat in the Senate, the resigna-
tion to take effect from the close of the 27th
Congress. The Legislature of South Carolina,
immediately upon the acceptance of the resig-
nation, unanimously nominated him a candidate for election as President of the United
States.

To-day nobody will question that Calhoun
was by far the superior of all his Democratic
competitors in intellect and in justly acquired
fame and character; and even at that time but
few failed to see this, though many did not see
fit publicly to acknowledge the fact. But in
spite of his great superiority in all the essential
qualities, no calm observer could doubt for a
moment that his hopes were sure to be disappointed. The second and third rate politicians
exerted, directly or indirectly, so great an in-

fluence upon the party nominations that the
chances of the first men of the nation to reach,
in ordinary times, the goal of the presidency
had become exceedingly small. The special interests of this class of people were better served
by sending one of their own chiefs into the
White House than by elevating to the chair a
leading statesman, whose renown and influence
were not based upon their cheap cunning and
petty arts. But even if this had been otherwise, Calhoun would have had no chance whatever. It was, to say the least, exceedingly
doubtful whether he could ever be elected, if
nominated by the party, and therefore it was
certain that he would never receive the nomination. It is true that he was not entirely without support in some of the Northern States.
The Irish especially manifested everywhere
some predilection for him, on account of his
pedigree, and in New York, where the Whigs
indulged very freely in their nativist and anti-
Catholic tendencies, this predilection could almost be mistaken for genuine enthusiasm. But
as the first commandment of the political dec-
alogue of the Irish masses was to vote the regular ticket, and as his Irish extraction was nearly
all they knew of him, their support was of very
 ittle avail, unless his other partisans were nu
merous and enthusiastic enough to scare his **op**

ponents within the party into submission. If
the Southern wing unanimously and emphatically declared themselves for him, the Northern
would, perhaps, not dare to resist.

But only ignorance or blind admiration could
suppose for a moment that the Southern Democrats could be marched up in serried ranks to
sustain his candidature. Ever since he had abjured his early national and latitudinarian bias,
and become an "honest nullifier" in the service of the slavocracy, he had unfitted himself
to be the leader of a great national party, because he had assumed the leadership of an extreme sectional faction. Perhaps this extreme
faction was destined, in the course of time, to
develop into a party, which would exercise despotic sway over the whole South. Nay, it was
sure to come to that, because the correct understanding of the slavery conflict must spread
with its own development. As yet, however,
ninety-nine out of a hundred saw the slavery
question through a mist, and therefore even
those who would have followed Calhoun through
thick and thin, to even out-Heroding Herod,
were now shocked and dismayed by his radi-
calism. There was probably not a single slave-
holder in the whole Union who was not glad to
have in the United States Senate such a champion of the peculiar institution, whose courage

and will were equal to any emergency; but outside of South Carolina, the number of those who were very anxious to see him at the head of the government was comparatively small.

The Calhounites fought stubbornly and carried their point in the first preliminary question, — the postponing of the national convention to the spring of 1844, — against the adherents of Van Buren, who had wished to set it for as early a date as November, 1843. In the other controverted previous question, however, the partisans of Van Buren were all the more unyielding. The Calhounites wanted the delegates to the national convention elected by districts, while their opponents would have the decision as to the mode of election left to the States. If the national convention was to represent, so far as possible, not the political log-rollers, but the party, the preference had undoubtedly to be accorded to the proposition of the Calhounites · but it was certainly somewhat strange that they, who believed themselves to have a monopoly of the pure states-rights doctrine, ventured to wish to give prescriptions to the "States."

So far as their course was determined by what they supposed to be the interest of their respective candidates, both factions might have saved their time and temper, and allowed this question to take care of itself. Van Buren was successful in the trial heat, but his final mortification was only the greater; for after all he lost the race, although his foremost competitor had taken the wise resolution to withdraw from it altogether on January 20, 1844.

South Carolina was dismayed, but she did not, as she had done heretofore, throw away her electoral votes by voting for some candidate of her own. This time she submitted to the party behest, although she did it with anything but good grace. The defeat of Calhoun's candidature had, however, but little to do with her anger. She indulged once more in a spasm of loud-mouthed passion on account of the double face which James K. Polk, the Democratic candidate, had seen fit to put on with regard to the tariff question, in order to secure for himself the electoral vote of Pennsylvania, without which his election was deemed impossible. Polk was accused of having gone over, bag and baggage, to the camp of the protectionists; indignation meetings and dinners, with an abundance of furious toasts, denunciations, and threats, were the order of the day ; the " Charleston Mercury " was not satisfied with urging " legislative nullification," but invited the people of the State to adopt " ulterior measures," in case hat " should prove inadequate."

There is always a fire where such volumes of smoke becloud the sky; but this time the quantity of smoke stood in no proportion to the size or heat of the fire. Calhoun disapproved of this wild ado about so little, and that now happened quite frequently which but a few weeks before had seemed impossible, — that his name was not mentioned at all at the political festivities of the radicals. He did not take this slight much to heart, nor had he any reason to do so. Not only was it a matter of course that Polk had not become a protectionist, but it was also perfectly evident that for the present the tariff was but a question of the second or third order. In both parties the opinions were far from being in full accord on this head, and in neither did the masses of those who were not most immediately interested in it feel very deeply about it. And now should a storm be artificially raised about a little more or less of duties, and thereby the gauntlet thrown into the face not only of the whole Whig party, North and South, but of all those who were too dull of comprehension to see the conservative force of nullification, and who clung to the old-fashioned idea that a law is a law, and has to be obeyed, — now, when the opportunity was offered of securing a prize of incalculable value to the democracy? Holmes and Rhett might amuse their followers by a revival of the nullification idea, " meditate ulterior measures," talk of dis-union, and declare that " to this complexion it must come at last;" Calhoun had packed away his thunderbolts, and thus far he alone knew how to use them effectually.

So early as 1839 he had, in the face of al-most countless declarations to the contrary, and yet apparently in good faith, astonished the Senate by the emphatic assertion that a dis-solution of the Union ever had been, and would remain in all future time, an imaginary danger. Replying to Mr. Buchanan, he had said : —

" The senator has done no more than justice to that measure [the compromise tariff]. It terminated honestly and fairly, without the sacrifice of any in-terest, one of the most dangerous controversies that ever disturbed the Union or endangered its exist-ence. Not the danger of dismemberment, as we learn from the senator, was anticipated abroad. No, the danger lay in a different direction. Dismemberment is not the only mode in which our Union may be destroyed. It is a *federal Union*, an Union of *sov-ereign States*, and can be as effectually and much more easily destroyed by *consolidation* than by *dis-memberment*. He who knows anything of the history of our race and the workings of the human breast best understands the great and almost insuperable difficulties in the way of dissolution. There is scarcely an instance on record of any people, speaking the same language and having the same government and laws, who have ever dissolved their political connec-tions through internal causes or struggles. . . . The constant struggle is to enlarge, and not to divide; and there neither is nor ever has been the least dan-ger that our Union would terminate in dissolution."

That was no bait thrown to " the political sopranos " of the North. He believed what he said, yet he did not mean to retract a single syl-lable of what he had declared so often before. The Union and abolition, as he had once ex-pressed it, cannot coexist. If the spirit of the fanatical visionaries of the North is not chained down, then the Union is irretrievably gone, for between the Union and slavery the South has no choice. But he is satisfied that the South will never be pressed before this alternative. In the letter, before mentioned, to the citizens of Athens, he had written : —

" Of all the questions which have been agitated under our government, abolition is that in which we of the South have the deepest concern. It strikes directly and fatally, not only at our prosperity, but our existence as a people. Should it succeed, our fate would be worse than that of the aborigines whom we have driven out, or the slaves whom we command. It is a question that admits of neither concession nor compromise. . . . There is one point in connection with this important subject on which the South ought to be fully informed. From all that I saw and heard during the session, I am perfectly satisfied that we must look to ourselves, and ourselves only, for safety. It is perfectly idle to look to the non-slave-holding States to arrest the attacks of the fanatics. . . . Nor would it be less vain to look to Congress. The same cause that prevents the non-slave-holding States from interference in our favor at home will equally prevent Congress. . . . But, if true to ourselves, we need neither their sympathy nor aid. The Constitution has placed in our power ample means, *short of secession or disunion,* to protect ourselves."

We have seen more than once that he had his hours of despondency, when this conviction was severely shaken, but it was never wholly relinquished. And now he thought that the day had come when a pillar of such gigantic dimensions could be put as an additional support under the dome of slavery that it would be able to withstand all the assaults of abolitionism. The annexation of Texas was to render the Union indissoluble by strengthening the slave power so much that it would have nothing more to apprehend.

CHAPTER VIII

TEXAS.

As early as May 23, 1836, Calhoun had declared in the Senate that he —

"had made up his mind not only to recognize the independence of Texas, but for her admission into this Union ; and if the Texans managed their affairs prudently, they would soon be called upon to decide that question. No man could suppose for a moment that that country could ever come again under the dominion of Mexico; and he was of opinion that it was not for our interests that there should be an independent community between us and Mexico. There were powerful reasons why Texas should be a part of this Union. The Southern States, owning a slave population, were deeply interested in preventing that country from having the power to annoy them."

Thus, but one month after the battle of Jacinto, he publicly and formally announced his programme with regard to the question which was to be the pivotal point on which the fate of slavery was to turn. No other single individual did so much as he to bring about the annexation. He himself has emphatically claimed that merit, and he considered it the greatest and most beneficent achievement of his public career. Perhaps it was, as things finally turned out, but he would have cursed the day on which he put his hand to the plough, if he had known what a dragon seed was to be planted. On February 24, 1847, when the harvesting of the fatal crop had already begun, he said in the Senate : —

"I trust, Mr. President, there will be no dispute hereafter as to who is the real author of annexation. Less than twelve months since, I had many competitors for that honor : the official organ here claimed, if my memory serves me, a large share for Mr. Polk and his administration, and not less than half a dozen competitors from other quarters asserted themselves to be the real authors. But now, since the war [with Mexico] has become unpopular, they all seem to agree that I, in reality, am the author of annexation. I will not put the honor aside. I may now rightfully and indisputably claim to be the author of that great measure, — a measure which has so much extended the domains of the Union ; which has added so largely to its productive powers ; which promises so greatly to extend its commerce ; which has stimulated its industry, and given security to our most exposed frontier. I take pride to myself as being the author of this great measure."

Though there is no positive proof for it, Benton's allegation is therefore probably true, that

Calhoun was also the real author of the intrigue which was to give the annexation wheel the necessary impetus, after several years had been spent in unsuccessful attempts to put it properly into motion. Other circumstances point in the same direction, and that he at first carefully kept himself concealed in the background is satisfactorily explained by the fact that the immediate purpose of the intrigue was to bring the still enormous influence of Jackson into play.

In the beginning of 1843 a Baltimore newspaper published a letter of Gilmer, dated January 10, to "a friend" (Duff Green) in Maryland, on the necessity of the annexation of Texas. Benton says that the letter was like a flash of lightning from a clear sky. The public, however, were allowed to settle down once more into indolent unconcern, for what followed was played under cover. The letter touched most strongly the two chords which were sure to find the loudest echo in Jackson's breast: preservation against England's ambitious desires and the strengthening of the Union. But as the name of Gilmer, as well as Green, awakened the suspicion that Calhoun was seated in the prompter's box, the letter was sent to the "Sage of the Hermitage" by Aaron V. Brown, of Tennessee, who was but an unconscious tool in

other hands. Jackson answered at once in the
tone desired, and although the letter had been
confessedly asked for only for the purpose of
working on the masses, it was now carefully put
away until the opportune moment for its publication should come. Those who held the
wires behind the curtain had attained their immediate end. Jackson had irrevocably engaged
himself for immediate annexation. Without
himself being aware of it, he had thereby de-
prived himself of the possibility of throwing his
whole weight into the scales in favor of Van
Buren; for immediate annexation was to be
made the leading issue of the presidential campaign of 1844. This was another reason for
the Calhounites to insist upon the postponement
of the nominating convention, for they needed
time to tie the South so closely down to this
programme that it could not afterward draw
back for the sake of a question of persons.

A few months later, one of the greatest obstacles in the way of the annexationists was
removed by Webster's exit from the cabinet.
Upshur, who, after a short interregnum under
Legaré, became Tyler's Secretary of State,
worked with his whole energy and with considerable skill at the solution of this problem. On
October 16, 1843, he proposed a treaty of annexation to the Texan agent. Texas, however,

was not now quite so eager to grasp the out-
stretched hand as she had been heretofore.
Thanks to the efforts of England and France,
there was an armistice between her and Mexico,
and negotiations tending to a formal peace had
been begun. Van Zandt, the Texan *chargé d'af-
faires* in Washington, in a letter of January
17, 1844, called the attention of Upshur to the
fact that, under these circumstances, a treaty of
annexation would drive Mexico to the immediate resumption of hostilities, and that it would
also cost Texas the friendship of the mediating
powers. He therefore confidentially inquired
whether, in case the proposal of annexation
were accepted by the Texan executive, the
President would, even before the ratification of
the treaty, protect Texas by a sufficiently strong
land and maritime force against all attacks.
Upshur dared not answer either yes or no. To
refuse the request was to drive Texas wholly
into the arms of England, while to grant it
was to pledge the President to assume, on his
own responsibility, as the price of Texas, the
war of Texas against Mexico.

The bursting of the cannon Peacemaker on
board the Princeton, on February 28, 1844,
ended the embarrassment of the Secretary. To
whose hands should the consummation of the
annexation now be confided? The answer to

this question was not given, as one would have expected, by the President, but by Henry A. Wise. Already, more than two years before, in a speech delivered in the House of Representatives, the hot-blooded Virginian had gone into ecstasy over the idea " of planting the lone star of the Texan banner on the Mexican capitol," of extending slavery to the Pacific, and of robbing the Mexican churches. Now he thought that the time had come to enter upon the realization of this sublime programme, and he was too great a man to let the trifling considerations of propriety, honesty, and right stand in his way. He had the effrontery to go to McDuffie and induce him to urge upon Calhoun the acceptance of the Secretaryship of State, causing him (McDuffie) to believe that he (Wise) had been sent by the President. Then he urged Tyler to offer the place to Calhoun. The President at first declined to comply with the wish, but he finally submitted, when he had been told what his devoted friend had presumed to do.

Calhoun accepted, declaring at the same time that he would resign the office so soon as annexation should become an accomplished fact. It was the universal understanding that it was only for this special purpose that he had been called to the helm, and that only for this reason

he consented to become a member of the cabinet
of the President, who had no party in Congress,
and but a corporal's guard of office-holders
among the people, to sustain him.   He afterwards fully confirmed this view.   On February
12, 1847, he said in the Senate: —

"According to my view, the time was not propi-
tious in one respect. The then President had no
party in either House.   I am not certain that he had
a single supporter in this, and not more than four or
five in the other.   It appeared to me to be a very
unpropitious moment, under such circumstances, to
carry through so important a measure.   When it
was intimated to me that I was to be nominated for
the office of Secretary of State, I strongly remon-
strated to my friends here; but before my remonstrance reached them, I was unanimously appointed,
and was compelled to accept.   I saw the administration was weak, and that the very important measure
would be liable to be defeated.   But circumstances
made action on it inevitable."

Niles's "Register" of March 23, 1844, said:

" The nomination of John C. Calhoun to the office
of Secretary of State, and the entire unanimity with
which that nomination has been approved, not only
by the Senate, but the public press of the country,
presents the incident, in our judgment, as one of the
most eventful, certainly in the life of that distin
guished and talented statesman, and very possibly

also, in the future and fate of the country, the inter
ests of which, to a vast extent, indeed, are thereby
confided to him, at a moment of exceeding delicacy."

That the Senate unanimously confirmed the
nomination of a man of Calhoun's standing was
a matter of course; but it would have been
strange indeed if it had with entire unanimity
" approved" it, and stranger still if the whole
press, and consequently also the whole people,
had rejoiced at it, — too strange to be believed,
although some years later he himself asserted
that he had been called "by the unanimous
voice of the country to take charge of the
State Department." Just because it was in
fact "a moment of exceeding delicacy" and
"the future and the fate of the country" were,
"to a vast extent," confided to his hands, the
nomination of this most thorough-going and
most daring partisan inevitably caused the deepest concern to all the opponents of annexation,
while it gave the greatest satisfaction to all its
advocates. And he fully justified as well the
expectations of the latter as the apprehensions
of the former; but in doing so he blurred his
fair fame. The man who had had the courage
to become "an honest nullifier" ought to have
had the courage to manage this annexation
ousiness with perfect honesty, though with a
high hand, and not stoop to sail under false col-

ors.   He would never have forgotten so far as he did what he owed to the dignity of his country and his personal honor, if he had not thought the annexation of such vital importance that almost anything seemed justifiable to render success more certain.

From the moment when Calhoun arrived in Washington, the negotiations, which had been rather stagnant during the interregnum, were resumed with zeal, while public opinion was aroused by the publication of Jackson's letter of February 12, 1843, postdated 1844.   John Nelson, who provisionally had charge of the State Department, had declined to accede to the before-mentioned condition of Texas, for the obvious reason that the President had not the constitutional power to employ armed force against a state with which the Union was at peace.   He had, however, assured the Texans that Tyler was "not indisposed" to make the desired disposition of the troops, in order that they might be able to protect Texas at the "proper time."   Calhoun now tried his luck with similar vague phrases, but the Texan agents would not be paid off in such a way.   On April 11 he yielded with a heavy heart, informing the two plenipotentiaries that an order had been issued to concentrate a powerful squadror in the Gulf of Mexico, and "to move the dis posable forces" on the southwestern frontier "to meet any emergency." The only object he attained was that he was allowed to evade the greatest difficulty by one word, which left a possibility open to him, not, indeed, to justify the action of the administration, but to defend it by dialectic subtleties. He declared that, "during the pendency of the treaty of annexation, the President would deem it his duty to use all the means *placed within his power by the Constitution* to protect Texas from all foreign invasion." On the following day the treaty was signed.

Ten days elapsed ere the treaty was submitted to the Senate. The reason of this, under the circumstances, very surprising delay was the wish of the Secretary to lay simultaneously before the Senate a copy of a letter, which was formally a reply to a dispatch of Lord Aberdeen, and addressed to Mr. Pakenham, the English plenipotentiary, but which in fact was a piece of special pleading in justification of annexation, directed to the people of the United States. A more remarkable and more revolting document has never been issued from the State Department of the country.

In the dispatch of December 26, 1843, which had been communicated by Mr. Pakenham to Secretary Upshur on February 26, 1844, Lord Aberdeen had said, —

" We desire to see [slavery] abolished in Texas.
With regard to the latter point, it must be and is
well known, both to the United States and to the
whole world, that Great Britain desires, and is constantly exerting herself to procure, the general abolition of slavery throughout the world. . . . With regard to Texas, we avow that we wish to see slavery
abolished there, as elsewhere, and we would rejoice
if the recognition of that country by the Mexican
government should be accompanied by an engagement on the part of Texas to abolish slavery eventually, and under proper conditions, throughout the
republic."

Calhoun declared in his letter of April 18,
1844, to Mr. Pakenham, that these avowals
of Great Britain had made it, in the opinion
of the President, " the imperious duty of the
federal government " to conclude, " in self-defence," a treaty of annexation with Texas as
the most effectual measure to defeat England's
intention.

" The United States have heretofore declined to
meet her [Texas'] wishes; but the time has now arrived when they can no longer refuse, consistently
with their own security and peace, and the sacred obligation imposed by their constitutional compact for
mutual defence and protection. . . . They are without responsibility for that state of things already
adverted to as the immediate cause of imposing on
them, in self-defence, the obligation of adopting the

measures they have. They remained passive so long as the policy on the part of Great Britain, which has led to its adoption, had no immediate bearing on their peace and safety."

It may not be correct to apply, without modification, the code of private ethics to politics; but, however flexible political morality be, a lie is a lie, and Calhoun knew that there was not one particle of truth in these assertions. Almost eight years before, on May 23, 1836, as we have seen, he himself had declared annexation to be necessary, and the first and foremost reason which he alleged for it was the interest which the Southern States had in it, on account of their peculiar institution. Two years later his colleague, Mr. Preston, had moved in the Senate, and Mr. Thompson, of South Carolina, had also moved in the House of Representatives, to declare annexation expedient. Several state Legislatures, as those of Mississippi, Alabama, and Tennessee, had agitated the question with hot zeal, unreservedly avowing that they did so "upon grounds somewhat local in their complexion, but of an import infinitely grave and interesting to the people who inhabit the southern portion of this confederacy." In December, 1841, it was a public secret in the political circles of Washington that Tyler had again taken up the annexation

project. It had, in fact, never been abandoned,
but only temporarily put off the order of the
day, because, for various reasons, the time had
not been deemed opportune. But on October
16, 1843, more than two months before Lord
Aberdeen's dispatch was written, and more than
four months before it was delivered, Upshur
had made the formal proposition of annexation.
Whether Calhoun had any knowledge of the
existence of this dispatch before he had consented to become the successor of Upshur we
do not know; but that he would have accepted
Tyler's invitation, and entered upon the office
with exactly the same programme, if Lord
Aberdeen's dispatch had never been written,
nobody has ever ventured to question. It is,
therefore, an incontestable fact that there was
not a particle of truth in those allegations of
the Secretary, and that he was fully conscious
of it.

To pervert the truth in such a manner required indeed a bold front. Even if the whole
world had not been familiar with the fact that
ever since the battle of San Jacinto the annexation of Texas had been but a question of time
with the whole South and the Democratic party,
Calhoun's assertion would have been simply ridiculous. Lord Aberdeen's dispatch contained
absolutely nothing to startle or even to surprise

the United States. The avowals which, according to Calhoun, the President regarded with such " deep concern," only stated a fact as notorious as the existence of slavery itself. That England's hostility to slavery and her desire to see it everywhere abolished was " for the first time " avowed " to this government " was evidently of no consequence whatever, for it did not add a grain's weight to the importance of the fact. Lord Aberdeen expressly declared that England's policy remained unaltered, and Calhoun did not pretend to doubt in the least the truth of this assurance. The mere fact that England had seen fit to state, in an official dispatch, what every school-boy already knew to be the case, could not be a cause of alarm, and the reason which had induced her to do it was calculated to have exactly the opposite effect. Lord Aberdeen had not indulged in any threats, but the only purpose of his dispatch was to dispel any apprehensions which the United States could possibly entertain. He said : —

" We should rejoice if the recognition of that country by the Mexican government should be accompanied by an engagement on the part of Texas to abolish slavery eventually, and under proper conditions throughout the republic. But although we earnestly desire and feel it to be our duty to promote such a consummation. we shall not interfere unduly, or with

an improper assumption of authority, with either
party, in order to assure the adoption of such a course.
We shall counsel, but we shall not seek to compel or
unduly control, either party. . . . She [Great Brit-
ain] has no thought or intention of seeking to act directly or indirectly, in a political sense, on the United
States, through Texas. . . . The governments of the
slave-holding States may be assured that, although we
shall not desist from those open and honest efforts
which we have constantly made for procuring the
abolition of slavery throughout the world, we shall
neither openly nor secretly resort to any measures
which can tend to disturb their internal tranquillity,
or thereby to affect the prosperity of the American
Union."

It did not require the keen intellect of a Calhoun to see that these emphatic disclaimers
were meant to be the essential part of Lord
Aberdeen's dispatch, and not the sentences on
which he based his reply to Mr. Pakenham.
Yet it would be a great mistake to suppose that
they only served him as a pretext, because he
could find no better one, and that his uneasiness
on account of England's policy was feigned.
His alarm was not only most real, but it was
also fully justified. In the course of the negotiations with Texas, Upshur had repeatedly
avowed that the alleged ambitious designs of
Great Britain, and especially her exertions for
the abolition of slavery in the republic, impera-

tively demanded that the annexation should no
longer be delayed. At the same time, however,
it was acknowledged on all sides that slavery
was doomed in Texas, independently of anything England might do. Leading Texans, *e. g.*
Ex-President Mirabeau B. Lamar, had frequently declared that the anti-slavery party
would soon acquire the ascendency, and that the
abolition of slavery could be effected " without
the slightest inconvenience." The most zealous
advocates of annexation in Congress had emphatically indorsed this opinion, and Upshur
himself had written to Mr. Murphy, "If Texas
should not be attached to the United States, she
cannot maintain that institution [slavery] ten
years, and probably not half that time." Calhoun held the same opinion. He informed Mr
Pakenham that the President had " the settled
conviction that it would be difficult for Texas,
in her actual condition, to resist what she [Great
Britain] desires, *without supposing the influence
and exertions of Great Britain would be extended
beyond the limits assigned by Lord Aberdeen ;*"
and he added, "and this, if Texas could not resist the consummation of the object of her desire, would endanger both the safety and prosperity of the Union."

An independent Texas without slavery and
the permanent continuance of slavery in the

Union were, however, irreconcilable. Even if
this had been a mistake, as it undoubtedly was
not, the opponents of the slavocracy had no reason to contest the truth of this confession, for
it was the most destructive judgment which
could be passed on slavery. The slavocracy declared through its most gifted representative, in
an official document, that between it and liberty there existed a conflict of principle so irreconcilable, that by the simple fact of the
neighborhood of independent States in which
slavery did not exist, it was brought face to
face with the question of life or death. Did it
not follow directly from this that its political
connection with free States was possible only
on the supposition of the complete subservience
of the latter? Was there a more forcible proof
needed, or even possible, than the very demand
which the slavocracy now made, in consequence
of that fact? Because the slave-holding States,
thought their peculiar institution endangered
by the existence of an independent free State,
it was declared to be the " imperative duty "
and a " sacred obligation " of the United States,
imposed by their constitutional compact, to ab-
sorb that State into the Union, in order to prevent the abolition of slavery in it. It was not
only a fact that Texas was to be annexed to
make the continued existence of slavery possi

ble there, but the fact was officially declared before the whole world by the executive of the Union. The democratic republic, which had based its existence upon the rights of man, was morally and constitutionally bound to prevent the breaking of the chains of the slave in a neighboring republic, though it could be done only by adding these very chains to those which already bound its arms. Calhoun's letter to Pakenham was the official proclamation of the "nationalization" of slavery, only, however, so far as it imposed duties upon the Union, but by no means with regard to any corresponding rights. "With us," the Secretary declared, the policy to be adopted in reference to the African race "is a question to be decided not by the federal government, but by each member of this Union, for itself, according to its own views of its domestic policy, and without any right on the part of the federal government to interfere in any manner whatever. Its rights and duties are limited to protecting, under the guarantees of the Constitution, each member of this Union in whatever policy it may adopt in reference to the portion within its respective limits." The slave-holding States had to say what was necessary to protect them in the policy they had been pleased to adopt, and the federal government had to act accordingly. The President had had no choice. The annexation of Texas was " the most effectual, if not the only means of guarding against the threatened danger," and therefore he had acted simply "in obedience " to the constitutional obligation of the Union. In other words, it was the constitutional obligation of the Union to engage in slavery propagandism in the defence of the interests of the slavocracy, and, confessedly, even at the risk of a war; for the Secretary declared, in an official dispatch to the American representative in Mexico, that the step had been taken " in full view of all possible consequences."

If the United States had indeed assumed such sacred obligations towards the slave-holders, in establishing the Constitution, there could be no impropriety in it that Calhoun concluded his letter with a short but enthusiastic exposition of his theory of the " positive good." But what were those to think of it who did not acknowledge those obligations? Surely, the history of the United States had entered upon a new phase, if the Secretary of State could dare, in an official communication and in the name of he federal Executive, to lecture a foreign state upon the blessings of slavery. And by his own testimony he stands convicted of having engaged in this whole correspondence partly for the very purpose of doing that, and of having

been grievously disappointed that the rejection
of the treaty prevented him from enlarging
upon this exalted theme. The "Charleston
Mercury" of November 28, 1860, published a
previously unknown letter, dated July 2, 1844,
in which Calhoun says : —

"If an opportunity should offer, I had hoped to
draw out a full correspondence by my letters to Mr.
Pakenham. They were, in part, written with that
view, and were intended to lay the foundation of a
long and full correspondence ; and I doubt not what
was intended would have been accomplished, had the
Senate done its duty [!] and ratified the treaty. Their
neglect to do so, I fear, will not only lose Texas to
the Union, but also defeat my aim in reference to
the correspondence. Had the treaty been ratified,
my last letter to Mr. Pakenham, which he transmitted to his government, would not have been left
without a reply, which would have brought on what
I intended. As it is, it will not be answered, as I
infer from Mr. Pakenham's conversation recently
His government is' content to leave to our Senate
the defence of its course, and is too wise, when it can
be avoided, to carry on a correspondence in which
they see they have little to gain. I regret it. It
will, I fear, be difficult to get another opportunity
to bring out our cause fully and favorably before the
world. I shall omit none which may afford a decent
pretext for renewing the correspondence."

Even ultra-Democratic papers and journals in

16

the North criticised the Pakenham letter in the severest terms. The "Democratic Review," though it advocated immediate annexation, and professed "exalted admiration, respect, and even attachment" for Calhoun, complained with bitterness that the President and his Secretary had not left a shred of the Southern doctrine, which was also that of the Northern Democrats, that slavery was a local institution, "with which the free States had nothing to do, for which they were in no wise responsible." It reproved with indignation the "volunteer discussion of the essential merits of this peculiar local institution through the peculiar organ of our collective nationality, for which, if for anything, the Union, and the whole Union, is emphatically responsible." Without reserve, it avowed that Calhoun had "nationalized" and "federalized" slavery, "actually pledging the military intervention of the country, by a simple unconstitutional executive promise, to plunge directly into war with Mexico if she should execute her threat of immediate invasion of Texas;" and all this "on the avowed ground, the almost exclusively avowed ground, of strengthening and preserving the institution of slavery."

Such language from a leading organ of their own party might well have induced the President and his Secretary to pause and ponder. Even if they succeeded, they were evidently playing a dangerous game. The deep-seated dissatisfaction in their own camp indicated that it would probably not be ended by their winning the stakes, and the sequel might be very far from corresponding with the beginning. But Calhoun, who so justly boasted of being wont to look to the farthest consequences of every question, had now neither ears nor eyes for anything except his immediate object. It is asserted that he obtained from Archer, of Virginia, the chairman of the Committee on Foreign Relations, the solemn promise that he would delay the Senate forty days with regard to the annexation treaty. The alleged reason for this wish was that Mexico's answer to the notification of the treaty was expected by the last day of that term. That was unquestionably an empty pretence, for in various ways this time might have easily been shortened a little; and, besides, it had been declared from the first that Mexico would not be allowed to interfere in any way whatever in this question. The term was evidently fixed with relation to the national convention of the Democratic party, which was to meet two days earlier at Baltimore. Calhoun wanted to make sure of the party with regard to the main question, ere he allowed the Senate

to come to a decision on the treaty. The "Spectator," the reputed organ of Calhoun in Wash
ington, had formally declared that Van Buren
was to be considered "as beside the presidential canvass," because he had refused to pledge
himself for immediate annexation. Therewith
the programme was announced which the annexationists were resolved to impose upon the
convention at all hazards. After a long and
arduous struggle over the preliminary questions,
they triumphed completely. The majority vote
which Van Buren received at the first ballot
was a bootless compliment. His partisans knew
that they had lost the game before the voting
commenced. On the eighth ballot the name
of Governor Polk, of Tennessee, appeared for
the first time, and on the next ballot he was
nominated. Polk was what, in the political
slang of to-day, is called "a dark horse;" but
as to the test question, he could have been im-
plicitly trusted, even if the platform had not
pledged the party to "the re-annexation of
Texas at the earliest practicable period."

The impatience, which Calhoun had betrayed
in the first stages of his annexation campaign
proved that he would have manœuvred with
more quickness and boldness if he had not had
good reason to apprehend that the Senate would
take serious objection to his policy. It was well

kwown that the treaty would not be supported
by all those who were in favor of speedy annexation. The Pakenham correspondence was a
two-edged sword. Calhoun had cut himself as
badly as he had cut his opponents. He had
succeeded in consolidating the South to the extent that he had expected; but, at the same
time, he had aroused the feeling of the North
to such a degree that even the best disposed
senators were afraid that they would commit
political suicide by voting for this treaty, after
it had been officially based on such grounds.
Besides, they did not see why such immoderate
haste should be necessary. Tyler's and Calhoun's interests might be well enough served
by it, but that was only another reason for them
to curb the over-zealous administration. While
there were but few, if any, senators who, under
any circumstances, would have been anxious to
smooth the way of either the President or the
Secretary in the pursuit of any personal ends,
the majority deemed it a duty to administer to
them a severe rebuke for their gross infringe-
ments upon the rights of Congress and the lack
of consideration for the Senate, which had characterized the whole transaction. Even zealous
annexationists indulged in searching and caus-
tic criticisms of the treaty and all the attendant
circumstances, and on June 8 it was rejected
by a vote of thirty-five against sixteen.

The dismay of Tyler and Calhoun was great, but they were not in the least daunted. They were bent upon attaining their end. If it was not to be secured in this way, nothing was to deter them from trying any other which promised success, though they might have to ride rough-shod over the Constitution and all the constitutional doctrines which they had heretofore professed. On the second day after the rejection of the treaty, the President sent a message to the House of Representatives, accompanied by all the documents relating to the question. The essence of the message was contained in the declaration that Congress was " fully competent, in some other form of proceeding, to accomplish everything that a formal ratification of the treaty could have accomplished." That was in fact an appeal from the Senate, which had the unquestionable right to reject a treaty, to the House of Representatives, to which no power has been given by the Constitution in relation to treaties. What was the sense of rendering the consent of two thirds of the Senate indispensable for the conclusion of every treaty, if, after a treaty had been rejected by the Senate, a simple majority of both Houses of Congress had the right virtually to ratify it, by accomplishing in some other form what the treaty was to have accomplished? Like a

French cavalier of the old régime, Tyler waived away this question with the bold reply, " The great question is, not as to the manner in which it shall be done, but whether it shall be accomplished or not." That such an answer would not have been given, unless it was fully approved by Calhoun, will not be doubted. But when had the most reckless Federalists ever dared to profess such an unblushing latitudinarianism, or to nationalize the Union to such an extent by pushing the Constitution aside, and giving the federal government *carte-blanche* in a question more important than any other ever submitted to it? Verily, the country had fallen upon strange times, if such a doctrine could be officially proclaimed by the President, under the sanction of the man who had come very near plunging the Union into a civil war, by pushing his states-rights theory to such extremities that he found, in the right of nullification, the mainstay of the Union and its great conservative principle.

The President had made no definite proposition to Congress, but the language of the message of June 10 was too plain to admit any doubt that the administration would not let matters quietly take their own course after the close of the session. The check which it had received had made it only more determined and bolder. Upon a notification from the Texan Secretary of State that Mexico intended a new invasion, Calhoun stated that his letter of April 11 had promised armed intervention only in case this emergency should occur while the *treaty* of annexation was pending. We have seen how loath he had been to give this promise, which his immediate predecessor, Nelson, had declared unconstitutional, and yet he now, September 10, after the treaty had been rejected, volunteered to extend the obligation to the whole time during which " the *question* of annexation " should remain " pending." In a formal and constitutional sense, however, annexation was not now at all a pending question. That the President had expressed the wish to see it ultimately accomplished, no matter in what way, and that some members of Congress had suggested this and that, did not and could not make it a *question* in this sense. The treaty had been rejected, the executive had not entered upon new negotiations with Texas for another treaty, and Congress was not even in session. The annexation of Texas was, therefore, no more a " pending question " than the tariff, the bank, or any other political problem in which the people took a lively interest. There was absolutely nothing to be found in the actual condition of things from which even the most subtle dialectics could deduce any international rights or obligations. Besides, the Senate had given it to be understood, in no very ambiguous manner, that, at least in what concerned the President's independent initiative, it did not approve of the promises made in the letter of April 11. Calhoun, therefore, forbore to announce, in express words, an armed intervention; but the declaration that the United States would feel themselves "highly offended" by a renewal of the war, and that they would not "permit it," virtually amounted to the same thing. When the news came that Mexican agents were agitating the Indians at the frontier, — news which never failed to reach Washington, whenever it was opportune that it should come, — Calhoun followed up his protest of September 10 by authorizing (September 17) the Union troops to enter Texas as soon as the Texans should desire it.

In their hot pursuit of the long-coveted prize, which had so unexpectedly slipped through their fingers, Tyler and Calhoun were, in fact, as ready "to assume the full responsibility" for any step which promised to bring them nearer the goal as Andrew Jackson had ever been when the constitutionality or legality of his acts was called into question. Perhaps they would have proceeded with a little more caution, if the

Southern annexationists had not set them the
example of an unblushing recklessness, which
was without a parallel in the whole history of
the Union. The threats of disunion, if the
North dared to resist this extension of the domain of slavery, were too common to make the
desired impression. Much more effect had the
announcement that the North would have to
choose between Texas and the abolition of the
tariff of 1842. There were many respectable
men in the North who honestly believed slavery to be a sin and a curse, but who loved their
pockets more than they hated slavery. With
others, again, their party attachment was
stronger than their hatred and fear of slavery.
They benumbed their consciences with the illusion that they could cleanse their skirts of all
responsibility by protesting against the annexation and recommending the election of anti-an-
nexationists to Congress, while they voted for
Polk. As to the office-seekers, a slight raising
of the party whip was, of course, sufficient to
make them all zealous annexationists, no matter
what their convictions had been before the Baltimore Convention ; their convictions had to be
stored away for the time being, for it would
have been foolhardiness to carry such heavy baggage in so hot a race, with so many competitors.
So the annexationists could count upon the

whole Democratic party of the North, though a considerable part of it either entirely disapproved of annexation, or, at least, thought immediate annexation inexpedient. Yet, in spite of that and of their complete control over the federal patronage, the annexationists would have lost the election, if the Liberty Party, instead of putting up a candidate of their own, had supported the Whigs, in order to bar the way to the former. The votes of that party caused the Whigs to lose the States of New York and Michigan, and with them the election. Polk was elected, but the history of the election proved beyond contradiction, that the majority of the people were opposed to immediate annexation. Tyler's annual message of December 3, however, not only asserted the contrary, but declared that both Houses of Congress had been instructed, — by "a controlling majority of the people, and a large majority of the States," — "in terms the most emphatic," to accomplish annexation immediately, and he therefore recommended it to be done in the most simple way, namely, by joint resolution.

How often had the holy anger of Calhoun's constitutional and political conscience been aroused by Jackson's daring to put such interpretations upon elections! Yet everything with which Jackson could be justly reproached in

this respect was mere child's play, in comparison with the monstrosity of the political heresy
of this assertion and with its brazen disregard
of truth; and that Tyler neither would nor
could have ventured to make it without Calhoun's consent nobody will contest.   It was
simply not true that the election had presented to the people for its decision " the iso-
lated question of annexation."   If it had been
true, the result could, perhaps, by means of
Benton's " *demos krateo* " principle, have been
tortured into an instruction " to both branches
of Congress, by their respective constituents;"
but neither the most searching chemical anal-
ysis nor the most powerful microscope could
discover the slightest vestige of *this* " *demos
krateo* principle" in the *Constitution*. Besides,
the theory of the message refuted itself in such
a way that not another word is needed to show
it up as a political counterfeit of the most
bungling kind. If the electoral votes of the several States were binding instructions to the respective senators, the eleven States which had
voted for Clay had instructed their senators,
" in terms the most emphatic," against annexation. The Union, however, consisted at the
time of but twenty-six States, and the least im
portant of treaties required the assent of two
thirds of the senators.   Thus the " instruc

tions " which the senators had received from the " States " made it impossible to accomplish annexation in the way which Tyler himself had acknowledged to be at least " the most suitable." Yet the " instructions " from a simple majority of States would, by the theory advanced, have made it the imperative duty of the Senate to conclude, without any further previous consideration, a compact with a foreign power, than which it is impossible to imagine one more important.   If the " people," by means of a presidential election, could oblige Congress to incorporate a foreign state, and if Congress could effect such incorporation by a simple majority resolution, the " consolidation " of the Union was complete, and its confederate character was completely and forever lost.   The theory of the message was, in fact, the subversion of all the underlying principles of Calhoun's political doctrines, upon which he had based his defence of the " peculiar institution."   In spite of that, however, he consented to this theory without any compunction, because the slavocracy would have to die, and to die beyond resurrection, if it could not get more land and create more slave-holding States.

Congress did not accede to the proposition of the President without a little more ado.   The House of Representatives, indeed, was satisfied

with having the line of the Missouri Compromise continued through Texas ; but, in the Senate, a back door had to be provided for the consciences of those annexationists who held that
the only constitutional way of effecting the annexation was by treaty. The resolution of the
House of Representatives was amended, by authorizing the President to negotiate another
treaty of annexation, if he should deem it more
advisable to do so than to submit the joint resolution to Texas. Benton and the other senators, who had sustained the above-mentioned
constitutional view, never deigned to inform the
people whence they derived the right to give
the President the choice to bring about the annexation either in the constitutional or in an unconstitutional way, as he should think best.
The crutch with which they limped over this
obstacle was McDuffie's declaration that Calhoun would not have the " audacity " to choose
the unconstitutional way, and submit the joint
resolution to Texas. Did they really so little
know the man who had dared to become " an
honest nullifier "? On March 1, 1845, the joint
resolution was approved by the President. On
Calhoun's advice " to act without delay," the
cabinet were summoned the next day, and concurred in the opinion of the Secretary of State,
who wrote his dispatch, inviting Texas to ac-

cept the terms of the joint resolution, the same night, and sent it off "late in the evening of March 3," a few hours before the expiration of Tyler's term of office. His reasons for acting thus he has repeatedly stated with a candor which proves that he would have been equal to a much greater "audacity," if it had been necessary to secure his object. In the dispatch to Mr. Donelson he wrote, " But the decisive objection to the amendment of the Senate is that it would endanger the ultimate success of the measure. . . . A treaty . . . must be submitted to the Senate for its approval, and run the hazard of receiving the votes of two thirds of the members present ; which could hardly be expected, if we are to judge from recent experience." And on February 24, 1847, he declared in the Senate, " I selected the resolution of the House in preference to the amendment of which the senator from Missouri was the author, . . . because I clearly saw, not only that it was every way preferable, but the only certain mode by which annexation could be effected. . . . That the course I adopted did secure the annexation, and that it was indispensable for that purpose, I have high authority in my possession."

Thus it was that ne triumphed over all obstacles, and succeeded in virtually accomplishing the purpose for which he had consented to become a member of Tyler's cabinet. What right had he to complain that the work was continued by his successors in the spirit in which it had been begun by him? Why should Polk's diplomatic conscience be more conformable to the code of private morals than his own? In order to get Texas, he, the sternest and most jealous partisan of strict construction, had loosened the bridle of the Constitution more than any of his predecessors had ever dared to do. What right had he to cry out and wash his hands of all responsibility, when his disciples refused to listen to his warning voice, and rushed on in mad zeal along the track upon which he had started them? He had hit the mark, but the ball pierced the target and continued its fatal flight.

Calhoun's friends expected that he would be called upon to finish the great work which he had directed with so much skill and energy, and it is asserted that he shared their opinion. We cannot prove the contrary, but are inclined to think that he judged Polk more correctly. If he really expected to remain at the head of the cabinet, the wish was father to the thought. Polk certainly never intended to tender him the office. Now, after the annexation of Texas was as good as accomplished, the whole party would probably have been rather dissatisfied to see the first place awarded to the leader of the small faction on its extreme left wing, which was so easily tempted to break through the bonds of party discipline and assume an independent position. Especially Jackson would have been deeply mortified, and Polk, who would never have reached the top of the ladder if he had not clung so faithfully to the heels of the general, was not inclined to array Jackson's still enormous influence against the administration. Besides, it was asserted that the offended politicians of New York had exacted the promise that, in consideration of their supporting the nominees of the Baltimore Convention, Calhoun should be discarded. But, above all, Polk was personally not at all desirous to put a political star of this magnitude and brilliancy in too close proximity with the rush-light of his own talents and achievements. Calhoun's character and whole political course absolutely forbade his honest subordination under another man's mind and will, and Polk was too ambitious and self-conscious to be a mere figure-head where it was his right and even his duty to be the real chief. On the other hand, he was well aware that openly to slight the Calhounites in the person of their leader would be the extreme of folly. He therefore offered him the first diplomatic office, the legation at the

Court of St. James, undoubtedly fully satisfied that the honor would be politely declined.

Many years before, at the end of 1819, when Mr. Gallatin had expressed the wish to be re-called from Paris, Adams had asked Calhoun whether he would accept the post. Calhoun had then answered " that he was well aware that a long and familiar practical acquaintance with Europe was indispensable to complete the edu-cation of an American statesman, and regretted that his fortune would not bear the cost of it. Calhoun devoted much time to the manage-ment of his estate, and he had the reputation of being an uncommonly experienced and effi-cient planter; but his pecuniary circumstances remained modest, though he lived with his nu-merous family in unostentatious but solid com-fort, and could indulge in the true luxury of always bidding a hearty welcome to the throngs of friends who came to enjoy the hospitality of his table and the pleasure of his genial com-pany. It is, therefore, very possible that he would have declined, under all circumstances, Polk's offer, for the same reason which had dic tated his answer to the overtures of Adams. But it is unquestionable that he would have taken the same course for political reasons, if he had been the wealthiest man on the continent. Polk knew perfectly well that he paid Calhoun an empty compliment, for it was certain that his going to London in such critical times would be considered by himself and by his political friends a kind of desertion. It was too late in the day to go to Europe in order to finish his education as a statesman. If he now accepted a diplomatic post, it could only be for one of two reasons: either because he wanted to gratify his ambition and vanity, or because he thought that he could render his country important services. This kind of ambition, however, though its fire had not entirely ceased to burn in his bosom, was no longer strong enough to determine his resolution in a question of such moment; and though it might soon become of great consequence who was the representative of the United States in London, yet he could evidently do much more to avert any dangers which might possibly arise if he should stay in his old place in the Senate, where he was not obliged to follow the instructions of other people, but was entirely free to be guided by his own opinion. His character and the peculiar part which he had played these last fifteen years in the history of the Union absolutely forbade his being an instrument in other men's hands; either he had to direct the policy of the Union, so far as that could be done by the Executive, or he had to remain the inde-

pendent senator, the foremost champion of the
slavocracy and the leader of the ultra states-
rights faction. The former he could not do,
and weighty reasons demanded that he should
once more return to the post which he had occupied so long with so much distinction. Un-
hesitatingly he had thrown his influence into
the scales for Polk, because he had only to
choose between him and Clay; but the late Governor of Tennessee and Speaker of the House
of Representatives would not have been his own
first choice, and he was far from being satisfied
that either the foreign or domestic policy of the
new President would entirely accord with his
own views. The wild denunciations in which
the radicals of South Carolina had indulged
during the campaign had been disapproved by
him, but he thought it wise not only to wait,
but also to watch. He therefore readily returned to his seat in the Senate, which was
vacated by his successor as a matter of course.
His position in his State was such that he might
consider the seat as belonging to him of right,
so long as he was willing to remain in public
life

CHAPTER IX.

OREGON AND THE MEXICAN WAR.

WHEN Calhoun was invited to become the head of Tyler's cabinet, the "Richmond Enquirer" said, "We cannot entertain a moment's doubt that he has been selected with a special regard to the question of Oregon and the annexation of Texas." The order of the two matters ought to have been reversed, but it was correct that, next to Texas, Oregon was the most important subject in the order of the day, and that it required a master's hand to bring the negotiations with England to a mutually satisfactory termination. Yet it is very unlikely that Calhoun himself harbored the delusion that he would add a new laurel leaf to his wreath by accomplishing that task. Everything that could be said in support of the claims of the United States he counted up with his customary ability, but he had no new fact and no new argument to add to what had been repeated already a dozen times. He, therefore, made no more impression upon Pakenham than Pakenham made upon him by reiterating for the

tenth time what England had to say in support of her claims. In this way it was evidently
impossible to advance a single inch on either
side. The two powers could go on telling their
respective stories to the end of days, and the
only result of it would be the heaping of proof
upon proof that nothing could be thus attained. The journals of the discoverers and
the legal arguments were certainly of some
weight, and an impartial examination of them
undoubtedly leads to the conclusion that of the
two incomplete and contestable titles that of
the United States was the better. But no log-
books and no principles of public and international law, as laid down by Hugo Grotius, could
avail anything against the simple fact that by
a solemn and repeatedly renewed agreement,
the Territory was held in joint occupancy by
the two powers, and that the possession of it
was deemed by both an interest of such moment that neither would ever voluntarily yield
.he whole ground to the other. As neither
wished to continue the *status quo*, and still less
to cut the knot with the sword, a compromise
was the only way to settle the controversy.
Great Britain therefore proposed to submit it
to an arbitrator; but on January 21, 1845, Calhoun, in the name of the President, declined
this offer, upon the ground that " it would be

unadvisable to entertain a proposal to resort to
any other mode, so long as there is hope of arriving at a satisfactory settlement by negotiation."

There the matter was allowed to rest for the
time. Tyler and Calhoun left it to their successors exactly as they had found it. Yet it is
to be supposed that Calhoun was tolerably well
satisfied, and thought that he had done the best
thing possible, under the circumstances, for the
interest of the United States. In the beginning
of 1843 a bill for the occupation and settlement of the Oregon Territory had been before
Congress. Calhoun opposed its passage, because he thought that the United States had no
right, under the convention of 1818–27, to offer
land bounties to settlers. With many others,
he apprehended that this might lead to a breach
with England, and he deprecated it as the greatest folly on the part of the United States to do
anything tending to provoke a decision by arbitrament of arms. In six weeks England could
bring a strong naval and military force from
China to the mouth of the Columbia River,
while the American fleet, which would have to
double Cape Horn, would need about six months
to reach that point; and the overland march
from Missouri would require at least one hundred and twenty days, if indeed it were possible

to sustain any considerable force in a region so destitute of supplies. The United States would, therefore, surely be worsted in a conflict of arms for the dominion over that distant country. On the other hand, the almost miraculous growth of the population of the United States and the impetus with which it was "rolling towards the shores of the Pacific" rendered it an absolute certainty that, in a comparatively short time, the United States would be as much stronger in Oregon than England as England was now stronger than they. Therefore Calhoun's advice was, "Let us be wise and abide our time; it will accomplish all that we desire with more certainty and with infinitely less sacrifice than we can without it." "All we want, to effect our object in this case, is 'a wise and masterly inactivity.'"

Calhoun had now acted in strict conformity to this programme, and, as a settlement of the controversy according to the wishes of the United States was as yet impossible, it is to be presumed that he was not exactly dissatisfied that the negotiation had had no result except to add another bundle of useless papers to the archives of the State Department.

President Polk's inaugural address made a sharp cut through this policy of "wise and masterly inactivity" by declaring the title of the United States to the Territory "clear and un-questionable."   The whole country was thrown into wild excitement by this declaration, for if Congress took the same view of the question the breach with England seemed almost inevitable.   That the President, in spite of his "blustering announcement," as Lord John Russell called that declaration, addressed a compromise proposition to England was a surprise; but the chances of an amicable settlement were not thereby increased, for in one of the earlier negotiations the United States had been willing to yield more than what was now offered by Polk.   Since England had then rejected the greater concession as insufficient, it was a matter of course that she would not now accept the smaller offer.   Besides, Polk had accompanied it with the declaration that "he would not have consented to yield any portion of the Oregon Territory had he not found himself embarrassed, if not committed, by the acts of his predecessors."   He therefore withdrew his offer after it had been rejected by England, and his annual message declared " that no compromise which the United States ought to accept can be effected."   At the same time he advised the abrogation of the convention of 1818–27.   The consequence was that, as Calhoun afterwards stated, " stocks of every description fell, marine insurances rose, commercial pursuits were suspended, and our vessels remained inactive at the wharves." General Cass, after previous consultation with the President and Secretary of State, poured oil into the flames by a violent speech (December 15, 1845), which culminated in the assertion that " war is almost upon us." Several senators expressed in strong terms their dissatisfaction with the course which the influential senator from Michigan had seen fit to pursue. It seemed, however, as if the majority of both Houses of Congress would only too willingly follow the lead of the administration. On December 18, Senator Allen, the chairman of the Committee on Foreign Relations, moved a joint resolution, advising the President " to give, forthwith, notice to Great Britain that the government of the United States . . . will terminate the convention existing relative to the joint occupancy of the Oregon Territory." And on January 5, 1846, the Committee on Foreign Relations of the House moved a resolution, peremptorily demanding " that the President of the United States forthwith cause notice to be given to the government of Great Britain," etc.

The right to give notice at any time they pleased, had been expressly stipulated by the high contracting powers in the convention of

1827. The adoption of those resolutions, therefore, would not have given Great Britain any just cause of complaint. The spirit, however, which actuated the hotspurs made the words almost equivalent to a declaration of war. The notice that the United States wanted the joint occupancy to terminate, was understood to be a notification that Great Britain must abandon her claims at once and absolutely, or take the consequences. " Fifty-four forty or fight " was the plain language of the radicals. A set of resolutions, introduced by Senator Hannegan, boldly denied even the power of the government to settle the controversy by any compromise or to concede one foot of the Territory to England. Calhoun, on December 30, 1845, introduced a set of counter-resolutions, asserting the power of the government which Hannegan denied ; stating the fact that, however clear the title of the United States to the whole Territory might be in their opinion, there were conflicting claims to the possession of the same between them and Great Britain; and declaring that the President, in proposing the forty-ninth degree as a compromise boundary, did not " abandon the honor, the character, or the best interests of the American people."

These counter-resolutions rolled a heavy load 'rom the breasts of all those in whose opinion

it was a criminal folly to treat this question in
a manner which, if it was not intended to provoke a war, actually pressed the British lion to
the alternative of crouching like a whipped
spaniel, or of using his powerful claws. It was
generally believed that it depended upon Calhoun whether passion and ambition or cool
statesmanship should rule the day, and though
the resolutions were clad in a strictly negative
form they left no doubt which side could count
upon his determined support.

To-day, probably, nobody will contest that
this is one of his best claims upon the gratitude
of his country, and yet it cannot be denied that
there was a good deal of solid matter in the
avalanche of bitter complaints and stinging reproaches which the Northwestern radicals hurled
against him and all the Democrats of the South.
Calhoun had carefully abstained from laying
down any positive programme in his resolutions, because his programme was now, as it
had been in 1843, to have none, — the policy
of "wise and masterly inactivity." And the
reasons which he had then adduced for this
course were now as good as they had been at
that time. He was probably right in supposing that a war would result in the loss of
"every inch" of the Territory; nor could any
body question that time was the ally of the

United States, and was working in their favor
with a force which Great Britain would ultimately be unable to resist. But this being so,
why did he not pursue his reasoning to the last
consequences? According to his argument, the
United States were sure to get the whole Territory, if they would but have patience and bide
their time; yet he did not contend for the continuation of the joint occupancy so long as
England could be prevailed upon not to give
notice. He still asserted that, in his opinion,
the title of the United States to the whole Territory was good, and that he wished to secure
the possession of the whole to them; but the
whole tenor of his resolutions, and especially
the last one, which declared that the offer of
the forty-ninth degree was not an abandonment of their " best interests," clearly indicated
that a fair compromise would meet with his
approval.

That was the wisest and therefore a truly
patriotic policy, but would he have advocated
it if Oregon had been situated south of Mason and Dixon's line? The history of the annexation of Texas answers this question in
an unmistakable manner. Only party passion
could doubt that the patriotism of the South
was strong enough to defend with energy the
rights of the Union, whenever these rights were

really " clear and unquestionable." But it is
equally certain that Calhoun and the other representatives of the South were not at all anxious
to assume any burdens and submit to any sac-
rifices in the defence of questionable rights,
if the North was to have the benefit of them.
As in the opinion of Giddings, the indomitable
enemy of slavery, the necessity to restore the
equilibrium between the two sections, which
had been disturbed by the annexation of Texas
in favor of the South, imperatively demanded
that the United States should maintain their
claims to Oregon at every hazard, so the South
apprehended that this equilibrium would be
disturbed in favor of the North by securing the
whole Territory to the Union, and therefore
was determined not to go a hair's-breadth beyond what the honor of the republic really required. Calhoun had openly avowed that, so
far as it depended upon him, the annexation of
Texas should be effected without delay, though
it should lead to a war, in which England might
be found on the side of Mexico. With regard
to the Oregon question, however, he was sure
to oppose with the utmost energy any policy
tending to endanger the peace of the Union
and the more energetically, the more that pol
icy was likely to result in an extension of the
Union territory in the north. For a war with

Great Britain would be, under all circumstances, most detrimental to the interests of the South, and might easily put the very existence of slavery into imminent danger. In and out of Congress, leading men of the South openly avowed that these considerations for the special interests of their section determined their course, and there was in fact no reason to conceal the truth. If the policy of the radicals was sure to do much harm to the South, and if it was, to say the least, very doubtful whether the United States as a whole would derive any benefit from it, the adoption of it would have been not only an act of folly, but a wrong on the part of the North. But, however sound the arguments of Calhoun and the other representatives of the South were, their sayings and doings, now that an interest of the North was at stake, did not agree with what they had said and done when they had contended for the interests of their "peculiar institution." The difference was the less justifiable because then the United States had had to deal with a *political* problem, while they had now to maintain, as they contended, an existing *right*. Besides, the South stood 'pledged," as Bedinger, of Virginia, admitted, to support the policy of the West with regard to Oregon, in consideration of what the West had done for the South with regard to Texas.

It is true, Calhoun had been personally no party to this bargain, which had been concluded and solemnly proclaimed to the whole world by the Baltimore Convention. The charge of "Punic faith," which Hannegan hurled against the South, was therefore too strong a term, so far as he was concerned. But he had not uttered a single syllable against this bargain, and the West had a right to infer from his silence that he approved and sanctioned it as well as the rest of the Baltimore platform. As he was the foremost leader of the annexationists, perfect candor would have required a declaration that he personally intended to stick to his policy of "masterly inactivity;" and now he even abandoned that; and declared himself in favor of a compromise. Public opinion and history have decided the controversy in favor of this policy. No blame rests upon Calhoun for what he did now. His annexation game had not been played entirely above board, and for this wrong he had now to pay the just penalty. What he had done then exposed him now to the charges of inconsistency and bad faith. And that was but the first drop of the bitter cup, which his own hand had pressed to his lips by the deed concerning which he declared to the last, "To no act of my life do I revert with more satisfaction."

On January 17, 1846, Webster had written to Mr. Sears, " Most of the Whigs in the Senate incline to remain rather quiet, and to follow the lead of Mr. Calhoun. He is at the head of a party of six or seven, and as he professes still to be an administration man it is best to leave the work in his hands, at least for the present." Seward was very indignant at this " ill-starred coalition of nullifiers with Whigs, to save slavery and free trade." Webster, however, was certainly right in believing that the surest way to check the wild policy of the Western radicals effectually and in time was to confide the lead of the opposition to a professed " administration man ; " and Seward labored under a great mistake in supposing that he and the Western radicals were fighting at the side of the administration, against this opposition, by contending in full earnest for the extreme views of President Polk's messages. Calhoun and his followers and allies would probably have succeeded in enlisting public opinion as strongly in favor of a sensible and sober policy, even if Polk had really wished to see the uncompromising course, which he officially advocated, adopted by Congress. But their task was undoubtedly rendered much easier by the fact that the President was secretly as anxious as they to see the fire quenched, which he had stirred up into so dangerous a conflagration. As to this question, Calhoun was a much better administration man than he was himself aware of. But in serving the President here, where he apparently crossed the policy of the administration, he also unwittingly promoted its ultimate designs, which filled his mind with the greatest apprehensions for the future of the country.

On March 16, 1846, Calhoun had said in the Senate, " A further inducement for dispatch in settling the Oregon question is that upon it depends the settlement of the question with Mexico." In this Polk perfectly agreed with him. Their ways parted only when they came to the question how and under what conditions the settlement with Mexico was to be effected. One of the main reasons why Calhoun so earnestly strove to bring about a compromise with England was the delusion that this was the surest way to avert a war with Mexico, while, in fact, the apprehension of a war with England was the only thing which, perhaps, could have deterred Polk from his aggressive policy towards Mexico. No more unjust accusation could be brought against Polk than that he wished a war with Mexico. He and his cabinet infinitely preferred the crooked ways of diplomacy to a war even with an enemy so weak that they could afford to despise him. They only were irrevocably determined to obtain from Mexico what they could not get without a war, and thus it became a " necessity " to " compel " Mexico, just as Calhoun had been " compelled " to accept the office of Secretary of State, because the annexation of Texas was a " necessity."

Calhoun had accompanied to the Mexican government the notification of the treaty of annexation with the assurance " that it is his [the President's] desire to settle all questions between the two countries which may grow out of this treaty, or any other cause, on the most liberal and satisfactory terms, including that of boundary." On March 31, 1845, his declaration was repeated almost literally by Mr. Shannon on behalf of President Polk. Calhoun, however, had intended to negotiate honestly with Mexico about the contested boundary of Texas, while, according to Polk, "the most liberal and satisfactory terms " were, that not a single inch f the territory claimed by Texas could, under any circumstances, be granted to Mexico, and that, in order to prevent future conflicts, New Mexico and California should be sold by Mexico to the United States. As Mexico could not be prevailed upon to see the question in the same light, the American army, under General Taylor, was ordered (January 13, 1846) to take possession of the contested strip of land, and to assume such an attitude that an appeal to the arbitrament of the sword was inevitable, unless Mexico had entirely lost her self-respect.

Calhoun heard of the fatal order only " a long time after " it had been given. He deprecated it, because he clearly foresaw its pernicious consequences, and wished the Senate to take some action forcing the President to recall it. But he himself refused to move in the matter, because, as he said, " it was important I should maintain the kindest and most friendly relations, in order that I should have some weight in bringing the Oregon question to an amicable settlement." That this was no afterthought is fully proved by his whole subsequent course with regard to the Mexican war. But it is equally certain that Calhoun here committed the greatest and most fatal political plunder of his whole career. Polk knew as well and better than he that Taylor's advance from Corpus Christi would lead to a war with Mexico, and it was folly to think it possible that a President of the United States could see a double war with Mexico and Great Britain in the same light as it would be seen by a demagogical stump-speaker, intoxicated by his own spread-eagle harangues. The order of January 13 1846, would never have been issued if Polk had not made up his mind to satisfy England with regard to Oregon. Calhoun could have crossed the way of the President in the most determined manner, without risking anything except his standing as an " administration man," and that he was sure to lose at any rate.

On Saturday, May 9, 1846, Polk received the welcome news that a skirmish had taken place on the eastern bank of the Rio Grande. On the following Monday he sent a message to Congress, which culminated in the assertion that " war exists, and, notwithstanding all our efforts to avoid it, exists by the act of Mexico herself." The House of Representatives at once indorsed the bold statement, without any examination of its truth, and without allowing the minority a single minute to develop their views of the question. In the Senate a short debate could not be avoided, but here, too, the administration party succeeded in preventing the minority from entering at all upon a previous examination of he main question. Calhoun demanded in vain at least one day " to consult the documents accompanying the message, " as containing the ground on which the bill ["for the prosecution of the existing war"] was to pass." In vain did he and those who acted with him repeatedly express their willingness to vote at once " the amount of supplies contained in the bill, or even

a greater amount," so that the succoring of Tay·
lor might not be delayed one hour, in case he
should really stand in need of it.   In vain did
Calhoun demonstrate that hostilities did not necessarily constitute a war, and that the President's
assertion was not and could not be true, because
the right to declare war was granted by the
Constitution exclusively to Congress.   In vain
was attention called to the fact that it was not
known as yet whether the Mexican government would approve of General Arista's crossing
the Rio Grande.   In vain was the majority reminded that the history of the United States
afforded more than one example of most outrageous hostilities, in which they had been the
assailed party, and which yet had not led to a
war, and much less had anybody ventured to
assert that these in themselves constituted a
war.   Like the President, the majority wanted
the war in order to conquer New Mexico and
California, and therefore no reasons, however
weighty and unanswerable, could be of any
avail.   On May 13 the war bill was passed by
a vote of forty against two.   Calhoun had abstained from voting, for " he could neither vote
affirmatively nor negatively," because " he had
no certain evidence to go on."   " He could not
agree to make war on Mexico by making war
on the Constitution."   Therewith he ceased to

be an "administration man," without joining
the opposition. More solitary than ever before,
he pursued his independent course. He neither
broke nor bent, but the furrows on his forehead
deepened, and his eyes looked more gloomy and
careworn than ever; for without abandoning a
single delusion as to the nature or future of
slavery, he saw but too clearly that the more
successfully the war was waged, the more the
" peculiar institution " and, in consequence, the
existence of the Union, became endangered.

Two presidential messages — one of August
4, 1846, addressed to the Senate, and the other
of the 8th of the same month, addressed to Congress — indirectly avowed the real purposes of
the war, which everybody had known from the
first. Polk asked two million dollars to negotiate a peace, in which he proposed to pay "a
fair equivalent" for some territory which Mexico was to cede, in order to adjust the boundary
by a line "securing perpetual peace and good
neighborhood between the two republics." The
House promptly acted on the suggestion of the
President, but on motion of Mr. Wilmot, of
Pennsylvania, a proviso was attached, by which
slavery and involuntary servitude were forever
prohibited in any territory which might be acquired from Mexico. An amendment, moved
by Mr. Wick, of Iowa, which divided the event

nal acquisitions by the line of the Missouri Compromise, was rejected by a vote of 69 against
54. The fulfilment of the dark forebodings
which had caused Calhoun to oppose the war
with all his energy had therewith begun. On
February 24, 1847, he said in the Senate : —

" Every senator knows that I was opposed to the
war ; but none save myself knows the depth of that
opposition. With my conceptions of its character
and consequences, it was impossible for me to vote
for it. When, accordingly, I was deserted by every
friend on this side of the House, including my then
honorable colleague among the rest [Mr. McDuffie],
I was not shaken in the least degree in reference to
my course. On the passage of the act recognizing
the war, I said to many of my friends that a deed
had been done from which the country would not be
able to recover for a long time, if ever ; and added,
It has dropped a curtain between the present and
the future, which to me is impenetrable ; and for the
first time since I have been in public life 1 am unable to see the future. I also added, It has closed the
first volume of our political history under the Constitution, and opened the second, and that no mortal
could tell what would be written in it."

For many years, he had been the trusted
leader of the South with regard to everything
relating to slavery, though but a small band
had kept pace with him. And in those porten

tous May days, when he, who had always rushed on in advance of all, the most radical of the radical slavocracy, cried Halt! beware! all dashed past him with indignant impatience, as if he had been the last and most insignificant among all the political apprentices. Now they began to ask themselves whether he had not after all been right. The day after the war bill had been passed by the House of Representatives, Giddings had said : —

" We sought to extend and perpetuate slavery in a peaceful manner by the annexation of Texas. Now we are about to effect that object by war and conquest. . . . Now I say to those gentlemen who are so zealous for this conquest that our slave States will be the last to consent to the annexation of *free* States to this Union. I know that Southern men are now, and have been, zealous in bringing on this war and for extending our territory ; but they will, at no distant day, view the subject in its true light, and will change their position, and will oppose the extension of our territory in any direction, unless slavery be also extended."

As soon as the words "territorial acquisitions" were officially pronounced, the verification of this prediction began. The din of war on the Mexican battle-fields was almost drowned by the vociferous passion with which the victors quarrelled over the expected spoils of the vanquished. The Southern President, acting in perfect unison with the slavocracy, had not been disappointed in the expectation that the bloody flag, which he had dug out of the graves of the Spanish *conquistadores*, could be carried to the shores of the Pacific with the hearty approval of the North. But had he quite forgotten that it was absolutely impossible to make any conquest simply for the *Union?* The United States had ceased long ago to be a Union merely of *States;* they were above all a Union of two heterogeneous *sections.* There was not a foot of Union territory which was not the legal domain of one or other of these two sections, and much less could an inch of new territory be acquired without legally assigning it to one or other of them. And now a stanch Democrat and an ardent supporter of the annexation of Texas met the intimation that new territory was to be acquired with the demand that the South should be at once legally excluded from all participation in the fruits of the common exertions. The South would not and could not submit to that, for it was not only not fair, but it was the death sentence of slavery. The balance of power between the two sections would be irretrievably destroyed, and that in itself would be the death knell of the "peculiar institution." And did the past history of the slavery conflict admit any doubt that the slavocracy would resist its doom to the knife? On the other hand, however, was it likely that the North would yield, if a man of the antecedents of Mr. Wilmot demanded such a proviso?

Every day brought new proofs how true Calhoun's prediction had been, that in the North the future belonged to the spirit of abolitionism. Just now it had received by the annexation of Texas a more powerful impetus than ever before, and the South undertook to force the North into a concession, in comparison with which all the other demands of the slavocracy were as nothing. Mexico had abolished slavery long ago. To allow the South to carry its "peculiar institution" into a part of the conquered territory was therefore nothing less than slavery propagandism with powder and lead. The Northern freemen were to allow millions of dollars, which they had earned with the sweat of their brows, to be spent, and the blood of their sons and of the Mexican patriots to be spilled like water, in order to open a new field of activity to the slave-driver's whip on a soil which was consecrated to universal liberty and legally protected against pollution by the tread of a slave. Were the descendants of the Revolutionary patriots willing to present the world with such a commentary on the Declaration of

Independence, and to hide their faces in shame before the semi-barbarians of Mexico? Thus the story of the treasure-digger, in whose hand the gold turned into glowing coals, had become true; but, unlike that fabled personage, who threw down the present of the evil spirit with a curse, the United States had to keep at least a part of their conquests. It was folly to expect that a war which, under false pretexts, had been undertaken for the purpose of making certain territorial acquisitions would, under any circumstances, be terminated by the administration and the majority of Congress without securing any compensation, after more territory than they had ever coveted had been actually conquered.

Here was a mass of difficulties boiling and seething in the caldron of the Mexican war, which was beyond the skill of any political cook. Perhaps some means could be discovered to let the steam escape, so that no explosion would ensue, but nothing could prevent the gradual corrosion of all the rivets by the poisonous fumes. Ardent Northern patriots helped the President to cover the whole width of the continent with the folds of the star-spangled banner, and thereby rendered the temporary destruction of the Union inevitable; hot-headed slavocrats sustained Polk's policy and urged him on, in order to realize the prediction of Henry A. Wise, that the " peculiar institution " would irresistibly press on, until the waves of the Pacific put a stop to its conquering march ; and thereby they sealed the fate of slavery.

Calhoun acknowledged that he was " unable to see the future, " and that he did not know what the second volume of the history of the United States under the Constitution would contain. If he had probed his own mind to the bottom, he would have been forced to add that he was glad of it. He would have shut his eyes with a shudder, if they could have pierced through the mist, for a voice, which nothing could silence, constantly whispered into his ear that it covered an unfathomable abyss. Now and then he tried to ease his heavy mind by reminding the South how earnestly and persistently he had raised his warning voice. But that could bring no comfort either to himself or others. On the contrary, his reproaches were met by the charge that he more than anybody else was responsible for the war, because it was the legit- .mate or even unavoidable consequence of the annexation of Texas. With hot indignation he repelled the charge as an absurd calumny ; for the annexation of Texas had been an impera- tive patriotic duty towards the Union, and he had been willing to meet Mexico with regard

to the boundary question in a most conciliatory
and liberal spirit.

The latter assertion was probably true, but
was it thereby proved that Benton's accusation
had absolutely nothing to rest upon? Let it
be granted, for argument's sake, that he would
have come to an amicable understanding with
Mexico, had it been certain or even likely that
the unravelling of this snarl would be left to
his discretion. The war was the legitimate
consequence of the annexation, though it might
have been prevented if the helm had remained
in his hands. He had taught the people that it
was not only right, but a national duty, to
make territorial acquisitions, if the slavocracy
declared its need of them for the safety of slavery, and that the stays of moral scruples might
be loosened to almost any extent for this laud-
able purpose. *He*, therefore, had no right to
blame Polk and the war party for anything, except that they were not satiated when he cried
Halt! enough! They were over-zealous and
maladroit disciples, but still they were his disciples. It was the old story: the wizard had
called the spirits merely to prepare a bath, and
his half-taught apprentices had them go on carrying water, till the house was flooded and destructive streams burst through every door and
window.

But what was the use of these criminations and recriminations? What had been done could not be undone. There the facts were, and they had to be dealt with. Calhoun did not retire to his tent like the irate Achilles. Just because Polk's policy had led the slavocracy into a dangerous defile, it was all the more sure that the shield and the spear of its veteran hero would be seen at their wonted place in the thickest of the fight. But to demand that he should now simply step into the ranks of the administration columns and obey the commands of their leader, and to denounce him because he refused to do so, was folly. Senator Turney, of Tennessee, charged that he was prompted by his presidential aspirations to obstruct the passage of bills necessary for the successful prosecution of the war. Calhoun repelled the charge (February 12, 1847) with passionate indignation: "If the senator speaks of me as an aspirant for the presidency, he is entirely mistaken. I am no aspirant, — never have been. I would turn on my heel from the presidency, and he has uttered a libel upon me. . . . No, sir. The whole volume of my life shows me to be above that." We have seen that as to the past the facts were pretty far from bearing out his self-laudatory assertion but as to the present the insulting intimation was indeed utterly unfounded.

It was a little too early after the last presidential canvass for him to declare, " At my time of life the presidency is nothing; " but the history of that canvass had taught him that to indulge any longer in such aspirations would be folly, with a tinge of ridiculousness. Never again would he have permitted his name even to be mentioned as a candidate. And even if he had not understood the lessons of that canvass as well as he did, he would have scorned every temptation, at this critical juncture of affairs, to allow his course to be in the least influenced by any personal considerations.

On the other hand, it is easily to be under-stood how the war party came to suspect him of personal motives. He was so deeply con-vinced that the war was a blunder and a calam-ity that he allowed once more the doctrinarian bent of his mind to get the better of his cool practical judgment. Turney had been pro-voked into his accusation by a speech, in which Calhoun had very elaborately advocated the policy of a " defensive line." The active mili-tary operations were to be entirely stopped. The United States should confine themselves to holding the conquered territory on a certain line, quietly waiting for Mexico to make up her mind to come to terms on this basis. This he declared to be " the policy best calculated to

bring the war . . . with *certainty* to a successful termination, and that with the least sacrifice of men and money, and with the least
hazard of disastrous consequences and loss of
standing and reputation to the country." The
difficulties which the enormous distances, the
climate, and above all the obstinate patriotic
pride of the Mexicans opposed to a successful
termination of the war, in spite of the brilliant
achievements of the American arms, were so
great, that one can understand how a clever
man could hit upon this strange plan, which
to-day must appear simply absurd to everybody who is not acquainted with all the details
of those countless embarrassments. Nevertheless, though the idea certainly could not stand
the test of a sober and somewhat close examination ; yet if the partisans of the administration
had been familiar with what had occurred behind the curtain, they would have felt less
tempted to ridicule it, and to give it a slight
coloring of that " moral treason " with which
they charged all the opponents of the war. The
President himself had been in favor of this
strange project of the " defensive line." The
original draft of his message had recommended
it to Congress. Calhoun had known this ; but
ne had not been informed of the alteration
which Polk had made at the instigation of Ben-

19

ton, who had convinced him that such a passive
policy of " masterly inactivity " was utterly incompatible with the genius of the American
people.

This was so true that probably neither Congress nor the people would have hesitated one
moment to reject the proposition as not only inexpedient, but also pusillanimous and deroga-
tory to the national honor, even if the administration had supported it with all its influence.
As the personal opinion of a single senator,
it was, therefore, of no consequence whatever.
The majority could have afforded very well to
pass it over with a few indifferent remarks, and
consideration for the man as well as policy ought
to have advised such a course.   With regard to
the main question, Calhoun had announced in
the same speech his complete acquiescence in
the unalterable facts : —

" It would be vain to expect that we could prevent
our people from penetrating into California. . . .
Even before our present difficulties with Mexico, the
process had begun.   Under such circumstances, to
make peace with Mexico, without acquiring a consid-
able portion, at least, of this uninhabited region, would
.ay the foundation of new troubles and subject us to
the hazard of new conflicts. . . . But it is not only in
reference to a permanent peace with Mexico that i
desirable that this vast uninhabited region should

pass into our possession. High considerations con
nected with civilization and commerce make it no less
so. We alone can people it with an industrious and
civilized race, which can develop its resources, and
add a new and extensive region to the domain of commerce and civilization."

Once admitted that extensive territorial acquisitions had become inevitable, the other question, how they should be disposed of with regard to slavery, had also to be met directly. If
Calhoun did not at once give a full answer to it,
his delay did not arise from any desire to conceal his views. The object of his speech was
to recommend the "defensive line," and for
that purpose it sufficed to say how the territory to be acquired should not be disposed of.
That he did with great emphasis : —

" We are told — and I fear that appearances justify
it — that all parties in the non-slave-holding States
are united in the determination that they shall have
the exclusive benefit and monopoly ; that such provisions shall be made by treaty or law as to exclude all
who hold slaves in the South from emigrating with
their property into the acquired country. . . . Be assured, if there be stern determination on their part to
exclude us, there will be determination still sterner on
ours not to be excluded."

" This known pointed division of opinion " as
to the ultimate disposition of the territory

seemed to him to render the vigorous prosecution of the war impossible : —

" Now, if I may judge from what has been declared on this floor, from what I hear on all sides, the
members from the non-slave-holding States, if they
were sure that slavery would not be excluded from
the acquired territory, would be decidedly opposed
to what they call vigorous prosecution of the war, or
the acquisition of a single foot of territory. Can they
then believe that the members of the slave-holding
States, on the opposite supposition, would not be
equally opposed to the further prosecution of the war
and the acquisition of territory ? "

Ten days after the delivery of this speech,
on February 19, 1847, Calhoun presented a set
of resolutions to the Senate, covering the whole
ground of the slave question with regard to the
Territories. The key-note of the remarks with
which he prefaced them was the assertion, that
" the day that the balance between the two sections of the country . . . is destroyed is a day
that will not be far removed from political revolution, anarchy, civil war, and wide-spread dis-
aster." This was not intended as a threat, nor
even as a warning, for he knew that it would
not be heeded. It was simply the statement of
the solemn conviction by which his course was
determined. In his opinion he had been forced
upon the position which he was about to assume

Adams's journal is documentary proof that he had not "always," as he now asserted, considered the Missouri Compromise a surrender of the "high principles of the Constitution." But it was of little consequence when he had come to that conviction. At all events, he now considered that compromise "a great error," and, in spite of that, it had been at his suggestion, as he informed the Senate, that the continuation of the compromise line had been proposed in the House of Representatives, as a settlement of the controversy about the territory to be acquired from Mexico. He had not wanted the Southern members to be "disturbers of this Union." But the proposition had been twice voted down by a decided majority; therefore his advice was now, "Let us have done with compromises. Let us go back and stand upon the Constitution!"

The resolutions affirmed: The Territories are the common property of the several States composing the Union. Congress has no right to do any act whatever that shall directly, or by its effects, deprive any State of its full and equal right in any Territory: a law which would prevent the citizens of certain States from emigrating, with their property, into any Territories would be such an act. Admission of a State into the Union may not be made

dependent upon any other condition, **except**
that its Constitution shall be republican.

A refutation of this doctrine cannot here **be**
attempted, for that would require a recapitulation of the whole slavery question and of the
doctrine of state sovereignty.   As to the question of constitutional law, it suffices here **to say**
that, whether Calhoun was right or wrong, the
whole history of the United States proved the
assertion to be an absurdity ; that what he
claimed to be a " high constitutional right " of
the slave-holders was "*not the less clear* because
deduced from the entire body of the instrument,
and the nature of the subject to which it relates, instead of being specially provided for."
If this " constitutional right " was as clear as if
it had been specially provided for by the Constitution, then all the Southern statesmen, ever
since the adoption of the Constitution, must
have been utterly devoid of brains or absolutely
nerveless, for the right had never been acknowledged or exercised.   Calhoun himself
opened " the second volume " of the history of
the United States " under the Constitution,"
and, by his resolutions, he marked a new era,
because they were not mere legal abstractions,
out a political manifesto, announcing a revolutionary programme of fearful import.

" The Constitution which we now present*

is the result of a spirit of amity, and of that mutual deference and concession which the peculiarity of our political situation rendered indispensable." Thus the framers of the Constitution had characterized their own work. North and South had always declared with one voice that the constitutional convention at Philadelphia would have labored in vain if the compromises concerning-slavery had not been agreed upon. Compromise had ever since been the unsteady compass by which the course of the Union ship had been directed in the slavery question. To that, and to that alone, it was due that the domain of slavery and the sway of the slavocracy over the national politics had constantly increased. And now Calhoun demanded that a heavy line should be drawn through this word "compromise," and that it should for all time to come remain expunged. It is true, he only wanted " to go back and stand upon the Constitution," but in the eyes of the North his interpretation of it absolutely divested it of the character of a compromise, and exacted the unconditional surrender of the Union to the slavocracy. Suppose he read the Constitution correctly : that did not change the fact that it was understood very differently by the North.

The Constitution in itself, however, was nothing but a dead piece of parchment, not even able to resist the attacks of moths and mice. There was no magical force in it, by which it could of itself make known and enforce its true will and intent. Like every other law, it became an active force only by the agency of the people and their several constituted organs. Whether right or wrong, that construction of the Constitution had to prevail which the people and their constituted organs believed to be correct. Was it, then, possible that they would ever adopt the doctrine of Calhoun's resolutions, according to which slaves could be brought into "any Territory of the United States, acquired or to be acquired," and according to which, in consequence, the slave-holders had been most grievously wronged, ever since the establishment of the Constitution, by excluding their human chattels from all the Territories north of Mason and Dixon's line?

The free States had by far the larger part of the population of the Union, and they went on steadily and rapidly gaining upon the South. Many years ago, however, Calhoun had declared with the utmost emphasis that, in the North, the future inevitably belonged to the spirit of abolitionism; and by this time the prediction was so far fulfilled that, according to his own testimony, all parties in the free States were united in the determination to exclude slavery

from the territory to be acquired from Mexico
The experience of the past certainly justifie‹
the hope that it would be possible to break up
this unanimity, but would it ever be possible to
unite the majority of the whole people, irrespective of Congress, upon the basis of Calhoun's
claim?   The acknowledgment of this claim
would have been nothing less than the renun-
ciation on the part of the Union of any policy
and will as to the future of its own political
nature; for the Territories were but inchoate
States, and experience had taught that, wherever slavery gained a firm foothold, it became
the paramount formative principle.   Calhoun
certainly believed in his own doctrine, but that
he should have expected ever to reconcile the
majority of the people to it seems hardly cred-
ible.   His idea probably was to obtain a good
deal by imperiously demanding all.   But he had
too carefully studied the history of the slavery
conflict not to know that, by thus demanding
all, the hatred of slavery and the opposition to
the slavocracy would be greatly intensified with
a very considerable portion of the Northern people.   The formation of a majority upon any
positive programme, therefore, evidently pre-
supposed the consolidation of the whole South
upon the slavery question, and the application
of very powerful levers to induce the rest of the

Northern people to support the slavocracy, in spite of the prevailing current of public opinion in their own section.

The framers of the Constitution had declared " the consolidation of the Union " to be " the greatest interest of every true American, in which is involved our prosperity, felicity, safety, perhaps our national existence." We have seen how ardently Calhoun professed the same faith in his earlier years. Now, he boldy proclaims the unrestrained expansion of slavery over all the Territories of the Union to be the shibboleth around which the whole South must rally.

" Henceforward, let all party distinction among us cease, so long as this aggression on our rights and our honor shall continue, on the part of the non-slaveholding States. Let us profit by the example of the abolition party, who, as small as they are, have acquired so much influence by the course they have pursued. As they make the destruction of our domestic institution the paramount question, so let us make, on our part, its safety the paramount question ; let us regard every man as of our party who stands up in its defence, and every one as against us who does not, until aggression ceases."

That is the only means to save slavery and with it the Union. It is the only means, but it s also infallible.

" But if we should act as we ought, — if we, by

our promptitude, energy, and unanimity, prove that we stand ready to defend our rights, and to maintain our perfect equality as members of the Union, be the consequences what they may, and that the immediate and necessary effect of courting abolition votes, by either party, would be to lose ours, — a very·different result would certainly follow. That large portion of the non-slave-holding States who, although they consider slavery as an evil, are not disposed to violate the Constitution, and much less to endanger its overthrow, and with it the Union itself, would take sides with us against our assailants ; while the sound portion, who are already with us, would rally to the rescue. The necessary effect would be, that the party leaders and their followers, who expect to secure the presidential election by the aid of the abolitionists, seeing their hopes blasted by the loss of our votes, would drop their courtship, and leave the party, reduced to insignificance, with scorn. The end would be, should we act in the manner indicated, the rally of a new party in the non-slave-holding States, more powerful than either of the old, who, on this great question, would be faithful to all the compromises and obligations of the Constitution ; and who, by uniting with us, would put a final stop to the further agitation of this dangerous question."

In truth, he was no novice in all the arts and artifices of party politics. How well he was acquainted with the most sterling political qualty of the Northern people, their unfaltering loyalty and their religious respect for the law, and how well he knew how to make use of that for his purposes! Still better was he acquainted with the doughty character of the professional Northern politician, and he knew more thoroughly how to profit by it for the benefit of the slavocracy. But there was still the old mistake in his calculation, which vitiated it from one end to the other. The more unanswerably he proved the irrepressible character of the conflict between slavery and liberty, and the more violently he pushed it to its climax, so much the more closely he shut his eyes to the fact that slavery *and* the Union could *not* be saved, and so much the more loudly he cried that this *could* and *would* be done. He was only too successful in the consolidation of the South, and the effect of that upon the Northern politicians probably surpassed his own expectations. The slavocracy achieved triumphs, in comparison with which all its former victories appeared almost ridiculously insignificant. But all these triumphs only hastened the last inevitable consequence of the consolidation of the South, namely, the corresponding consolidation of the North. The perfecting of the consolidation of the two sections upon the slavery issue, however *was* the breaking up of the Union.

The left wing of the Northern Democrats

which used to be called "Copperheads," throws
the moral responsibility for the civil war upon
the Republicans, because they forced the South
into secession by forming a sectional party.
This view of the case takes the symptom for
the cause. The Union was not broken up because sectional parties had been formed, but
sectional parties were formed because the Union
had actually become sectionalized. The beginning of this process dated back to the constitutional convention at Philadelphia, and its
roots were imbedded in the slavery compromises
of the Constitution. The abolitionists — that
is to say, the abolitionists proper, and not all
whom Calhoun was pleased to call so — had
been the first to recognize this fact, but they
were not, properly speaking, a *political* party,
because they refrained by principle from acting
as such. The slavocracy was the first to proclaim the principle that the slavery issue must
be the division line of the political parties. It
did this with full consciousness of the import of
the declaration; it carried the principle much
farther than the Republicans did, until long
after the beginning of the civil war; and Calhoun was in this respect, as in all others, the
foremost leader of the slavocracy. The Republicans only opposed the extension of slavery.
Calhoun, however, demanded that the South

should unite in making the slavery question in all its forms and bearings the main plank of its political platform, and, in this shape, he wanted "to force the issue upon the North." He writes to a member of the Legislature of Alabama, " I would even go one step farther, and say that it is our duty — due to ourselves, to the Union, and our political institutions — to *force* the issue on the North. . . . I would regard any compromise or adjustment of the [Wilmot] proviso, or even its defeat, without meeting the danger in its whole length and breadth, as very unfortunate for us. It would lull us to sleep again, without removing the danger, or materially diminishing it." And how did he propose thus to meet the danger? " There is and can be but one remedy short of disunion, and that is to retaliate, on our part, by refusing to fulfil the stipulations in their favor, or such as we may select as the most efficient." He proposed a convention of the Southern States, which should agree that, until full justice should be rendered the South, all the Southern ports should be closed to the sea-going vessels of the North. The northwestern States would be detached from the northeastern by leaving open the trade by river and railroad, and the northeastern States would surely come to terms, for " their unbounded avarice would, in the end, contro' them." To-day, the South knows whether the avarice of the northeastern States is quite so unbounded as Calhoun thought, and whether the northwestern States are willing to let it depend upon the gracious good-will of the South whether the national rivers, and especially the mouth of the Mississippi, shall be open to their trade.

One thing, however, Calhoun ought to have known already at that time, namely, that the North would never acknowledge such a measure to be a " retaliation." He said, " That the refusal on their part would justify us in refusing to fulfil those [stipulations of the national compact] in their favor is too clear to admit of argument." It was, in fact, too clear to admit of argument that, in the most essential point, the two cases had no more in common than yes and no. The opponents of slavery were convinced that Congress had the constitutional right, or even that it was in duty bound, to prevent slavery from entering the free territories to be acquired from Mexico; and even Calhoun forbore to charge them directly with doing violence to their consciences and acting against their better knowledge. He, on the contrary, unreservedly acknowledged that he intended to deprive the North of its *constitu-*
'ional rights.

Benton very correctly said that such a resolution on the part of the South *was* the breaking up of the Union; and now, as before, there were not lacking people who maintained that it was this that Calhoun was aiming at. They understood the man the less in proportion as the crisis and catastrophe more nearly approached. In the same letter, above quoted from, he said:

"This brings up the question, How can it [the danger] be so met, *without resorting to the dissolution of the Union?* I say without its dissolution, for, in my opinion, a high and sacred regard for the Constitution, as well as the dictates of wisdom, make it our duty in this case, as well as all others, not to resort to, or even to look to, that extreme remedy, until all others have failed, and then only in defence of our liberty and safety."

That he honestly and ardently wished the preservation of the Union is, indeed, as certain as it is certain that his remedies had the effect of sledge-hammer strokes. The consciousness of weakness drove him to the desperate resolution to burn the ship of compromise, which had carried the slavocracy so far, and to demand the unconditional submission of the North. "We are now stronger relatively than we shall be hereafter, politically and morally." He thought the last moment had come, when it was stil' possible to chain down the North so absolutely by positive law that slavery could scorn all the assaults of the brutal facts and the spirit of the times. In truth there never had been a time when that could be done, and it grew every day less possible to do it, because this growing weakness of the slavocracy was no secret to the North. The forging of new chains for the Northern States made them feel more than ever the weight of those which they already wore; and in shaking these, while listening to the complaints of the Southern States that their political and moral strength was irremediably on the wane, they learned better to know their own strength. The will and the ability of the North grew to do what, in its opinion, every political and moral consideration bade it do. The more the South succeeded in chaining down the North by positive law, the louder and the more energetic the protest of the spirit of the times and of the facts became. And had Calhoun quite forgotten that many years ago he himself had declared that the ultimate decision would be given not by the law, but by the facts? So far from swinging the fire-brand of sectional agitation without cause, and only to further secret treacherous designs, as so many accused him of doing, he now, as heretofore, shrunk back from drawing the last conclusion from his own premises, because he would not believe that slavery and the Union could not both be saved. With every new contest, it became more apparent that the curse resting upon slavery was, that every new success of the slavocracy was another step towards the judgment and doom of the "peculiar institution." This curse, therefore, necessarily weighed most heavily upon the thoughts and the deeds of him who, in all the tremendous exertions of the slavocracy against the onslaughts of the spirit of the times and of the facts, proved himself to be alone "a host." With the consolidated South, he now drove the North from the battle-field of the Wilmot proviso, but the quiver on his back was almost empty, the bow in his hand was cracked, and the field proved to be a barren conquest, so that the ultimate effects of the victory were those of a crushing defeat.

Benton, in his "Thirty Years View," lays great stress upon the fact that Calhoun never called up his resolutions to be acted upon by the Senate, because they had been received with general disfavor. It is hard to imagine how Benton, after witnessing the further development of the controversy, could still think that this afforded any reason for exultation. Calhoun continued to oppose, with the utmost energy, the giddy agitators of unbounded territorial aggrandizement, though the contemplated acquisitions lay so far to the South that the slavocracy would probably have been able to secure the prey for the "peculiar institution." When there seemed to be some danger that it would be impossible "to conquer peace" unless the whole Mexican republic was taken possession of, he still advocated his "defensive line," and he sternly put himself against Polk's recommendation of a temporary military occupation of Yucatan. But while he did his best to prevent the sea of difficulties, into which the Union had been thrown by the craving for more land, from being agitated even more profonndly, he did not recede one inch from the position which he had taken with regard to the equal right of the Southern States to all the Territories. He had refrained from calling up his resolutions, but the number of converts to his doctrines increased at such a rate that the " abstractions " rapidly changed into a positive programme.

A bill for the organization of the Oregon Territory had been passed by the House of Representatives at the second session of the 29th Congress. The Senate committee, to which the bill was referred, moved to strike out the clause which, in conformity with the provisional laws enacted by the inhabitants of the Territory, prohibited slavery. As this motion would have led to endless debates, the bill was laid on the table, and Oregon remained unorganized. Benton asserts that the motion to strike out was made at the instigation of Calhoun. However, that be, at all events the fate of the bill in the Senate lay in the announcement on the part of the South that Oregon, although lying entirely north of Mason and Dixon's line, should not without more ado be given up to the North, and the resistance was based upon the doctrine of Calhoun's resolutions.

When the subject was taken up again by the 30th Congress, it was openly avowed that slavery was not expected to gain a firm footing in these high latitudes. The South declared itself to be contending merely for the principle. To force upon the North the acknowledgment of the principle was, however, evidently an utterly hopeless undertaking. The slavocrats, Calhoun not excepted, knew that well enough, and they were not such doctrinaires as to risk their bones in charging windmills. Calhoun was undoubtedly thoroughly convinced of the soundness of his theories, but the practical aim and end of his struggle for the principle was to wring from the North acceptable concessions with regard to all present and future Territories which were sufficiently well adapted for slave labor. So far from receding from the position which he had taken in his resolutions, he now

tarried their doctrine to its last legitimate consequence by denying the binding force of the
former compromises. In his speech of June 27,
1848, on the Oregon bill, he said of the Missouri Compromise, —

"A compromise line was adopted between the
North and the South ; but it was done under circumstances which made it nowise obligatory on the latter. . . . The South has never given her sanction to
it, or assented to the power it asserted. She was
voted down, and has simply acquiesced in an arrangement which she has not had the power to reverse,
and which she could not attempt to do without dis-
turbing the peace and harmony of the Union, to
which she has ever been averse."

Calhoun was too candid and daring a man, he
had too much of the fanatic, and, above all, he
understood this question too thoroughly to approve of the covering up and concealing of the
depth of the antagonism which necessarily aggravated the evils. He shares with the abolitionists the merit of having always probed the
wound to the bottom, without heeding in the
least the protesting shrieks of the patient. The
return of the left wing of the Northern Democrats into the service of the slavocracy was acknowledged by him with a gracious smile, but
he spurned the cunning device which made
the bitter morsel palatable to the peace-crav

ing masses. As his immediate purposes were
served by it, he of course received with satisfaction the announcement that the reintegra-
tion of the Democratic party could and should
be effected upon the basis of his doctrine of
" non-interference." But no blame rested upon
him for the fact that it was a reunion over the
bottomless chasm of a conscious falsehood, because the " non-interference " as understood by
the Northern Democrats had nothing in common with the " non-interference " demanded by
him and the Southern radicals, except the abandonment of the right to have a national policy
with regard to slavery in the Territories. When
Cass and Dickinson now proclaimed the doc
trine of squatter sovereignty, the cudgel of his
logic with a few strokes smashed into atoms the
coarse and bold sophisms. Whatever of legislative powers the Legislatures or the inhabitants
of the Territories had, was derived from an act
of Congress. If, therefore, Congress had no
right to take any action whatever in respect to
the introduction of slavery into the Territories,
the former evidently could do so much less.
Calhoun called the doctrine of Dickinson and
Cass " the most absurd of all the positions ever
taken." " The first half dozen of squatters
would become the sovereigns, with full dominion and sovereignty over them [the Territo-

ries]; and the conquered people of New Mexico and California would become the sovereigns
of the country, as soon as they became the Territories of the United States, vested with the
full right of excluding even their conquerors."

Calhoun's own doctrine was certainly more
logical, and he was perfectly consistent in denying to Congress, to the territorial Legislatures,
and to the squatters, as well the right to establish slavery as the right to prohibit it. But
nevertheless his theory also had a logical hitch.
He claimed for the slave-holders the right to
bring their human chattels into all the Territories as a right *under* the Constitution, but he
did not dare to assert that the Constitution *established* slavery either in the Territories or any-
where else. It had, however, thus far been uni-
versally acknowledged that, wherever slavery
existed, it was the creature of municipal law.
Whence, then, should slavery derive its legal
existence in Territories where it did not actually
exist, or where thus far it was even expressly
forbidden by law, as in New Mexico and California? Was it now to be denied that slavery
could only be the creature of positive, though
perhaps unwritten, law, — *i. e.* was the right
to hold slaves in any Territory to be derived
from the law of nature? If so, by what process
of logic could this natural right be limited to

negroes, and even to negroes who were already slaves in certain other places ? This course led no less to sheer absurdity than the doctrine of squatter sovereignty ; and yet there was no other course, unless the Constitution was to be construed to *establish* slavery in all the Territories.

Conclusive as this logical hitch in the "non-interference" doctrine was, it dwindled down into absolute insignificance, when compared with the political absurdity of the theory. Calhoun's doctrine made it a solemn constitutional duty of the United States government and of the American people to act as if the existence or non-existence of slavery in the Territories did not concern them in the least. If they could not help taking an interest in it, at least that interest had to be purely academical, as if the Territories had been situated on some distant planet. The question was not allowed to be a question at all. Yet the fact was that North and South were perfectly agreed in considering it *the* question, in comparison with which everything else was as nothing. Thus the theory and the facts clashed in a most ridiculous manner ; and in such a conflict between theory and facts the former has always to yield, though it be written in giant letters and with living fire in the Constitution. No people with the least vestige of political vitality ever will or can turn their backs upon a question which they consider of paramount importance to their whole future, look at the sky and whistle, because the Constitution says that the matter must not be touched ever so lightly with a single finger. And if the Constitution does not say that in so many words, but only an endless string of hotly contested assertions, deductions, and conclusions leads to this result, then the sole effect will be that another huge monument of human folly has been erected.

Nothing shows in so drastic a light the fearful embarrassment into which the policy of territorial aggrandizement had thrown the country, as the recommendation of a committee of the Senate to solve the problem by adopting this ostrich policy. On July 18, 1848, Mr. Clayton, with the consent of Calhoun, who was a member of the select committee, introduced a compromise bill, which acknowledged the provisional laws of Oregon " till the territorial Legislature could enact some law on the subject of slavery." New Mexico and California were to be organized as Territories by the appointment of a governor, secretary, and judges, to compose a temporary Legislature, "but without the power to legislate on the subject of slavery; thus placing that question beyond the

power of the territorial Legislature, and resting
the right to introduce or prohibit slavery in
these two Territories on the Constitution, as
the same should be expounded by the judges,
with a right of appeal to the Supreme Court
of the United States. It was thought that by
this means Congress would avoid the decision
of this distracting question, leaving it to be
settled by the silent operation of the Constitution itself."

By acquiescing in this arrangement, Calhoun
abandoned his position on the "rock" of the
Constitution, and took once more the old track
of compromises. No better proof can be exacted that he had claimed all in order to get
enough. But this comparative moderation was
not yet to be rewarded. Even Democratic organs
emphatically protested against "the cowardly
conduct of Congress in seeking to shove [the
responsibility of the decision] upon the Supreme
Court." By the Senate the bill was passed, but
in the House it was laid on the table, on motion
of Alexander H. Stephens. Calhoun was of
course free to climb again to the top round of
the ladder of principle, but his doing so could
no longer produce the same effect as heretofore.
He knew this well enough, and his discomfiture
was the greater because a leading Southerner
had felt himself called upon to move the rejec

tion of the compromise. The consolidation of
the South on the basis of the slavery question
had indeed so far been effected that every Southerner peremptorily demanded for his section
some share of the Mexican spoils; but the representatives of the South were very far from being agreed as to the arguments on which to rest
the claims, or as to the means with which their
realization should be attempted. Calhoun had
yet one arrow left in his quiver, and he did not
hesitate to take it out; but its point was broken
off by Southern hands ere he could shoot it.

After a most tenacious resistance on the part
of the Senate, the first session of the 30th
Congress was brought to a close by the passage
of the Oregon bill as it had come from the
House; that is, with the exclusion of slavery.
California and New Mexico, however, had remained unorganized. The rapid and most ab-
normal development of the former, in consequence of the discovery of gold, imperiously
demanded that Congress should at last do its
duty towards the newly acquired possession.
From all sides the cry was raised that it was
a shame and an inexcusable wrong to give up
the Territory to anarchy, because Congress
would not come to a decison on the slavery
question. But there seemed to be little chance
that the knot would be unravelled by this Con-

gress at its second session. The South showed
no more disposition to yield than before, and
the North had good reason to hope that a decisive victory could be gained, if it but braced
up its strength and persisted. California had
as yet only two newspapers, and both declared
that the population was unanimously of opinion that " the simple recognition of slavery "
in the Territory would be the greatest misfortune. " The people of New Mexico, in convention assembled " at Santa Fé, sent a petition to
Congress, emphatically asking protection against
the introduction of slaves. Calhoun called the
petition most impudent, and Westcott thought
it an abuse of the right of petition. But that
did not change the fact that, if the introduction
of slaves into these Territories should be permitted, it would be done against the solemn
protests of the inhabitants. Squatter sovereignty, however, was the utmost limit to which
the Democratic politicians of the North could
hope to lead their constituents in the service of
the slavocracy. The determined opponents of
the slave power, therefore, felt sufficiently elated
to take the offensive. In the House of Representatives, several motions with a view to the abolition of the slave-trade, and even of slavery itself in the District of Columbia, were made, and
it was with some difficulty that the more mod

erate of these attacks were repelled by the South.

These signs of the times appeared to Calhoun so ominous that he deemed it necessary to prove to the North by an extraordinary demonstration that in this question the South thought, and eventually would act, as one man. At his instigation, sixty-nine senators and representatives from the South met for deliberation on December 23, 1848, in the Senate chamber. A committee of fifteen was appointed, which appointed a sub-committee to draw up an address. When this sub-committee met, Calhoun submitted to it the draft of an " Address of the Southern Delegates in Congress to their Constituents." Of its object the address itself said that it " is to give you a clear, correct, but brief account of the whole series of aggressions and encroachments on your rights, with a statement of the dangers to which they expose you. Our object in making it is not to cause excitement, but to put you in full possession of all the facts and circumstances necessary to a full and just conception of a deep-seated disease, which threatens great danger to you and the whole body politic." It did not pretend to have any new facts or arguments to lay before the people. It was throughout the old story, which, in and out of Congress, had been repeated many thousand times. Nevertheless, a short recapitulation of it in calm but incisive and even bitter language could of course produce a great effect. Calhoun, however, did not rely principally on that. The fact in itself, that all the Southern members of Congress united in addressing their constituents in such a solemn form, was to make an overpowering impression not only on the South, but also on the North. Men of all parties believed that his designs went much farther and were of much darker complexion. The old charge was renewed that he was driving directly at a dissolution of the Union, and some of the accusers had evidently some apprehension that this time he might possibly succeed. So far as his wishes were concerned, however, the suspicion was now as unfounded as it had been on all former occasions. The possibility — and, in his opinion, perhaps no more an improbable one — of the withdrawal of the slave-holding States from the Union, he kept steadily in view. There is no question about that, for he had often declared it in express words, and he had not now made the concession to his more moderate colleagues to conceal it in the least in the address. As the address was to impress the people with the gravity of the crisis, it was a matter of course that this eventuality had to be pointed to in a forcible manner. Nay, more. One of his purposes undoubtedly was to prepare the South for it, and to make the South equal to the emergency, if it should come to the worst. But a calm and attentive perusal of the curious document cannot fail to satisfy every reader that its main object was exactly to prevent this dire eventuality from becoming an actuality.

The assertion that if the North was allowed "to monopolize all the Territories" "she would emancipate our slaves, under the color of an amendment of the Constitution," and then the white population would " change conditions" with the slaves, absolutely excluded the possibility of submission, if all the Territories should be closed to slavery by the verdict of the majority. " As the assailed you would stand justified by all laws, human and divine, in repelling a blow so dangerous, without looking to consequences, and to resort to all means necessary for that purpose." But, at the same time, the address declared it probable that the calamity could still be averted by the South. " If you become united, and prove yourselves to be in earnest, the North will be brought to a pause, and to a calculation of consequences; and that may lead to a change of measures, and the adoption of a course of policy that may quietly and peaceably terminate this long con

flict between the two sections." This expectation caused Calhoun to leave the last decisive
word unpronounced. He had no positive measures of any kind whatever to propose. The address, so to speak, lacked an end. It was a long
string of premises, which suddenly broke off
without a conclusion. All the advice it had to
give was, " We earnestly entreat you *to be
united*, and for that purpose to adopt all necessary measures. Beyond this, we think it would
not be proper to go at present."

On January 13, 1849, the sub-committee reported to the committee of fifteen. A long and
animated debate ensued. The Whig members
showed very little inclination to follow the lead
of Calhoun, and they afterwards avowed that
they had consented to help dig the mine only
in order to pour water on his powder. The address was adopted with a majority of but one
vote. Two days later, over eighty members of
Congress met and deliberated with closed doors.
Considerable excitement prevailed in Washington, for " many of the most intelligent men "
believed, as Horace Mann wrote on the same
day, that " Mr. Calhoun is resolved on a disso
lution of the Union." They were mistaken.
" We hope that, if you should unite with anything like unanimity, this may of itself apply a
remedy to this deep-seated and dangerous dis

ease; but if such should not be the case, the time will then have come for you to decide what course to adopt." This last paragraph of the address stated with perfect truthfulness what he intended. To unite the South, — that was his purpose, neither more nor less, — to unite the South for good or for evil, as the case might be. He "*hoped*" that the North would yield when it should be convinced, by the unanimity of the South, that "the refusal of justice" would be promptly followed by the dissolution of the Union. This calculation was not to be submitted to the test of facts. Washington's anxious expectations came *post festum.* The reception which the address had met from the committee had already proved that the South could not as yet be united on the slavery question in such a manner that thereby the Union could either be saved or destroyed. The attempt to form a Southern party had completely failed. The address was finally issued, but among the signatures were the names of only two Whigs, while even several Democrats had refused to sign it. The whole number of signatures was forty, just enough to save the movement from ridicule.

If the private correspondence of Calhoun should still exist, and some time see the light, we shall perhaps be authentically informed of

the effect which this signal and probably unexpected defeat had on his mind. His public
utterances contain no explicit answer to this
question. But we can form a conception, probably nearly correct, of his frame of mind, if we
direct our attention principally to what he did
not say and do. Nothing betrays the least personal disappointment. There is left hardly a
glimmering spark of the fire of ambition, which
once burned so fiercely in his bosom, for he
knows that he stands on the brink of the grave.
He is wholly and exclusively devoted to the
cause with which he has absolutely identified
himself. As faithful and determined as ever,
he stands at what he considers his post of duty,
— of duty towards his section, and therefore
also towards the Union. Every device calculated to hinder the North yet a little longer in
securing a " monopoly " of all the Territories, or
to open a new chance to the South, by means
direct or indirect, could count upon his earnest
support, provided it appeared to him not derog-
atory to the honor of the South, and to promise at least a postponement of the evil day, on
which the balance of power would be irretrievably lost. Once (February 24, 1849) he had a
sharp passage of arms with Webster on the question whether the Constitution extends of itself
to the Territories, and it was one of the stranges'

incidents in the strange story of the slavery conflict and states-rightism, to see the affirmative of
this proposition sustained by the "great nulli
fier" against the great "defender of the Constitution." Upon the whole, he unquestionably
got the better of his antagonist in this contest,
which, short as it was, fully proved that his
mental vigor was absolutely unimpaired. Yet a
certain languor had evidently taken possession
of him. The last weeks of the 30th Congress
were the stormiest of Polk's stormy administration, but Calhoun refrained from increasing the
excitement by a set speech. He had nothing
new either to say or to propose. Too deeply
was he convinced of the justice of his cause to
despair of its ultimate triumph; but care sat
heavily on his brow, for nothing would silence
the voice which night and day whispered the
maddening question into his ear, How is this all
to end? Every day he found himself less able
to answer the problem. Yet there was no.halt.
ing; for something must be done, and he had
become thoroughly convinced that nothing more
was to be expected from Congress, unless an irresistible pressure from outside was brought to
bear upon it. The time had come to write the
omitted end of the "Address of the Southern
Delegates in Congress to their Constituents,"
— to draw the practical conclusion from the
premises therein enunciated.

The public did not know what snare he had in the new movement. Even a leading politician like Henry S. Foote had no knowledge of it, though he himself was one of the principal instruments in the hands of Calhoun. So late as February 8, 1850, Foote indignantly rebuked Senator Houston for intimating that "the sovereign State of Mississippi, in the incipient movement towards the Nashville Convention, . . . was instigated by South Carolina, or her statesmen." And he added, "I know that what he has said will be understood as intimating, at least, that this Conventional movement of ours was stimulated by South Carolina, and was the result of concert between certain South Carolina politicians and certain politicians in Mississippi, with a view of having that movement originate in the State of Mississippi instead of South Carolina, in order to avoid any odium that might thereby arise. I am sure he did not intend to be so understood, and yet he will be, if he does not correct his remarks." Mr. Houston replied, "I can assure the honorable senator that this is a very delicate and complicated question. But I believe that if South Carolina had never existed, and if it had not teen for her disposition and the movement which began there, Mississippi would never have thought of it." The senator from Texas probably was not himself fully aware at the time how true this assertion was. In December, 1851, Foote had to retract his former passionate and haughty disclaimer, and to excuse himself by stating that, at that time, "I did not believe that any human being in the world had received a letter from Mr. Calhoun on the subject, except one which I myself received." He now had to avow not only that Calhoun had "had a pretty extensive correspondence with persons" in Mississippi, but also that his (Foote's) mind had become satisfied by the perusal of these letters "that the *modus operandi* of the Convention was more or less marked out by his great intellect." Nay, he even declared with considerable pride, "It was through me, in the first instance, that Mr. Calhoun succeeded in instigating the incipient movements in Mississippi, which led to the calling of the Nashville Convention."

Foote, in the above-quoted rejoinder to Mr. Houston, has stated correctly the reason which prompted Calhoun to assign the part of ostensible leader to Mississippi, and which made him so anxious not to let anybody see that his hand held and pulled all the wires. The best proof of the consummate skill with which he played his game is the fact that even the chief actors had not the slightest suspicion of their being but tools in his hands. The details of the intrigue are not likely ever to be unveiled, because the greatest part of that secret correspondence is probably no more in existence. The loss is, however, of comparatively little importance, as one of those letters, — dated July 9, 1849, and addressed to Collin S. Tarpley, of Mississippi, — which came to light some time after his death, fully informs us about his intentions. He says : —

"In my opinion there is but one thing that holds out the promise of saving both ourselves and the Union, and that is a Southern convention; and that, if much longer delayed, cannot. It ought to have been held this fall, and ought not to be delayed beyond another year. All our movements ought to look to that result. For that purpose, every Southern State ought to be organized with a central committee, and one in each county. Ours is already. It is indispensable to produce concert and prompt action. In the mean time, firm and resolute resolutions ought to be adopted by yours, and such meetings as may take place before the assembling of the Legislatures in the fall. They, when they meet, ought to take up the subject in the most solemn and impressive manner.

"The great object of a Southern convention should be to put forth, in a solemn manner, the causes of our grievances in an address to the other States, and to admonish them, in a solemn manner, **as to the con** sequences which must follow, if they should not be redressed, and to take measures preparatory to it, in case they should not be. The call should be addressed to all those who are desirous to save the Union and our institutions, and who, in the alternative, should it be forced on us, of submission or dissolving the partnership, would prefer the latter.

"No State could better take the lead in this *conservative* movement than yours. It is destined to be the greatest of sufferers if the abolitionists should succeed; and I am not certain but by the time your convention meets, or at farthest your Legislature, that the time will have come to make the call."

It is the old programme; only the way of executing it is somewhat changed, and changed exactly in the manner which he had repeatedly pointed out in his speeches and addresses. It was another attempt to save the Union, but, at the same time, another step forward towards its final dissolution, if the North should persist in rejecting the conditions of the South. Calhoun's last great speech in the Senate proves that he had not intended the Nashville Convention to present an *ultimatum* to the North, though, for greater effect, he had perhaps wished to see its propositions clad in the most peremptory language. Whether or not he would have liked to come at once to "an end with terror" rather than to endure still longer "the

terror without end," he knew that the South
was not yet ready to act. Therefore he did not
expect from the Nashville Convention what the
faint-hearted and weak-kneed peace fanatics of
the North apprehended from it, and it was very
far from fulfilling even what he expected. He
did not live to drink this new cup of bitterness, but he lived long enough not to derive
any consolation from the vain hope that this
last attempt to save the Union by rendering
slavery absolutely safe *in the Union* would be
successful. His eyes were too keen not to see
the fast-accumulating indications that another
disappointment — more bitter than all the disappointments he had experienced heretofore —
was in store for him. His weary limbs longed
to stretch out and rest, but he knew only too
well that so long as his mortal eyes saw the
light of the sun there was no rest for him. By
their very keenness, these eyes became his worst
tormentors.

How often had he told the country that, by
everything dear to man and making life worth
living, the South would be compelled to sever
its connection with the North, if its equal rights
in the Territories were not recognized! But he
had never ventured to assert that, if this were
done, the peace of the country could never
again be disturbed by the slavery question, be-

cause slavery would thereby be absolutely secured against all attacks. His arguments were
always presented in such an ingenious form
that to the blunt logic of many of his hearers
this would appear to be the self-evident conclusion; but though he certainly deceived himself
to some extent in this respect, he had never directly and expressly asserted the fact. On the
contrary, all his speeches were replete with irre-
futable arguments, proving that the slavery
question could not be decreed out of existence,
because the moral, economical, and political antagonism between slavery and freedom was a
fact, and would assert itself as a fact in all eter-
nity. The people, therefore, neither would nor
could acquiesce in it, if Congress should attempt
to ignore it, or even forbid noticing it. No matter how high the "peculiar institution" was
placed on "the rock of the Constitution," the
waves of the sea of facts unceasingly beat against
it, and gradually washed it away.

In his great speech on the Oregon question
(March 16, 1846), Calhoun had said : —

"But I oppose war, not simply on the patriotic
ground of a citizen looking to the freedom and prosperity of his own country, but on still broader grounds,
as a friend of improvement, civilization, and progress.
Viewed in reference to them, at no period has it ever
been so desirable to preserve the general peace which

now blesses the world. Never in its history has a period occurred so remarkable as that which has elapsed since the termination of the great war in Europe with the battle of Waterloo, for the great advances made in all these particulars. Chemical and mechanical discoveries and inventions have multiplied beyond all former example, — adding, with their advance, to the comforts of life in a degree far greater and more universal than all that was ever known before. Civilization has, during the same period, spread its influence far and wide, and the general progress in knowledge, and its diffusion through all ranks of society, has outstripped all that has ever gone before it. The two great agents of the physical world have become subject to the will of man, and have been made subservient to his wants and enjoyments; I allude to steam and electricity, under whatever name the latter may be called. The former has overcome distance both on land and water, to an extent which former generations had not the least conception was possible. It has, in effect, reduced the Atlantic to half its former width, while, at the same time, it has added three-fold to the rapidity of intercourse by land. Within the same period, electricity, the greatest and most diffuse of all known physical agents, has been made the instrument for the transmission of thought, I will not say with the rapidity of lightning, but by lightning itself. Magic wires are stretching themselves in all directions over the earth, and when their mystic meshes shall have been united and perfected our globe itself will become endowed with sensitiveness, so that whatever touches on any one point will be instantly felt on every other. All these improvements, all this increasing civilization, all the progress now making, would be in a great measure arrested by a war between us and Great Britain. As great as it is, it is but the commencement, the dawn of a new civilization, more refined, more elevated, more intellectual, more moral, than the present and all preceding it. Shall it be we who shall incur the high responsibility of retarding its advance?"

Could he altogether refuse to see how much the advance of this new civilization was retarded by the "peculiar institution"? The most exaggerated eulogies on its conservative virtues could not banish from his sight the glaring contrasts between the two sections; the most positive assertion that these were wholly due to the unjust and unconstitutional economical policy of the federal government could not conceal the fact that, no matter what this policy was with regard to tariffs and internal improvements, these contrasts became more glaring every year. No ingenuity, displayed in the attempt to prove that the North would lose infinitely more by a disruption of the Union than the South, could disprove the fact that these contrasts indicated the increasing weakness of the South, not only morally and polit-'cally, as he had himself avowed, but in **every**

respect; no prophecy that, after the breaking
up of the Union, the economical development
of the unfettered South would be unparalleled,
could cover up the fact that whatever touched
any one point of the civilized part of the globe
was instantly felt on every other, and that this
economical, moral, and mental consolidation of
the civilized world rendered the perpetuation
of the "peculiar institution" impossible, because slavery, whether in itself good or bad,
grew every day more incompatible with all the
laws governing the life of this civilized world.
Much duller eyes than his had begun long ago
to be struck and alarmed by the fast-accumulating proofs of this all-important fact, furnished by the under-currents in the slave-holding States themselves. The non-slave-holders
had begun to doubt the heretofore unques-
tioned identity of their interests with those of
the slave-holders. In the border States the old
creed was revived that slavery was a "mildew" and a "curse"; in some of them an
earnest agitation for its gradual extinction was
entered upon. The old cotton States, and
among them principally South Carolina, not
only bitterly complained of the heavy drafts
which the emigration as well to the northwestern as to the Mississippi States constantly made
upon their wealth and their population, but

they also saw the day approach on which a modified abolitionism would boldly raise its head actually among themselves, if nothing should be done to improve the miserable condition of their poor white people. But all the proposed remedies proved, upon closer examination, to be deadly poisons. The man who had been the zealous advocate of the first great Southern railroad, and who still bitterly accused the federal government of having crippled the South economically, now gave it as his opinion that the South would commit suicide by introducing factories and stimulating all sorts of industrial pursuits, because the artisan and mechanic are born enemies of slavery.

All this could not shake in the least Calhoun's conviction that slavery was " a good, a positive good." But how could he have seen all this, and failed to perceive that, even if all the Territories were thrown open to the slave-holders, the " peculiar institution " would be as far as ever from being safely anchored in haven ? The future was still completely hidden from his view, and had forever to remain so ; for, as his theory of slavery had become with him a *dogma,* he was determined not to see it, and had become incapable of seeing it, unless he lived to see the dogma crushed by the accomplished facts. But he could not help seeing that the entanglements

of the slavery question grew ever more laby-
rinthine, and he could not help feeling that the
whole ground was thickly strewn with thorns.
Wearily he turned away from the facts, which
he neither would nor could understand any
more.

The 30th Congress had expired, leaving the
question of the disposal of the newly acquired
Territories where it had found it, and a Whig
President had taken possession of the White
House. Nine long months the people had to
go about their business in this thick and sul-
try political atmosphere, ere their law-makers
returned once more to the well-nigh hopeless
task of solving this problem. Calhoun did not
pass this time in idleness. The world of stub-
born facts he had been unable to master, but
he still thought himself able to prove on paper
that he was nevertheless right. In these months,
the " Disquisition on Government " and the
" Discourse on the Constitution and Government of the United States " were in the main,
if not entirely, penned. That he expected to
exercise an influence on the decision of the impending question by these essays is hardly to be
supposed. His idea seems rather to have been
to leave an authentic exposition of his political
creed as a political testament and solemn warning to posterity. At all events, it is only in this

quality that they can claim a place in the history of the United States. Unlike so many of his speeches, they were not political deeds, and did not help to shape the course of events. Besides, when they appeared in print, he already rested in his grave, and every day the futility of the attempt to smooth down the wild breakers of realities by pouring on the oil of abstract theories became more apparent. To the student, these two essays will always remain among the most curious books of the political literature of the United States, and they may be read with great profit, though for the most part not exactly in the spirit intended by the author. The people have passed judgment on them without reading them; and have repudiated states-rightism, as Calhoun understood it, that is, state supremacy, as emphatically as they have repudiated the doctrine of the " positive good " of slavery.

When the 31st Congress met, December 3, 1849, the slavocracy was smarting under a defeat, the importance of which could not be overestimated. California, with the informal sanction of the President, but without any authorization from Congress, had adopted a state Constitution prohibiting slavery and involuntary servitude, and this clause had received the unanimous vote of the constitutional convention,

although many of its members were Southerners. This was a commentary on the doctrine
of the " positive good " of slavery which told
more than all the abolition speeches ever made.
California was irretrievably lost to the slavocracy, for to think that Congress could be compelled to force slavery upon her would have
been sheer madness. Therefore it had become
only the more necessary to struggle with the
utmost energy for the rest of the Mexican
booty, and for the principle, upon the acknowledgment of which those Territories which might
be acquired at some future time could depend.
The formal irregularities with which the proceedings in California were tainted furnished
the South with a position of sufficient tactical
strength to continue the struggle, with the hope
that, after all, the strenuous exertions would be
ultimately rewarded at least by a partial success. California was not to be admitted into
the Union as a State until the North had
made satisfactory concessions on all the other
controverted points. At last, the slavocracy was
apparently unanimous in the determination " to
resist the aggressions of the North " to the last
extremity. In the House of Representatives,
the very same Southern Whigs who had so
recently defeated Calhoun in his attempt to
form a Southern party seemed ambitious to

assume the leadership of the "fire-eaters." The
gigantic edifice of the Union trembled to its
very foundations, and, for a while, many patriots hardly dared hope that its proud pillars
could be steadied once more. Week after week,
the storm of debate raged on with unabated
fury. Now and then the dark clouds were torn
by a compromise proposition, but in the next
moment they were again blown together by a
counter-blast, and the darkness seemed but the
greater for the passing ray of light.

No one watched the progress of the storm
with intenser interest than Calhoun, though
his voice had as yet hardly been heard at all in
the Senate hall. The hand of death lay heavily
on his shoulder. His body was sadly bent under its weight, so that the tears involuntarily
pressed into the eyes of those who remembered
what an image of strong and noble manhood
he had been. A dying man he was, though his
mental faculties were still unimpaired. But it
was not hope that fed the flickering flame of
his mind, so that it shone to the last in all its
original brightness. The knitted brows and
the deep lines, which care had chiselled into his
fleshless face, told with most impressive eloquence with what a heavy load he stepped into
his grave. Two years ago he had repelled
the charges of Mr. Turney with the proud as-

sertion, " For many a long year, Mr. President,
I have aspired to an object far higher than the
presidency ; that is, doing my duty under all
circumstances, in every trial, irrespective of
parties, and without regard to friendships or
enmities, but simply in reference to the prosperity of the country."   The sense of duty was
now the strong staff on which the expiring
man leaned, and his iron will bade death stay
its hand till he had done and the country had
heard his parting words. Surely, he had a
right to demand that the country should at-
tentively listen to them. Now nobody could
accuse him of being actuated by presidential
aspirations, and his most embittered adversary
could not dare to intimate that he was a fiend
in human shape, who would willingly and wittingly kindle with his dying hand a fire which
was to consume his country's peace, prosperity,
and glory. Perhaps his political testament contained the best proof that what he had proclaimed to be white was black, and that what
to him appeared black was white, but he certainly revealed in it his solemn conviction, and
he could not have anything in view but what,
in his innermost heart, he believed to be con
ducive to the true welfare of his country.

Calhoun had suffered for some time from an
acute pulmonary affection, which had recently

become aggravated by a heart disease. He himself was no more able to address the Senate for
any length of time. On March 4, 1850, his
carefully prepared speech was read by Mr. Mason, of Virginia, to the Senate. Every senator
listened with profound attention and unfeigned
emotion; the galleries were hushed into the
deepest silence by the extraordinary scene,
which had something of the impressive solem-
nity of a funeral ceremony.

"I have, senators, believed from the first
that the agitation of the subject of slavery
would, if not prevented by some timely and
effective measure, end in disunion." What a
melancholy satisfaction for the man who, for
nearly forty years, had been one of the bright-
est stars of the federal government, in one capacity or another, thus to open his last speech!
He had contributed his full share to the glory
and greatness of the republic, and now the last
question which he had to argue in the federa
Capitol was, "How can the Union be pre
served?" Every line of the speech bears wit
ness how thoroughly he himself is pervaded
oy the consciousness that it is "the greatest
and the gravest question that can ever come
under your consideration." Every word is carefully weighed; not one syllable of angry and
passionate declamation is to be found in it,

— nothing that the most sensitive mind can construe into a threat. A " widely diffused and almost universal discontent " pervades the Southern States, caused by the belief " that they cannot remain, as things now are, consistently with honor and safety in the Union," because " the equilibrium between the two sections . . . has been destroyed," — these undeniable facts are the basis of his argument. He admits that if this destruction of the equilibrium had been " the operation of time, without the interference of government, the South would have no reason to complain ; " but he denies that such is the fact.

The facts and assertions on which he based this denial are familiar to us, and therefore need not be repeated here. Nor is it necessary to recapitulate his version of the story of the antislavery movement, and the reasons why this hostility of the North to the " peculiar institution " would inevitably subject the Southern States " to poverty, desolation, and wretchedness," after " all the power of the system " had been concentrated in the federal government, and the North had " acquired a decided ascendancy over every department of this government." He declared " the views and feelings of the two sections " in reference to slavery to be " as opposite and hostile as they can possi

bly be," and he avowed once more that "all
the elements of influence on the part of the
South are weaker," while "all the elements in
favor of [the antislavery] agitation are stronger
now than they were in 1835, when it first commenced." He therefore asked, "Is it, then,
not certain that, if something is not done to arrest it, the South will be forced to choose between abolition and secession?" And he added,
"Indeed, as events are now moving, it will not
require the South to secede, in order to dissolve
the Union. Agitation will of itself effect it,
of which its past history furnishes abundant
proof."

This startling assertion was probably deemed
by many one of those wild exaggerations, verging upon the absurd, of which he had so often
been guilty in the eyes of all the moderates and
conservatives. Upon more mature reflection it
could, however, not be denied that the split in
several of the great religious denominations, to
which he principally alluded, went far to warn
the people that this opinion was not a day-
dream of the diseased imagination of a fanatic.
Just now he proved, in a manner most unexpected to most of his hearers, that he judged
the situation with more calmness and sobriety
of mind than the great majority of them. "It
is a great mistake," he said, 'to suppose that

disunion can be effected by a single blow.
The cords which bound these States together
in one common Union are far too numerous
and powerful for that. Disunion must be the
work of time. It is only through a long process,
and successively, that the cords can be snapped,
until the whole fabric falls asunder." The history of the next ten years decided in an unmistakable manner the question whether he was
right, or those who thought that the 31st Congress would be the last of the old Union. At
the same time, the sentences just quoted are
proof absolute of the injustice of the accusation
that Calhoun was consciously aiming at the dissolution of the Union, in order to become President of a part, since he could not become President of the whole. Even if he had been such
a black traitor at heart, he knew that his foul
designs could not be executed in time to gratify
such a mad and petty ambition. Who can tell
what "the second volume of the history of the
United States under the Constitution" would
contain, if the conservatives of the North had
known as well as he knew how strong the Union
was? He was no more thoroughly convinced of
the inevitability of its disruption than of the
impossibility to "snap the cords" in this moment and by one blow. And so far from wish-
ng that it could or should be done, his last

bequest to his country was an answer to the question how the Union could and should be saved.

Ere he proceeded to answer this question, he stated how it could not be done. "Nor can the plan proposed by the distinguished senator from Kentucky [Henry Clay], nor that of the administration, save the Union." The course of events has proved the correctness of this opinion. Such compromises could postpone the evil day, but the catastrophe became only the more certain and terrible. No more could eulogies on the Union and appeals to Washington's warnings in his Farewell Address avert the danger. "The cry of 'Union, Union,—the glorious Union!' can no more prevent disunion than the cry of 'Health, health,—glorious health!' on the part of the physician, can save a patient lying dangerously ill." The only way to cure the disease was to remove its causes. Sure enough; but could that be done? He answered, "Yes, *easily;* not by the weaker party, for it can of itself do nothing,—not even protect itself,—but by the stronger. The North has only to will it to accomplish it; to do justice by conceding to the South an equal right in the acquired territory and to do her duty by causing the stipulations relative to fugitive slaves to be faithfully fulfilled; to cease the agitation of the slavery question, and to provide for the insertion of a provision in the Constitution, by an amendment, which will restore to the South, in substance, the power she possessed of protecting herself, before the equilibrium between the sections was destroyed by the action of this government."

Now, if that was needed to save the Union, and nothing less would do, then the Union could not be saved. For the first time, Calhoun directly asserted that, if the North would but follow his advice, "discontent will cease; harmony and kind feelings between the sections be restored, and every apprehension of danger to the Union removed;" and he followed up this assertion by demanding what was in the strictest sense of the word impossible. The members of Congress from the North could not only concede to the South an equal right in the acquired territory, b·.t even abandon it entirely to the slavocracy, and they could bid the people deliver fugitive slaves "with alacrity," as Webster afterwards did; but the North *could* not cease agitating the slave question, because it *could* not *will* it. It *was* a *question*, as Calhoun himself had correctly called it, and it is a physical impossibility to *will* a great economical, moral, and political question out of existence; and if it had not been physically impossible, the North

*s*ould not have overcome the moral impossibility
to will what it actually did not will; that is to
say, she could not will to change or annihilate
her economical, moral, and political convictions
relative to slavery, — she could not will it, simply because they were convictions.

Nor is that all. Calhoun did not say in
his speech how the Constitution ought to be
amended, in order to restore and secure to the
South, for all time to come, the lost equilibrium,
but the answer to this question is to be found
in the second of the above-mentioned essays.
He had the candor there to admit that a constitutional amendment would in itself not be
sufficient. The necessary preliminary step was
to expunge from the statute-book all the laws
by which the *federal* Union of the Constitution
had been changed into a *national* Union. Suppose this was granted: would the actual consolidation of the Union, with its nationalizing
tendencies, which had been uninterruptedly going on ever since the adoption of the Constitution, be also wiped away thereby? Calhoun took
good care not to propound this question. He
confined himself to the statement that the lost
equilibrium between the two sections could not
be thus restored. But if it was impossible to
undo what had been done, it was at least possible to prevent the sins of the past from hav-

ing any practical effect in the future. This
he proposed to do by giving to the weaker section "a negative on the action of the [federal]
government." He admitted that the government might thereby "lose something in promptitude of action," but he asserted that, "instead of being weakened," it would be "greatly
strengthened," for it would "gain vastly in
moral power." As the surest and simplest of
the various ways in which the desired object
could be effected, he recommended a reorgani-
zation of the executive power,

"so that its powers, instead of being vested, as they
now are, in a single officer, should be vested in two;
to be so elected that the two should be constituted
as the special organs and representatives of the respective sections in the executive department of the
government and requiring each to approve all the
acts of Congress before they shall become laws. One
might be charged with the administration of matters
connected with the foreign relations of the country,
and the other, of such as were connected with its
domestic institutions; the selection to be decided by
lot. . . . As no act of Congress could become a law
without the assent of the chief magistrates representing both sections, each, in the elections, would choose
the candidate who, in addition to being faithful to its
interests, would best command the esteem and confidence of the other section. And thus the presiden
tial election, instead of dividing the Union into hos

tile geographical parties, — the stronger struggling to enlarge its powers, and the weaker to defend its rights, as is now the case, — would become the means of restoring harmony and concord to the country and the government. It would make the Union a union in truth, a bond of mutual affection and brotherhood."

That was the " conservative principle " of nullification in its highest perfection, coupled with the total abandonment of the federal structure on the basis of state sovereignty. The Constitution, as has been stated before, knew nothing whatever of sections, and their actual formation was in itself the first step towards the dissolution of the Union. The Union was endangered, not because the original equilibrium between the sections had been destroyed, but because, by the agency of the slave question, it had been actually split into two geographical sections, of unequal strength. And now this fact, which ran directly counter to the constitutive principle of the Union, as established by the Constitution, was to be made its determining principle; that is to say, the disease was to be cured by making the cause of the disease the vital principle of the body politic. Nothing, absolutely nothing, was left of the equality of the States, which was the basis of the states-rights doctrine, and in a modified form also of the Constitution, if a permanent minority of the States forming a geographical section had an absolute veto against the majority in all federal concerns. It was a misnomer — nay, one might justly say, it was a bold abuse of the name — still to speak of a *Union*, if the constituent members of the commonwealth were to be constitutionally consolidated into a permanent geographical minority and a permanent geographical majority, which, in every question, had to come to a complete understanding, ere the body politic became capable of political action in any manner whatever. Calhoun's remedy, which was to effect the cure so "easily," was in fact nothing less than the actual dissolution of the Union, thinly covered by some artificial contrivances, which could not serve any purpose except to keep it for a little while mechanically together, and to expose it to the scorn and ridicule of the whole world.

" Having faithfully done my duty to the best of my ability, both to the Union and my section, throughout this agitation, I shall have the consolation, let what will come, that I am free from all responsibility." Those were the last words of the last speech of the great and honest nullifier. He could no more support himself. Two friends had to lead him out of the Senate chamber. Slowly and heavily the curtain rolled down to shut from the public gaze the last scene of the grand tragedy of this brilliant life. For nearly twenty years the suspicion and even the direct accusation had weighed on his shoulders, that he was systematically working at the destruction of the Union. By doing more than any other single man towards raising the slavocracy to the pinnacle of power, he had actually done more than any other man to hasten the catastrophe and to determine its character, and yet he labored to the last with the intense anxiety of the true patriot to avert the fearful calamity. But the last efforts of his powerful mind were a most overwhelming refutation of all the doctrines whose foremost champion he had been, ever since the days of nullification. It would have been impossible to pass a more annihilating judgment on them than he himself did in his speech of March 4, 1850, and in the Discourse on the Constitution. Yet he had been absolutely sincere in everything he had said. On March 5, in a short running debate with Mr. Foote, of Mississippi, he declared, "As things now stand, the Southern States cannot remain in the Union;" and a few minutes later he asserted, "If I am judged by my acts, I trust I shall be found as firm a friend of the Union as any man within it."

Calhoun closed this colloquy with the remark, If any senator chooses to comment upon what

I have said I trust I shall have health to defend my own position." This hope was not to be fulfilled, though he still spoke in the Senate as late as March 13, and in a manner, as Webster stated in his eulogy, "by no means indicating such a degree of physical weakness as did in fact possess him." On the last day of the month, the " magic wires " carried the tidings into every part of the Union that John Caldwell Calhoun was no more. To the last moment, he manifested the deepest interest and concern in the troubles of his country. " The South! The poor South! God knows what will become of her!" murmured his trembling lips; but he died with that serenity of mind which only a clear conscience can give on the death-bed. On February 12, 1847, he had said in the Senate, "If I know myself, if my head was at stake, I would do my duty, be the consequences what they might." It was his solemn conviction that throughout his life he had faithfully done his duty, both to the Union and to his section, because, as he honestly believed slavery to be " a good, a positive good," he had never been able to see that it was impossible to serve at the same time the Union and his section, if his section was considered as identical with the t avocracy. In perfect good faith he had undertaken what no man could accomplish, because

It was a physical and moral impossibility: antagonistic principles cannot be united into a basis on which to rest a huge political fabric. Nullification and the government of law; state supremacy and a constitutional Union, endowed with the power necessary to minister to the wants of a great people; the nationalization of slavery upon the basis of states-rightism in a federal Union, composed principally of free communities, by which slavery was considered a sin and a curse; equality of States and constitutional consolidation of geographical sections, with an artificial preponderance granted to the minority, — these were incompatibilities, and no logical ingenuity could reason them together into the formative principle of a gigantic commonwealth. The speculations of the keenest political logician the United States had ever had ended in the greatest logical monstrosity imaginable, because his reasoning started from a *contradictio in adjecto.* This he failed to see, because the mad delusion had wholly taken possession of his mind that in this age of steam and electricity, of democratic ideas and the rights of man, slavery was "the most solid foundation of liberty." More than to any other man, the South owed it to him that she succeeded for such a long time in forcing the most democratic and the most progressive commonwealth of the universe to bend its knees and do homage to the idol of this " peculiar institution ; " but therefore also the largest share of the responsibility for what at last did come rests on his shoulders.

No man can write the last chapter of his own biography, in which the *Facit* of his whole life is summed up, so to say, in one word. If ever a new edition of the works of the greatest and purest of proslavery fanatics should be published, it ought to have a short appendix, — the emancipation proclamation of Abraham Lincoln.

INDEX.